THE DEVIL'S WORKSHOP

Musings of an Idle Mind

J.T. NAYAHAM

notionpress
.com

INDIA · SINGAPORE · MALAYSIA

Notion Press

Old No. 38, New No. 6
McNichols Road, Chetpet
Chennai - 600 031

First Published by Notion Press 2018
Copyright © J.T. Nayaham 2018
All Rights Reserved.

ISBN 978-1-64324-081-7

This book has been published with all efforts taken to make the material error-free after the consent of the author. However, the author and the publisher do not assume and hereby disclaim any liability to any party for any loss, damage, or disruption caused by errors or omissions, whether such errors or omissions result from negligence, accident, or any other cause.

No part of this book may be used, reproduced in any manner whatsoever without written permission from the author, except in the case of brief quotations embodied in critical articles and reviews.

The Devil tempts all humans.

Idle humans tempt the Devil!

-Anonymous

I dedicate this book to the memory of my late grandmother

Marybeth.

To me, she was a little bit of a parent, a little bit of a teacher

and most of all, my best friend.

She would fondly call me her 'little devil'...

If only she could have known how prophetic she was!!

CONTENTS

1. TO DIE OR NOT TO DYE — 1
2. MICHAELPET — 4
3. THE DAY EVERYTHING WENT WRONG — 9
4. YOGI AT SIXTY-EIGHT — 14
5. THE LIGHTER SIDE OF YOGA — 20
6. BHANUMATI — 26
7. THE AFFAIR — 33
8. ALL IN THE MIND — 72
9. A GASEOUS TALE — 82
10. THE TRAIN CALLED LIFE — 86
11. ALBERT PINTO KO KYUN GHUSSA AATA HAIN -1 — 92
12. ALBERT PINTO KO KYUN GHUSSA AATA HAIN-2 — 100
13. ALBERT PINTO KO KYUN GHUSSA AATA HAIN-3 — 105
14. AN EERIE EXPERIENCE — 112
15. AJJI'S CRICKET — 127
16. GHOSTS AND OTHER APPARITIONS — 132
17. THE TURNING POINT — 136
18. FOWL PLAY — 147

CONTENTS

19. INS AND OUTS	150
20. IT'S A WONDERFUL LIFE AFTER 65	153
21. FATE IS THE HUNTER	156
22. LUNGI DANCE	205
23. NO-FRILLS AIRLINES	214
24. THE CROSSWORD PUZZLE	217
25. THE GHOST IN THE GRANDFATHER CLOCK	236
26. THE EVIL EYE	251
27. ONE BRIGHT SUNDAY MORNING	256
28. THE SHIRT-TALE	262
29. WHO'S THERE?	269
30. A HAIRY TALE	273
31. THE CHALLENGE	285
32. FISH OUT OF WATER	307
33. HAVE A HEART	313

TO DIE OR NOT TO DYE

To dye or not to dye...that is the question that had been bugging me for several years...in fact from the day when the first grey hair had surreptitiously appeared in my jet-black mop of hair. But somehow, I had managed to push it so far back in my memory, that I had all but forgotten how it had gravely vexed me in days gone by. In fact, I had hoped that I would not have to ponder over it until the day I would die. Dear readers, don't get me wrong...it is not that I wanted to dye my hair just at the precise moment that I was 'giving up the ghost' or 'kicking the bucket' or 'croaking' or 'attaining lotus feet' or (just) 'breathing my last.' No...that is not what I implied. I therefore respectfully entreat you to read on, and I shall endeavour to enlighten you on this distressing incident.

Getting back to where I started, my resolve never to consider dyeing – or at least not to do so as long as I lived – was rudely shattered a few days ago, when a dear friend of mine (at the Park where I walk), suddenly popped the question, "Why don't you dye?"

To say that momentarily I was struck speechless, would qualify as the under-statement of this millennium. My look of absolute shock and astonishment at her utterly rude and patently insensitive query probably betrayed my thoughts, for she immediately tried to cover up her gaffe. "Oh," she said, "I just meant that I wish you would dye."

Now this was getting quite intriguing, if 'intriguing' is indeed the word I am looking for. I was totally and absolutely at a loss as to why she was so insistent that I make arrangements to depart to my Heavenly Abode post-haste. Here I was, minding my own business, having briskly walked around the park for the mandatory five kilometers, and suddenly being confronted with this weird injunction from someone, whom I had all along considered my friend. For a moment, I thought I could understand what Julius Caesar must have felt like on that fateful day, when Brutus so treacherously inserted the sharp, glistening, 8-inch steel blade of his dagger into his unprotected back!

Not being one to take such unreasonable demands lying down, I turned to my erstwhile friend and most vociferously voiced the most obvious question that sprung to my mind, "Hullo, hullo, hullo," I yelled, "and just why do you want me to die?"

To put it mildly, she was stunned at my somewhat violent reaction, and looked at me as if seeing me for the first time. "Why are you getting so angry?" she asked. "Do you think you are too young to dye?"

By Jove, I thought...this was getting more and more personal! Who the dickens was anyone (even a close friend) to decide at what age I should take the long walk or hang up my boots or assume room temperature?

Although my gentlemanly upbringing strictly forbade me from getting into even a modicum of an argument or skirmish with a lady, I think something snapped within me (I was told later that I was drooling like a hungry hyena). "Madam," I said, as icily as I possibly could, "you have either gone totally bonkers, or are mistaking me for someone else. Just because I have a crop of grey hair on my head does not mean that I should be setting a date to meet my Maker."

I was not even into half of my planned diatribe, when I was interrupted by my tormentor. "Wait...wait," she said, waving her hands in my face. "That is what I have been asking you: why don't you get your hair dyed? You are far too young to have grey hair."

I could have died of the embarrassment!!

MICHAELPET

Stories of ghosts, apparitions and other supernatural occurrences were quite commonplace in Michaelpet, the small town that I lived in when I was a child. Indeed, it was the rule, rather than the exception, that most folks could relate to some personal experience or the other with the paranormal.

The town itself was very plain and non-descript, consisting mainly of red tile-roofed bungalows, with lots of trees and sprawling compounds. The residents were mostly Anglo-Indians – engine drivers, firemen and such-like. In those days, locomotives were all steam powered, and it was every boy's dream to become an engine driver; the biggest building in town was the Railway Institute, where grand functions were held at least once in three months. Several old and retired folks had also made this sleepy town their home. For most of them, one of the highlights in their otherwise mundane life was attending Sunday morning Service in the small Church, which stood in the middle of the town. Everyone knew everyone else, and after the Service, they would share news and gossip while sipping hot coffee, thoughtfully provided by the parson's wife. Of course, the other major occasion for meeting in Church was when there was a funeral service, and the subsequent burial in the tiny, quaint cemetery behind the Church.

As children, many of us attended the small Railway School, whose Head-mistress was also the parson's wife. By today's standards it wasn't much of a school and was able to sustain itself all those years only because it was run by the Railway Department. However, for us children, it was where we spent most of our days and made all of our friends. It was also the place where we learnt geography and English, traded catapults, played hopscotch and – most importantly – swapped stories. Bear in mind that in those days, we did not have televisions or video games or even a library which could provide us any excitement. So, it was no surprise that there were dozens of spooky stories making their rounds, embellished with more and more scary details every time they were recounted.

****

Michaelpet had several old houses, some of them in ruins and uninhabited. These decrepit buildings were invariably termed 'haunted' and made ideal locations for us children to explore, fantasize in and play hide and seek. Our parents and elders mostly did not approve of our adventures – they were more worried about us getting bitten by the odd snake or stung by black scorpions (which were fairly common, especially during the rainy season) than by the fear that we would come to harm from the resident spirits.

However, for us children, it all added to the excitement.

One such broken down house had belonged to the Pereira's and had been lying in that dilapidated condition from the time that I could recall. Malcolm Pereira had been a retired engine driver and lived with his wife Constance in that house for many years. Both were just 19 they had got married, and now, at the fag-end of their lives, had crossed well into the nineties. He always called her Connie, and to her, he was Mally. Despite their age, they were considered the most loving and beautiful couple in Michaelpet. They would not miss a single ball in the Institute, where, everyone agreed, they could out-dance couples several decades younger than them! Indeed, as the years went by, Malcolm and Constance only became closer, and loved each other all the more.

It was a few days after Malcolm's 96th birthday that the old couple had been to the May Queen Ball at the Institute. They were the toast of the party and had spent almost the entire evening in each other's arms...waltzing to some lovely music. By and by, around 10:00 pm, they decided to go home, and went to sleep shortly afterwards, after kissing each other good night.

The next morning, as always, Constance was up first and went into the kitchen to make coffee. Invariably, the faint noises from the kitchen would rouse Malcolm, and he would go in and kiss Constance good morning. However, on this particular day, he did not come to the kitchen even as the water was about to come to a boil. Mildly surprised, Constance went to the bedroom and tried waking him up, calling him at first, and then gently shaking him. When there was no response, she realized with total disbelief that her beloved Mally had gone. She was absolutely heartbroken and quite inconsolable and seemed incapable of accepting her loss.

The funeral was a sombre affair and held the same evening. Constance had somehow managed to get herself together and accepted the condolences from friends with great poise. Malcolm was buried wearing his favourite suit in the Church cemetery.

Constance was very sad that night, when she realized that for the first time in nearly 80 years she would be going to bed all alone. She dropped into a fitful sleep, tired out from the events of the day.

Sometime later that night, Constance woke up with a start. There was a severe storm raging outside – typical for the season. Flashes of lightning shed eerie light into the room, and thunder rolled across the sky. The small bedside clock with its luminous hands and dial showed that it was 11:48 pm.

****

The summer storm passed as quickly as it had come, and it was very quiet, except for the sound of water flowing down from the roof. The sudden rains had cooled the room, and Constance pulled the blanket over herself, turning over and trying to go back to sleep. She may have dozed off for a few minutes, when the sound of the telephone ringing woke her up. It was exactly midnight. Reaching across through the bed clothes, Constance picked up the receiver and said, "Hello?"

She clearly heard a voice at the other end… "Connie…" It was Malcolm! "Connie, I could not say goodbye last night and tell you that I love you…"

Constance screamed. The phone dropped from her lifeless fingers. She felt a tremendous pain in her chest and she collapsed to the floor.

She was dead.

****

It was said that from that day onwards, one could hear the sound of a telephone ringing exactly at midnight, followed by a long scream.

For all I know, the house still remains in Michaelpet, but the truth of the matter will never be known. The one thing that I can vouch for is that this story was narrated to me by none other than my grandmother – a lady who was known for her total absence of mischievous intent and for her absolute honesty.

THE DAY EVERYTHING WENT WRONG

It was one of those days when just about everything went wrong.

As soon as I woke up and got out of bed, I noticed that one of my slippers was missing. A brief search revealed that it had been chewed up by my puppy, Bozo, and dumped unceremoniously near the bathroom door. As a result of which, I had to go bare feet to the kitchen to make myself some tea.

On my way to the kitchen, I tripped over the other slipper and lost my balance, stubbing the small toe of my left foot. "Damn!" I said, although I was not one given to swearing. I hobbled back unsteadily and sat down on the chair beside the bed, examining my toe, which had begun to swell up and turn a deep shade of purple. "Damn!" I said again, flexing my toe, to see if it was broken. Fortunately, it did not seem to be, because I could move it, despite the sharp pain.

After a while I got up, and gingerly proceeded into the kitchen, careful not to put my full weight on the left foot. I filled a saucepan with a little more than a cup of water, and set it on the gas stove, and turned the knob to get the burner going. Being an automatic burner, it went 'click-click-click,' but did not light up. I tried again, with the same result. Reaching for the box of matches kept on the kitchen shelf, for just such an emergency, I took out a match stick and struck it on the side of the box. It broke into two. Irritably, I extracted another, and standing well away from the burner (the gas having been turned on all this while), attempted to light the match stick. This time the match lit up with a small 'pop,' and I moved it close to the burner, expecting the gas to burst into flame. But nothing happened. I held the match stick closer to the burner, at the same time turning the gas knob anti-clockwise and then clockwise. Same result – no flame! "Aarg!" I said in frustration. Obviously, the gas cylinder was empty. There was no choice but to go to the Utility area and change the gas regulator on to the spare cylinder.

All this time, I had not noticed that Bozo had come into the kitchen and had been sitting just behind me. As I turned around, I must have stepped on his leg, for he let off a blood-curdling yelp, which made me jump up and land on my left foot, once again stubbing the injured toe. I think I must have screamed louder than Bozo, because he vanished from the kitchen, whining and yelping as though the devil was after him.

After about thirty seconds, I managed to gain some control, and limped my way out of the kitchen into the balcony, which also served as the Utility area. Reaching the gas cylinders, I took off the regulator from the empty one, and set about installing it onto the spare cylinder. To do this, I had to remove the plastic seal which was around the neck of the cylinder, held by a safety clip. Now, as is common knowledge, the safety clip is removed by pulling the string attached to it..and this is precisely what I did. I got hold of the string and pulled. Nothing happened. Wrapping the string around my fingers, I pulled again, using more force. Again, nothing happened. This was getting to be really frustrating. But I wasn't about to give up and concede defeat. More determined than ever, I got a firm grip on the string, I gave an almighty tug. This time, something happened..and happened big time. The string snapped, and I went reeling backwards, falling heavily on my buttocks. "Aaaaaarg!" I screamed.

As I struggled to get myself off the floor, I got a glimpse of Bozo, peeping out of the kitchen door, looking at me with a quizzical look on his face. At any other time, I would have laughed at him, but presently I was so irritated that I growled at him like an injured tiger, making him whine and beat a hasty retreat.

I returned to the cylinder and stared at the obstinate clip with unmitigated abhorrence. It stared back at me with an attitude of utter disdain. This mutual staring would probably have gone on interminably, had I not remembered that I had not had my tea as yet, nor Bozo his milk.

I now realised that I needed a pair of pliers to extract the clip. In the absence of the string, it was impossible to get a grip on the clip. So I limped back into the house, heading for the loft of my bedroom, where the tool box was kept.

Although I stand almost 6 feet tall in my socks, I needed the ladder to reach the handle of the loft. I retraced my steps to the Utility area (where the ladder was normally kept) and proceeded to the corner reserved for it. However, on reaching there, I realised that it was not there. I did a thorough search of the 4 × 10 room, but the ladder remained elusive. "Very strange," I muttered to myself, my mind working overtime to figure out where the ladder could have vanished.

The mystery, however, was soon solved when I remembered that the ladder had been borrowed by my neighbour, and who had (conveniently) forgotten to return it. I also remembered that my neighbour, along with his family, had left on a holiday for three weeks just the previous day. "Damn!" I said loudly, venting my anger. "Damn...damn...damn, and double-damn!"

I realised that if I had to open the loft and take out the tool box I had no choice but to resort to utilising my ancient three-legged stool to try and reach the loft handle. How the stool became three-legged is another story, and I will not go into that at present. Anyway, I pulled out the 'specially-abled' stool from under my bed, propped it up with a dictionary and two packs of playing cards, and gingerly ascended it, standing on my uninjured right foot. The stool was a bit wobbly, but I felt it seemed stable enough for my purpose.

I managed to straighten up, and reach the handle of the loft shutter, which I proceeded to tug. It would not budge. "Must be a bit warped," I said to myself. Using more force, I tugged a bit harder. At this point in time I felt the stool tilting to the right, much like the Titanic did, after making the disastrous contact with the iceberg. I tried balancing, putting more weight on my injured left foot, but I guess that the stool had already gone beyond its limits of stability. I felt myself falling and hung on to the handle with all my strength.

The handle must have been fixed to the loft shutter extremely well, and it did not separate from the wood. However, it seemed that the hinges that held the shutter were not fixed as firmly. With a loud, creaking sound, both hinges hastily parted company with the frame to which they were mounted, causing me to free-fall with the shutter over my head.

Fortunately, I had the presence of mind to fling the shutter backwards, before I landed with a massive thud on my left foot, collapsing in immense pain. The shutter, meanwhile, flew across the room and hit the alarm clock kept on the dressing table, causing it to fall to the floor, come to life, and go 'brrrrrrrrrrrrr..brrrrrrrrrrrr..brrrrrrrrrr.'

I don't know if I passed out, but I may well have..for the next thing I remember was Bozo standing next to me, licking my face.

YOGI AT SIXTY-EIGHT

I am over 67 years old and perilously close to stepping into my 68th year on this Earth! I live in Bangalore and am considered a 'short-tempered, cranky old man' by some, a 'nut-case' by others and a 'pain in the neck' by most. Well, that is a cross that I have to bear, and believe me..it is not doing my cervical spondylosis any good. Oh..and I may as well mention here that in my youth (I guess, about a million years ago) I was a pilot in the Indian Air Force. Having retired (prematurely) in 1990, I was connected with civil aviation for several years after that, until one fine day, my poor heart said, "Enough is enough," and decided to pack up. Fortunately, modern medical magic got the errant organ back on line, and I am still around to bore people with stories about my life.

My tryst with yoga happened quite unexpectedly – and that too, just about six months ago. No..actually that is not entirely correct. Having been goaded by my daughter to venture into the hitherto (at least for me) untested realm of yoga, a couple of years ago, I had joined a *yogashram*, which claimed to teach the basics of this ancient art. More importantly, it was located a mere stone's throw away from where I reside. Having paid the fee and enrolled, I was absolutely thrilled that

I would finally learn to sit cross-legged on the floor like most of my fellow countrymen (and women!).

That I was unable to sit cross-legged may surprise most of my readers, but the fact of the matter is that right from my childhood, I had gotten used to sitting on chairs (even to partake of meals). This was thanks to an awfully flawed notion in my parents' minds that doing so was the 'proper' and 'sophisticated' thing to do. As if the parental influence was not enough, I joined the Indian Air Force at the age of twenty, and for the quarter of a century that I donned the uniform, there was absolutely no question of sitting on the floor – cross-legged or otherwise.

Anyway, coming back to my first encounter with yoga, I must, in all honesty, say that it was an unmitigated disaster. The (so-called) *guru* at this reputed *yogashram* was a seasoned contortionist, who would have given Baba Ramdev a run for his money. Now, that was fine by me, but my impassioned pleas that I was over sixty years old and could not even bend my knees to tie my shoe-laces, fell on deaf ears. He insisted that I be part of a class, where the other students were scarcely a year or two older than my grandchildren!

Not only that, right from the first session, he made me contort myself into horribly grotesque positions, most of which I had not experienced even in the wildest nightmares that I used to have as a child, after watching horror movies.

However, having been a soldier for most of my adult life, I made a valiant attempt to please my *guru* for all of two sessions. That was when I realized, that for me to continue to endure this torture, would be a toss-up between (a) a slipped disc, and (b) having to permanently ambulate in a wheeled chair. Not being particularly enamoured with either choice, I decided to quit..and also decided to permanently banish the word 'yoga' from my vocabulary.

All that was until one bright, sunny morning, when loitering outside Thoms Supermarket, waiting for my wife to finish her (seemingly endless) shopping, I noticed a hand-bill on the notice board, advertising yoga classes by someone called Megha Rao. Going by my earlier catastrophe, my first reaction was to totally ignore the poster. However, I was absolutely intrigued by the fact that the person offering the yoga lessons claimed to be an 'M.Sc. in yoga!' Honestly, until that moment, I was not even aware that yoga was a taught in College..let alone being a subject for post-graduation! My curiosity got the better of me, and – believe it or not – I took a snapshot of the poster on my cell-phone, since I did not have the luxury of having pen and paper at that moment to note down the contact details.

After several days, when I had all but forgotten about this incident and was deleting unwanted stuff from my cell-phone, I got to see the photograph I had clicked of the yoga poster. I was all set to delete it, but, succumbing to my inherent penchant for all things mysterious, I decided to call Ms. Megha Rao, M.Sc., on the number given. And the rest (as is often said) is history.

I met Ms. Megha Rao the next day. If I had been expecting to meet someone like my erstwhile tormentor at the *yogashram*, I was in for a very pleasant surprise indeed. Presumably, going purely by my past experience, I was mentally prepared to see a stout, *paan*-chewing, old, ugly ogress with missing teeth. On the contrary, Ms. Rao turned out to be young and pretty, with a full set of teeth – and definitely did not chew *paan*! More importantly, when I told her that I was 67 years old and that all I was interested in was learning some 'breathing exercises' (and definitely wanted to avoid contortions!), she did not glare at me as though I was insulting the hoary traditions of yoga. Instead, she seemed genuinely intrigued by the fact that someone as ancient as me was interested in learning the art, and agreed to take me in. She even promised that she would set up a regimen to suit my aching, creaking, Jurassic joints. In hindsight, I think that perhaps it may have been as much of a challenge for her as it was for me.

I must confess that I went for my first session with a sense of enormous trepidation…possibly because of my earlier episode with the contortionist. However, I soon realized that my fears were absolutely unfounded.

My petite yoga teacher put me through a few simple exercises like balancing on one leg, balancing on both legs, looking left, looking right, not looking left or right (i.e., closing my eyes) and lying flat on the floor. I guess I passed with flying colours, because she pronounced me 'fit to learn yoga!'

And so..here I am today, absolutely enjoying the *'asanas'* which I have learnt thus far. Not only can I go through *'Surya Namaskara'* with surprising élan, I have also become somewhat of an expert in imitating animals – I can do the Dog Pose, Rabbit Pose, Camel Pose, Cow-face Pose, Cat Pose, Cobra Pose, Fish Pose and (hold your breath) even Crocodile Pose! Oh..and I must reveal that, without batting an eyelid, I can breathe fast, breathe slow, inhale through one nostril and exhale through the other and make the sound 'aum' without opening my mouth! I can be a 'bow' at one moment, and a 'boat' in the next..a 'plow' now and a 'stick' soon after! It seems that the possibilities are infinite.

How has all this helped me? Well..basically, it has taught me that it is NEVER too late to learn something new. It has also been very useful in making my geriatric joints more flexible..I can very nearly bend and touch my knees, which would have been impossible barely few months ago. My lung capacity has shown a remarkable increase..and so has my patience. Thanks to the breathing exercises, I am certainly calmer and composed now – believe me – I have not screamed at demonic auto-rickshaw drivers or called into question the parentage of suicidal two-wheeler riders in a long time!

Has all of this come with a price? Of course, it has. Nothing in this world is free, right? And, what is the 'price,' you may certainly ask. Well, my wife swears that I keep saying words like *'paschima-uttanasana,' 'urdhva-mukha-svanasana,' 'baddha-konasana,' 'paschima-*

namaskara,' 'suptha-padangushtasana' and *'gomukhasana'* in my sleep. She even asked me if I was learning black-magic to counter her snoring!

I have noticed lately that her barbs and taunts do not irritate or annoy me, though – all thanks to yoga. I am sure that someday, in the not-too-distant future, I will learn to switch my mind off, snap my eyes shut and sublimely relax in my favourite pose – *'shavasana!'*!

THE LIGHTER SIDE OF YOGA

You may have read my earlier narrative –Yogi at Sixty-Eight. After reading it, some of you probably thought that it was just a fib...others may have thought that the enthusiasm would have lasted for all of one week, after which it would have died a natural death. I even think that a few of you may have been convinced that this was the nuttiest thing to do for someone close to seventy and would probably have scoured all the obituaries to see if I had indeed attained lotus feet/reached Heavenly Abode/gone to be with my Maker...or simply, expired due to excess *shavasana*. Let me hasten to reassure you that this is not the case, and I am very much alive and kicking (and certainly not the bucket!).

Having said that, I must confess that I have been sorely tempted on several occasions to take a deep breath (through both nostrils), turn around and walk away from it all. However, whether it is because of my innate obdurate and obstinate nature of never throwing in the towel, or the fact that the three-days-a-week routine has become more of a habit, I am still persisting at it.

Perhaps it could also be to a large extent on account of my instructor. Readers may recall the remarkable circumstances under which I started my initiation into yoga with my present tutor, who is not only young, pretty and petite, but also extremely persuasive and – believe it or not – has an M.Sc. in yoga to boot! So here I am..barely a couple of years shy of the Biblical age of 'three-score and ten years,' actually enjoying every moment, and contorting myself into shapes and positions that I would never have imagined that I was capable of!

During the course of these six-odd months that I have been 'practicing' yoga, there have been some hilarious moments – at the yoga class as well as outside it. At my age it is difficult to remember each and every amusing episode, but I will still try and get a few smiles out of you. If you do not find any these anecdotes funny...well, enrol for yoga classes. Perhaps then your sense of humour will be awakened!

****

One incident that I distinctly remember, happened at the third session that I attended. There were three of us in the class – two young ladies and I. The ladies had already attended more than a dozen classes, and therefore were 'veterans' as compared to me. Hence their exercises were not the rudimentary stuff that I was being put through, but rather more advanced. In this particular instance, both ladies were doing *Pranayama* (or breathing exercises), sitting on the floor in the classic *Padmasana* (or Lotus pose), with their eyes closed. I had been asked by my tutor to stand as straight as possible, with eyes closed, feet together and hands by my side. If you ask me, I was rather amused that I was asked to do this *asana* – which I later came to know was *Tadasana* – because I felt that there was nothing to it. But, as things turned out, I couldn't have been more mistaken.

I must have stood in this pose, perhaps for all of thirty seconds, when (I was told later by my tutor) I started swaying..gently at first, but more violently as the seconds ticked by. The best part of it was that I was blissfully unaware of my swaying, and in my mind, was as steady as the Qutab Minar! All of a sudden, I lunged to my right and stumbled over, falling smack onto the lap of the young lady sitting closest to me, who (I presume) was in the middle of breathing in through her left nostril. One moment there was complete silence, and the next, a banshee scream rent the air, as my co-pupil shrieked and took off vertically, dislodging me from her lap in the process.

Things may have abated there, and *shanti* prevailed, but my sudden and rapid eviction from the lap only served to propel me at great velocity onto the next young lady. Fortunately, she had broken her breathing cycle and opened her eyes when she heard the scream. Having lightning-quick reflexes, she swerved aside, and I flew past, missing her nose by a whisker. Thankfully, the side wall put an end to my uncontrolled flight, and I landed rather heavily on the floor, with arms and legs all over the place. (I still wonder if they have a name for that ridiculous pose!).

****

Another incident which will always stay etched in my mind happened a good two months after I started learning yoga. One of my favourite *asanas* was – and still is – *Supta-baddha-kon-asana* (or *S-B-K-A*, as I have come to call it). In this, the person has to sit on the floor, bring both feet together so that the soles touch each other, with the sides of the small toes in contact with the floor. Once this is done, one reclines backwards and lies on the floor, with hands on the side of the body. To help in achieving this position, beginners (like yours truly) are encouraged to use yoga belts. These are canvas strips, about an inch wide, and with a buckle at one end which is used to make a loop of the belt. This looped belt is put around the lower waist, the feet being inserted into the other end of the loop, and the belt tightened to keep the feet in place.

As I mentioned earlier, this was one of my favoured poses, and I was determined to excel in it (and perhaps impress my tutor?). I therefore borrowed one of these belts from her and took it home to practice over a weekend.

That particular Sunday, I woke up at around 5.30 in the morning, and tip-toed out of the bedroom shutting the door behind me, making sure that my wife would not be disturbed by my eccentricities. As was my habit, I went to the Study Room (which is situated a fair distance from the Master Bedroom), put on some soothing music, shut the door, and after limbering up for a few minutes, proceeded to do my yoga routine. No surprise then, that I started with my favourite pose. I sat on the yoga mat, put the belt around me and inserted my feet into the loop. I was extremely happy that I was able to get my feet really close in and tightened the belt to its maximum. Then I reclined backwards and went into *S-B-K-A*, absolutely relaxed and happy.

After about six minutes, I decided to get up and try something else. But, try as much as I did, I just could not get up and sit on my buttocks. I tried turning to the right…then to the left – but it was of no use. I was stuck in that position. I knew then that unless I removed the belt, I would not be able to get up. Now, that was proving to be impossible, as I had tightened it too much! I vaguely remembered my tutor saying "Don't tighten the belt too much…" but clearly, remembering her words was not of much help at this stage.

After struggling for about ten minutes – by which time my legs were cramping up – I realized that I just had to get help, if I was not to be forever stuck in this weird pose.

But that was easier said than done…my wife continued to sleep, oblivious to the fact that her dear husband was about to set a world record in *S-B-K-A*. My shouting for her help was of no avail, as (a) the music was on, (b) the study room door was closed and (c) the bedroom door was closed too! I did not need to have a degree in rocket science to deduce that I was in deep s**t!

Well…to cut a long (and painful) story short, here I was, as helpless as a turtle on its back. To keep myself busy, I did a few *Anulom-Vilom*, two dozen *Brahmiri* and some *So-Hum*. After that, I did not know any more variations to breathing. So, I just lay there, until my wife found me about two hours later.

Believe you me, I had never been happier to see her (that is, since we first met 48 years ago!!).

BHANUMATI

I had met her quite by chance.

It had been raining the entire day, and I had no plans of going to the Park for my routine evening walk. I had cursed the weather, and was getting thoroughly bored, sitting around at home and doing nothing – well, not exactly 'nothing'... I had been twiddling my thumbs so vigorously that they had become numb. Literally numb-thumbs!

Anyway...sometime around four in the evening, the weather suddenly cleared – perhaps our own Goddess Indira...or the mighty Greek God Zeus...or whosoever is in charge of the rain – decided to take a break. The clouds that had been hanging over the area, like an unending grey blanket, suddenly decided to do a disappearing act, and, in fact, one or two adventurous rays of evening sunshine tentatively sneaked through, casting a mellow, diffused light all around.

Those stray streaks of light were sufficient to awaken my nearly dormant brain and set it in motion. Without further ado, I quickly got out of my bean-bag (no...that is a bit of an exaggeration – I can never get out 'quickly' bean-bags...not at my age!) and did a hasty status-check of the weather. To my great relief, I saw that there was a perceptible change in the scene..in fact, the drip-drip-drizzle had indeed stopped.

Wasting no time, I donned my Nike sneakers, and in a jiffy, was ready to 'just do it'...which, at that point in time, was to get the hell out of the house, and head towards the Park. I hoped that there would not be too many water-patches, and that I would be able to do my three kilometers of brisk evening walk.

Reaching the Park, I took out my cell-phone, and turned on the Pedometer, before setting off on round one. Going around the first corner, I was just beginning to accelerate into my 6.5 kmph stride, when I felt a small drop of water fall directly on my nose. I promptly dismissed it as a drop of water falling from one of the several trees inside the park and brushed it off perfunctorily with the back of my right hand.

What happened next could only be termed 'unbelievable.' In a matter of seconds, the sky, which had fast been turning blue, was once again obscured from view by an uniform layer of greyish-black cloud, which to my professional aviator's eye, could only have been nimbo-stratus – the type which is notorious for discharging copious amounts of precipitation. At the same time, I noticed that the wind had also picked up, and was blowing from a South-Westerly direction, and that certainly was not good news. If I had hoped to complete at least three to four rounds before it started raining, I was in for a rude shock.

In a matter of seconds, it had become dark, and king-sized drops of rain pelted down with great force. At that moment, I realized that this was the end of my walk..at least for that day. On a more urgent note, I knew that I just had to get under some shelter – and that too – ASAP, unless I enjoyed having a shower in my track-pants and tees – which I most certainly didn't.

The only shelter in the park was the bandstand, situated right in the middle of the grounds. Incidentally, this bandstand had been a water tank in the good old days, when this locality of Bangalore, known as Richards Town, was home to folks, mainly of British origin. However, things had changed over time, and not only had the water tank become defunct, but had been turned into a bandstand, at some point in time, where various bands (Army, Air Force, Police, etc.) used to perform, providing entertainment to the now predominantly Anglo-Indian citizenry, who had replaced the original residents of the area.

It is often said that the only certainty in life is change. As if to prove this, the bandstand had also changed and had fallen silent with the passage of time, mainly due to the fact that the older residents of Richards Town either moved 'underground' on a permanent basis..or had sold their properties and migrated 'Down Under.' Anyway, these days, the majestic structure – that had at one time provided precious drinking water, and in later days soothed a million ears with wonderful music – just stands as mute testimony to its glorious past. Oh..and it also provides emergency shelter to hapless walkers caught unawares in pouring rain..like yours truly, on this particular day.

Thus, it was to this century-old edifice that I hastened, in order to escape the fury of the storm. I did not check my Pedometer (since the cell-phone would have gone kaput had it got wet), but I am sure I must have touched at least 8.5 kmph during the period of transition from the walking track to the bandstand. Understandably, I was totally out of breath, and panting, by the time I was safely under the canopy of the bandstand. It took me a moment to catch my breath, and to adjust my eyes to the relative darkness within the bandstand. I did not see anyone, and it seemed that I was the only one, marooned on this lonely island.

The rain, meanwhile, was coming down heavily, and it looked as though I would have to spend a considerable amount of time waiting for it to stop. I took out my handkerchief, and was vigorously wiping the water from my face, my head and my misted-up glasses, when I suddenly had this weird feeling that I was not alone. Since no one had overtaken me, nor did I overtake anyone while I was making hasty tracks for the bandstand, I thought that this was quite strange. I quickly wiped my glasses, and put them back on, and turned around to see if there was indeed anyone behind me.

It was at that moment that I spotted her. Obviously, she must have been under the shelter before me, and I noticed that she was as wet as me. In the dim light, she looked frightened, and cold..and totally lost. But what attracted me to her were her eyes – large and brown and beautiful. They were gentle eyes..and at the same time, appeared very sad...so much so, I just couldn't take my own eyes off them! I wanted to tell her not to be afraid...that I would not harm her in any way. But I just knew deep inside me that it would be of no use...

I smiled at her and beckoned to her to come closer. But this only seemed to make her more nervous, and she retreated a few steps, edging back towards one of the supporting pillars of the bandstand. Much as I was tempted to reach out to her, I refrained from doing so, for I did not know how she would react. And so we just stood there, two rain-soaked strangers..immersed in our own thoughts, and shivering a bit in the chill breeze that was blowing through the bandstand.

Suddenly, and as quickly as it had started, the rain eased in its intensity and a hint of blue skies reappeared. My fellow being too had noticed the change, and with one final, fleeting glance in my direction, turned and walked quickly away down the path, and out of the Park gate. I waited just a few more minutes to make sure that I would not get caught in the rain again, then walked to my car and drove back home.

Once home, I completely forgot about the incident at the park, and went about my routine activities, had my usual two drinks, followed by a light dinner, and went to bed.

The next day, I was up early as usual, and went for my morning walk to the Park. I think I was on my third round, when I suddenly realized that my fellow-being from the bandstand was walking beside me..matching me pace for pace and looking intently into my eyes. I was able to study her eyes better today..feeling fresh and clear-headed in the morning, and in better light conditions, than on the previous occasion. They were indeed the most beautiful pair of eyes that I had ever seen, and it seemed that they were lined with just the faintest outline of black *kajal*, making them look at once, traditional as well as exotic. But, as I had observed the previous day, they were indeed sad eyes..eyes that said a million things, without a word being spoken..eyes that had probably seen happiness at some point in time, but now were forever consigned to sorrow, loneliness and fear.

She was quiet..but (seemingly) happy to walk beside me. I knew that she wouldn't talk..but still I tried... "Hello," I said. There was no reply..just a slight tilt of the head, and I thought I saw a faint glimmer of light in those magnificent eyes. And so we continued our walk, somehow completely – and inexplicably – comfortable in each other's company. I think I was in my eighth round, when she – either by accident, or on purpose – faintly brushed against me, and the next moment..she was gone.

This pattern of things carried on for nearly two months...until one day, she came along with someone else. Ooh..this guy seemed young, sporty and handsome..although a tad overweight. But then, what the hell – who was I to judge?

She walked beside me, looking me in the eye, as she always did. But this time, there was a sparkle..a new passion in her beautiful *kajal*-lined eyes, and they seemed to say..thank you..thank you my friend, for being there, when I needed you most.

And then…she was gone. I never saw her again.

****

Several months later, I was on my usual morning walk, with another friend, when I mentioned about this incident. Naturally, curiosity got the better of my friend, who asked, "But..if you both were walking together every day for two months…why the hell didn't you ask her name, or find out who she was?"

"Hello," I said, laughing so loud and long that the other walkers gave me quizzical looks. "I think you've got it all wrong. Did I forget to mention that she was just another stray dog…who had either lost her way…or had been dumped at the park by her owners?

Oh..and by the way, she had a blue collar around her neck with the letter 'B' on the locket. So I had named her Bhanumati."

THE AFFAIR

PROLOGUE

The sound of running water woke him up. With a great effort, Vinod managed to open one eye a wee bit...but quickly shut it back, the bright light from the table lamp hurting him.

His head felt as though a million nails were being driven into it. The sound of the water was making it even worse. He tried turning over, covering his ears with his palms. But it was no use...the throbbing in his head was quite unbearable.

Slowly, very slowly, he opened one eye again, taking care not to look towards the light from the lamp. Instinctively he held his left wrist a few inches away from his face and tried to see the time on his watch. Annoyingly, he could not see the watch, and he brought his arm even closer to his face. As his wrist came closer, he sensed the sensual perfume that she had worn. Vinod smiled...his mind recalling the events of the previous evening, culminating in the most exciting and wonderful night that he had ever spent in his life. He shut his eye again, wondering where he had found the strength to make love three times, each time more thrilling, more passionate and more fulfilling than the time before. Just thinking of it now sent shivers up his spine and he could feel himself getting delightfully aroused all over again. Oh yes..Sunaina was definitely the sexiest woman that he had ever known!

Sunaina...

CHAPTER - 1

Vinod Chawla, at forty-five, was a success in life. He had a booming business, a beautiful wife, and two wonderful, smart children. It was not as if he had had all the good things in life handed to him on a platter. Indeed, he was extremely proud of how he had achieved success and would readily recount his early days of struggle and strife to anyone who cared to listen.

His father, Raminder Chawla had been a refugee who had crossed over into India in 1947, along with his wife, Guddi, and three young children. The initial years were a nightmare, with the family barely able to keep body and soul together. Having worked as a lathe operator in Peshawar before coming to India, Vinod's father managed to get a job in a machine shop in Ludhiana. His hard work and honesty paid off, and he soon became a supervisor of sorts. Vinod's mother too was very enterprising and contributed her share to the family's meagre income by supplying tea and snacks to the workers at the numerous machine shops that had sprung up in Ludhiana.

Vinod was the eldest child. Every day he would watch his parents' desperate efforts to earn enough money to feed, clothe and educate him, and to look after the needs of his younger brother Vikas and their little sister Laila.

The typical day in the Chawla household (the 'house' itself was nothing more than a dilapidated, disused shed, with an asbestos roof and a corrugated iron sheet for a door) would begin at 4:30 am, when his mother would get up to go out and fetch water from the nearby well. She would carry the two battered and disfigured aluminium pots – one on her waist and the other precariously balanced on her head – to the corner of the shed where the earthen *angheeti* (hearth) stood. She would then start a fire with twigs (collected the previous evening), pieces of cardboard and old newspapers. At times, especially when the rains came, the twigs would be soaked, and would not light up easily. Vinod would see his mother blowing and coughing..blowing and coughing...desperate to get the fire going. It was a frantic race against time...the first cups of tea and snacks had to be ready to serve to the workers, who would soon be trudging up to work the first shift at the machine shops.

The rest of the family too would be up by now, for all of them slept together in the single room. Winter mornings were particularly difficult, with the harsh cold seeping up from the rough stone floor, through the thin *chhattais* (mats) on which the family slept. Laila would invariably be the last to wake up, having snuggled as close to the *angheeti* as possible to keep warm.

By the time the first tentative slivers of sunlight emerged, Vinod's father would have gotten ready for the day. As the 'super,' he had to be present at the machine shop by seven in the morning to check on the progress of the work allotted to the night shift and to plan the schedule for the day. The *seth-ji* (owner) of the machine shop would come in around 9:30 am and would expect a full report. Working hours were long and tedious, and the old man would plod wearily home, much after the children had eaten their *daal-roti* and turned in. At times Vinod would be half awake when his father came in and would hear the whispered conversation of his parents..always – always – on how to give the children a better quality of life. In his state of half-sleep, Vinod would promise to himself that he would one day ensure that his parents' desires were fulfilled.

Vinod studied in the Government School, which was about four furlongs from their house. It was a long walk, especially on cold winter days. He was not the most brilliant of students, but he more than made up for his shortcomings by his hard work and the zeal to succeed. He managed a first class in his School Final examination and was determined to become a graduate.

His parents, on the other hand, had been desperately hanging on to the hope that once Vinod completed school, he would get a job somewhere, and would supplement their meagre income. So, when he told them of his plans to do his graduation, it was as though their small world had shattered into a million pieces. It was not that they did not share in his ambition to study more and go ahead in life...they were truly proud of his achievement in High School. But they also knew that it was futile to aspire for the unattainable.

Vinod's father was not a man of many words and was one who lived from day to day...the past eleven years of constant struggle had also made him a cynic. His reaction to Vinod's plans was typical of his rustic nature. *"Paagal ho gaya kya?"* (Have you gone mad?) he shouted at Vinod. *"Apne aap ko kya samajthe ho. Laath sahib?"* (Just what do you think of yourself...a gentleman?) And before Vinod could even think of replying, he had stomped out of the house.

Vinod just stood there, looking pleadingly at his mother, who, at this moment, was praying to God that the situation would not go out of hand. Slowly, she came to him gently taking his arm and holding him close. It was as if she knew intuitively that their life would never be the same again. After what seemed an eternity, she let go of her firstborn, and went to tend the *chulha* and make *rotis* for the evening meal.

The next few days were utter agony for Vinod. His father chose to completely ignore him, and sitting down with the family during meal times became such an ordeal, that Vinod would gladly have gone to sleep on an empty stomach. But he knew that if he did not at least make a pretence of eating, his mother too would have gone hungry. Also, he did not want Vikas and little Laila to witness any unpleasant scenes between him and his father.

Vinod knew that his parents were deeply saddened that they were unable to afford his college education. But he could also see that they were becoming more and more frustrated to see him hanging around the house, moping all day. Nothing would have pleased them more than if he could get some small job – any job – and bring in some income to mitigate their precarious pecuniary situation. However, neither of them had the courage to broach the subject, lest it flared up into a major issue.

CHAPTER - 2

Vinod started remaining out of the house more and more. Most of the days, he would go and sit on the parapet wall of the clock tower near the bus station, wistfully staring at the buses that brought in affluent passengers. At times he was sorely tempted to just jump into one of the buses and hitch-hike his way out of this miserable existence. But he knew that this was a futile idea..he would soon be discovered by the Conductor and thrown out in some god-forsaken place. Worse still, he could land up in jail for traveling without a ticket!

Summer had passed, and the monsoons had set in. The seasonal rains brought further misery and hardship to the already beleaguered family – even getting sufficient dry twigs to keep the *chulha* alight was becoming a major daily challenge. The strain of keeping the family going, as well as keeping the fragile peace between her son and her husband had taken its toll on Vinod's mother. Looking at the gaunt, weary face of his mother each morning as she struggled with the household chores, made Vinod want to cry.

One day, matters came to a head. It had been raining heavily, and his father had not gone to the factory at the usual time. He had been sitting on the stool with three legs (the fourth having broken off and used as firewood long ago), and staring out of the door. Guddi had made some gruel for breakfast, and carefully divided the food for each of her children. As she was handing the bowl of gruel to Vinod, he noticed his father glaring at him. It was a look that Vinod had never seen before – red, unblinking eyes, filled with emotions which he could not put into words. Vinod stared back at his father, hands lifted to take the bowl from his mother. At that instant, he seemed to understand what his father's eyes were saying...it was not anger or pity or sorrow – rather, they conveyed his father's absolute loathing for him.

Vinod turned to his mother and with a barely perceptible shake of his head refused the gruel. *"Kya hua beta? Nashtha le lo."* (What happened son? Have your breakfast), said his mother. He could not speak...so choked was he with guilt and sorrow and frustration. He shook his head again and slowly got up from the mat. *"Chalo Vinod...thoda sa kha lo."* (Come on Vinod...eat a little bit), his mother was pleading.

"*Bas kar, Guddi!*" (Stop it, Guddi!), his father suddenly shouted...so loudly, that the two younger children cringed in fear.

Vinod knew right then and there, that he was no longer welcome in this house.

It was the first defining moment in his life.

CHAPTER - 3

Vinod walked out of his home that very day. His mother had cried and pleaded with him not to leave, that she would placate his father, and that things would be alright. But Vinod had made up his mind...the three words that his father had uttered before setting off in the rain, echoed and reverberated in his head endlessly.

With one last hug for his mother, a kiss each for Vikas and Laila, two faded, weather-beaten shirts, one spare trouser, and the Timex watch (which his father had gifted him for his 15th birthday), Vinod set off on the next chapter of his life, not knowing where he was headed to, or what he was going to do. It was the 16th day of December, 1958 and he was almost sixteen years old.

Fortune, the saying goes, favours the brave. Vinod did not consider himself to be particularly brave, and felt intense fear and anxiety in the days following his exodus from the security of his home. This was especially so when, by the end of the first week, he had all but run out of the money he had got by selling the watch on the first day itself. He had travelled far from Ludhiana, and had reached Chandigarh, the bustling capital city of the Punjab and Haryana.

He had tried to get some job or the other for the past seven days – even toiled as a porter in Chandigarh Railway Station. But that had lasted just one day...the mafia elements that controlled the workforce were just too intimidating. And so, here he was sitting on a bench, staring at Sukhna Lake – tired, hungry and demoralized.

Sukhna Lake was a popular destination of Chandigarh residents, especially in summer. Several families would drive up and sit around the water body, enjoying the cool breezes that offered welcome respite from the blazing temperatures of the season. Today was no exception. On the bench next to the one where Vinod was sitting, there was this family of four – a man (perhaps in his thirties), his wife and two young children (both boys around six and four years of age). They were clearly from South India – Madrasis – although Vinod could not fathom from which state (for North Indians, all South Indians were Madrasis!). They must have been having a picnic the whole day, and now they were all packed and set to go home. The kids were obviously tired, and both wanted to be carried. After much coaxing and cajoling, the elder boy agreed to walk holding his father's hand, while the mother carried the younger one. Vinod watched the family – his mind recalling the days he had spent with his younger brother and baby sister – and he heaved a great sigh...a sigh of despair, loneliness and hopelessness. Well..he too had better move and find himself some place for the night – tomorrow he had planned to go to the bus station early and try and get a porter's job there.

As Vinod was about to get up, something caught his eye from beneath the bench recently vacated by the Madrasi family. At first, he was inclined to dismiss it as a silver foil, probably from a bar of chocolate. But curiosity got the better of him, and he walked across and reached down for the shiny object. It took some effort to reach beneath the bench, and he was about to give up, when his fingers touched something solid. Crouching even lower, Vinod stretched his hand as far as possible and managed to get a grip on the object. Slowly he straightened up and looked at the silvery object he now held in his fingers. Lo and behold..it was a sleek, Sony camera! Vinod turned it round and round with his fingers and realized that the Madrasi family must have dropped it below the bench by accident.

Initial surprise gave way to exhilaration. Although he had never seen – much less, held – a camera in his life, Vinod realized that this Sony camera must be very valuable. His mind raced with the idea of having a whole lot of money than what he presently had.

As much as his mind kept screaming at him to make a bee-line to the nearest *kabadi mandi* (flea market) and make his fortune, something in his heart told him that he should find the owners and return the camera. Perhaps it was just his innate honesty...or perhaps it was his subconscious recalling the sense of right and wrong that had been instilled by his mother ever since he was a child. Whatever it was, Vinod made up his mind to find the Madrasis and return their camera.

Little did he know at that moment, that within the span of one week, he would reach the next defining moment in his life.

CHAPTER - 4

Vinod headed towards the direction that the family had taken just a few minutes ago. But in the crowd of people making their way towards the exit, he did not see them. He increased his pace, pushing himself through the milling mass of humanity, frantically looking around. After what seemed eternity, he reached the small turnstile leading to the car park and squeezed himself through. He seemed a man possessed..something within him making him desperate to find the family.

There must have been at least a hundred and fifty cars parked there, and he couldn't be sure if they had already got into their car and left. But he kept going, desperation bordering on anxiety. And then, just when he was about to give up...he saw them!

It is often said that God works in mysterious ways..and it definitely must have been one of those days as far as Vinod was concerned. He stared in astonishment as he saw the Madrasi family all crowded around a dark blue Fiat car. The man was on his haunches and labouring hard to fix a flat tyre. The woman was doing her best to keep the children occupied – both the boys were obviously very tired and sleepy.

Something must have caught the woman's attention, for she turned and looked in Vinod's direction. She instinctively clutched both her children closer to her, even as she recognized Vinod as the young man who had occupied the bench next to theirs. She could not be blamed for her reaction, what with the recent spate of kidnappings and other atrocities in the City. Vinod could sense the apprehension in her eyes, as she said something to her husband. The man too looked in Vinod's direction and at the same time picked up the tyre-rod and braced himself.

Just for a brief moment, Vinod considered turning around and running away, but he dismissed the thought even as it occurred. It was as though someone – or something – was guiding his steps towards them, regardless of the consequences. For a moment, he was quite unsure as to how he was going to calm their fears...tell them that he meant no harm. He was not even sure if they would understand his language, and his English was, at best, rudimentary.

When he was just about twenty feet from them, he took out the camera from his pocket and held it out for them to see. "*Namaste sahib,*" he said, "camera yours."

For a moment, it seemed as if the man did not understand what Vinod was trying to convey, or even recognize what he was holding in his hand. But then, abruptly, his look changed to one of surprise, and he turned to his wife and said something in their language. She in turn let go of the children and hastily opened the air-bag that was next to her. After a brief search, she realized that the camera was not there.

The man got to his feet, and walked towards Vinod, a faint smile on his lips, perhaps recalling that just a few moments back, he was all set to use the heavy tyre rod on the young man. "Thank you," he said, reaching out to take the camera from Vinod.

As soon as he had handed over the camera, Vinod turned around and started walking away. He would have probably taken a dozen steps when he heard the man say in Hindi, "*Suno...idhar aao!*" (Listen...come here). Vinod stopped and turned around, to see the man holding out a hundred rupee note to him. Much as he was tempted to take the money, Vinod shook his head, indicating that he did not want it. If the man was surprised at this, he did not show it. Instead, he put the money back in his wallet and walked up to Vinod.

CHAPTER - 5

What happened from that point onwards would be a mystery to Vinod for the rest of his life. As a child, he had heard of the miracles that God had worked in people's lives – stories of how poor, hungry and destitute persons had found untold riches or how paupers had become princes. But these were only fairy tales..fables told to little children by their mothers to make them forget the cold and damp and hunger.

In Vinod's case, such a miracle did happen...and neither was it God who appeared to him in a dream, nor was it some treasure that he unearthed while digging the ground. It came in the form of a Madrasi family, who had chanced to be at the same place as Vinod was at that particular point in time.

****

The man's name was Kanchipuram Girija Srinivasan – known as Srini to his friends. He was a Squadron Leader in the Indian Air Force and stationed at the Chandigarh Air Base. His wife's name was Shanti, and she too had a military background, her father being a retired Group Captain. Srini had met Shanti whilst posted to Tambaram, near Madras, where her father was the Chief Instructor in the Flying Instructors' School. They got married shortly thereafter, and now had two children – Akshay, who was six years old and Ajay, who had just turned three.

At the time that they met Vinod at Sukhna Lake car park, Srini and Shanti were on the lookout for someone to work for them as an orderly...who would be a sort of personal valet for Srinivasan, a general handyman around the house, and most importantly – someone whom they could entrust the children with when they were out of the house. Many persons had been interviewed, but none had come up to their expectations.

That is, until the incident with the camera. Instinctively, Srinivasan knew that they had found the person they were looking for. As for Vinod, it was as though he was being led by some unknown force..some mysterious motivation drawing him to this Madrasi family.

And so it was that Vinod joined the Srinivasan family. He was paid a sum of 400 Rupees a month, besides being given free board and lodge.

From the day he started work, he was an absolute hit with the children, and would keep them occupied for hours on end. For them, 'Vinod *bhaiyya*' was a super hero – who could fly kites, ride a bike, climb trees and do magic with cards.

He was also meticulous in his job and quick in learning all that was taught to him. Srinivasan realized that he had the potential to be much more than a menial servant, and when Vinod told him of his dream of becoming a graduate, he was more than willing to enrol him in a correspondence course to fulfil his ambition. Vinod was overwhelmed and grabbed the opportunity with both hands. Every night, after completing the chores for the day, he would sit and study until the wee hours of the morning.

The Srinivasans were posted to Agra after about a year, and he went along with them to the new place. In his quest to further his studies, he received tremendous encouragement and support from Srinivasan and Shanti, who now looked upon him as one of their family.

Three years later, he graduated from Delhi Open University. It was indeed the proudest moment of his life.

CHAPTER - 6

Although Vinod continued to work for the family, Srinivasan and Shanti knew that it was only a matter of time before he would leave and seek better prospects. At the same time, they were hesitant to bring up the topic, lest he felt that they were asking him to leave.

The matter was, in fact, resolved surprisingly easily, with Srinivasan receiving his posting orders from Agra to Bangalore. When they told Vinod about it, he hesitatingly told them that he had been planning to go back to Ludhiana for a while to visit his family, and thereafter to try and study for a Diploma in Management through evening school in Delhi. Obviously, he was thinking of taking up some employment in Delhi and continuing his studies.. although he did not spell it out, so as not to hurt their feelings. Srinvasan and Shanti were thrilled with the idea, and told him as much.

And so, after living with them for a little more than four years, Vinod was on his own again, but this time with a tidy sum of money in his pocket and – more importantly – a degree to his name.

He had not been to his home all these years, although he had thought of doing so several times. Perhaps he felt guilty running away, or perhaps he wanted to go back only when he had achieved something worthwhile. Whatever it was, he decided that he would go there now.

Although he had anticipated that his parents would have grown older in these four-odd years, it came as a terrible shock when he saw them. His father had become virtually blind, and had long since left his job at the factory. Now he just sat all day on the *charpoy* outside their hut, listlessly chasing the flies that buzzed around him. Vinod's mother had become even thinner than what he remembered of her, and her cough had become worse. But somehow, she still managed to carry on her pitiful trade of supplying tea and snacks every morning, rain or shine. His brother, now quite tall, was studying in the eighth class, and little Laila too had grown into a pretty young girl.

After the first awkward moments, the family had been overjoyed to see him, and plied him with so many questions, that he was hard-pressed to answer them. He had brought a woollen shawl for his father, a blue nylon saree with red flowers for his mother, a wind-sheeter for Vikas and a pair of tiny ear-rings for Laila. When he gave his mother five thousand Rupees, she was speechless: she had never seen so much money at one time in all her life! It was as though the Gods had finally heard her supplications, and after many years, there was some joy in the little hovel, and all of them revelled in the warmth of togetherness.

The happiness, though, was short-lived. When he told his parents that he was leaving for Delhi soon, they were heartbroken. But he had made up his mind much earlier to pursue his ambitions. Now, looking at the woeful condition of his family, his resolve only became stronger. If at all he wanted to help his family, he just had to get a decent job, and be able to support them financially for the rest of their life. He was also determined that Vikas should be able to study as much as he wanted. Then of course, there was the matter of keeping some money aside for his little sister's marriage.

Vinod stayed in Ludhiana for a week. When the day of departure finally arrived, the parting was painful. He tried his best to keep a brave face, especially when he hugged his frail mother good bye. He dutifully touched his father's feet, kissed his brother and sister, and with a final glance at his mother, walked out.

CHAPTER - 7

Delhi in the late sixties was not exactly a haven for job-seekers, what with literally thousands of migrants from the neighbouring states crowding the City. For the first two days after his arrival, Vinod lived in the New Delhi Railway Station – checking in his suitcase into the Left Luggage facility, and managing to sleep in the Waiting Room, after bribing the attendant. The daylight hours he spent searching for a job, returning tired and worn out as darkness fell. At the end of the second day, he had not found a job, and he could sense a feeling of desperation and defeat creeping in. What little money he had was also fast dwindling. It was only the thought of his family that motivated him not to give up.

His perseverance and determination paid off on the third day. He managed to get a job as a booking clerk cum supervisor in one of the numerous road transport companies in Chandni Chowk. The business was owned and run by a burly Sardar – Satnam Singh – who himself came from a family displaced by the Partition. That, and the fact that Vinod could read, write and speak English, went in his favour, and he was employed for a monthly salary of Rs. 2,000, which was actually on the lower side. But Vinod did not want to push his luck, especially when his employer graciously allowed him to put up in the godown, when Vinod told him that he had no place to stay.

Working hours were long, and there was hardly any rest throughout the day. If it was not writing 'Way Bills' for consignments, it was checking stuff that had come in, or going to the Traffic Check Post, if there was any problem with incoming trucks (which, incidentally, happened quite often, with the policemen at the Post invariably holding up the trucks unless *mamool* (bribe) was paid). Vinod learnt the job fast, and it was not long before he was practically handling the business single-handedly, much to his boss's admiration.

Once he settled into the routine, Vinod enrolled himself for a Diploma in Management, in a night college nearby. Every evening after closing time, he would hastily have a wash, and literally run to attend classes. In spite of all his efforts, there were days when he would miss sessions, because of some delay or the other at work. He bought himself the necessary books and religiously studied for at least two hours every night, immaterial of what time it was. It was all very tiring, but sheer will power kept pushing him towards his ultimate goal.

He tasted success in his endeavours in the month of July 1967, when he obtained a Diploma in Management. It was a moment that he had eagerly looked forward to, these past four years. Strangely, now that the moment had arrived, it somehow did not set off the euphoria that he had expected.

Vinod continued working for the Transport Company, where he had risen to the post of Manager. He was now drawing a salary of Rs. 10,000 of which he dutifully sent half to his mother. His family was now living in a *pucca* two-room house, and finally had enough money for his mother to give up her 'business' of tea and snacks. His father's vision too had been partially restored in his left eye after undergoing cataract surgery. Vikas was in his final year of College in Ludhiana, and Laila had just passed her Pre-University Examinations.

It was while working in the Transport Company that Vinod first toyed with the idea of starting his own business. It was a period when tourism was catching on in the Capital, and travel agencies were just coming on to the scene. Vinod saw a great potential in this and decided to try his hand. He applied for a loan from a Bank, and after a couple of months, it was sanctioned.

He finally took the plunge in 1969, after quitting his job with Satnam Singh. He had a reasonable amount of money saved from his earnings, which he now utilized to rent a tiny house with two small rooms, one in which he would stay and the other, which would be his office. After much struggle to procure a telephone connection, investing in a second-hand Remington typewriter and buying a weather-beaten almirah (from a budget furniture shop in Karol Bagh), he was ready for business. He named his Company 'Vitra Enterprises' – Vitra being the abbreviated form of Vinod Travels.

Vitra Enterprises opened its doors for custom on the auspicious day of Diwali in 1969.

CHAPTER - 8

The first year of business was the most difficult, as he had had no experience in the line, and had to learn the ropes mostly by trial and error. But by sheer grit, and instinctive business skills, he was able to make a small profit by the end of the second year. He managed to lease another office space, and employ an assistant, who was trained in the travel business.

During this time, he met Neelu, whom he would later marry. She was a Section Officer in the Department of Transport in the Delhi Administration, and whom Vinod had to interact with on a regular basis while getting various official clearances and permits.

The department was 'renowned' for its corrupt staff and bureaucratic hurdles, and Vinod was profoundly ignorant of these devious methods. He could still vividly remember his trepidation when he went to get the all-important NOC (No Objection Certificate) to start the agency. As with any Government department, his file was shunted from desk to desk, and he would desperately follow it, each time parting with money, but getting nowhere closer to the elusive, but vital, document.

It was on his sixth visit to the Department that he found himself in front of a young lady, in a deep blue salwar kameez, and with the most captivating eyes that he had ever seen. For a moment, he seemed to forget what he had come for, and stood staring into her eyes. This would have probably continued until eternity, had not the lady cleared her throat and asked him, "*Haan ji...aapko kya chahiye?*" (Yes Sir, what is it that you want?). The question snapped Vinod out of his reverie, and he managed to convey his requirement, albeit with much stuttering and stammering. At the end of his submission, he broke out in cold sweat, wondering how he was going to offer '*chai-pani*' (bribe) to a lady. As if sensing his discomfiture, she smiled, and asked him to leave his papers with her and return the next day.

Vinod promptly reported to the Department at 10:30 am the next day and went straight to her desk. He half expected that she would take her time coming around 11:00 am, as did most of the other staff. But to his surprise, she was already at her desk and had his file opened in front of her. He was now more or less convinced that he would have to fork out a hefty sum to this lady.. and this caused him extreme anxiety. She looked up from the file, and said, *"Kripya baithiye,"* (Please be seated), *"aapka* NOC *tayyar hain."* (your NOC is ready).

That was the start of the relationship between Vinod and Neelu. Every evening he would be at her office to pick her up on the ramshackle Lambretta scooter that he had bought, and they would go and sit in some park or the other, until it was time for her to go to her hostel in Munirka. She had also struggled through life, having lost her parents at a young age and growing up in the care of an elderly aunt.

It was not long before friendship turned to love and they decided to get married. He knew that no one from his family would be able to come, but still, he informed them by letter. With three friends from his side (which included his previous boss Satnam Singh), and an equal number from hers, Vinod and Neelu were married in the Arya Samaj on 18th May, 1973. She moved in with Vinod on the same day.

CHAPTER - 9

It is widely believed in India that a man's life or career would succeed or fail depending on the kind of luck and good fortune the wife (the *'Laxmi'* of the family) brings with her. In Vinod's case, it seemed as if Neelu was Goddess *Laxmi* personified. Literally, from the day that Neelu came into his life, Vitra Enterprises grew at a phenomenal pace and within a span of five years, had for its clients several 5-star hotels in Delhi and other major cities. The business had grown to such an extent that Vinod had shifted his offices to up-market Chanakyapuri, and now had a staff of eight working for him.

Success did not change Vinod's commitment to his family. He had bought a three bedroom flat in Ludhiana, where his parents and siblings lived in comfort beyond their wildest dreams. For himself and Neelu, Vinod had acquired two flats in Delhi, one in Greater Kailash (where they lived) and another in Safdarjung Enclave. Their first child was born in 1975 – a son, whom they named Akshay. After a gap of four years, they had a second child..a daughter this time, whom they named Shanti. It was Vinod's way of remembering the Srinivasans.

Vinod was a very loving husband and a devoted father, who enjoyed nothing better than just hanging around with his wife and children. He simply adored his wife and would take great pride in showing off her beauty and good taste to his friends. He was especially proud of the beautiful house she kept, and the lavish parties that she hosted.

Neelu, on her part, had stopped working when she was expecting her first child, and had not gone back thereafter. She was a very caring mother and a passionate wife, who revelled in her husband's success. Her only grouse in life was the frequent traveling that her husband did. Having grown up for the most part of her childhood sans parents, she would have liked him to spend more time with the children in their growing years. But she also knew that in this line of business, personal contact with clients and potential customers was of vital importance. So, just as much as she disliked his absence from home, she rationalized that this was a very small price to pay for the success and prosperity that they were enjoying.

CHAPTER - 10

It was 1987, and there was tremendous excitement in the air about the upcoming International Health Conference to be held in Bangalore in December that year. It was expected that delegates from more than fifty countries would be attending the conference and would be also visiting several cities in the country. The meeting was being touted as not only an important forum in the field of Medicare, but also as a great bonanza for tourism.

Vinod was very excited with the prospect of garnering a huge chunk of the travel requirements of the delegates. He had worked diligently for the past couple of months exploring and short listing the parties that he would target. He knew that such an opportunity came only once in a blue moon, and if he could project Vitra as a player of repute, the Company would well and truly be catapulted into the world of international travel agencies.

Much as he was looking forward to the success of this endeavour, he also had an iota of regret to contend with. Neelu and he had planned to take the children on a holiday to Rajasthan in July and take a ride on the fabulous Palace on Wheels train. Now he would not be able to go, as he would be required to travel to Bangalore. Perhaps for the first time since their marriage, Neelu seemed visibly upset that he was giving priority to business over family. But it soon passed, and she seemed her normal happy self, once it was decided that the trip would not be cancelled, but that she would take the children and travel to Rajasthan. Nevertheless, Vinod did feel that she should have been more sensitive to the issue, and not displayed petulance, especially in front of the children.

Neelu and the children left Delhi on the 6th of July, on a holiday that would keep them away for nearly three weeks. The children were highly excited, and Neelu too was caught up in the moment, and looked forward to having a great time. Vinod had been to the station to see them off, and honestly wished that he too could have gone along. He stood watching, until the train disappeared from sight, and slowly walked to his car and drove back to his office.

CHAPTER - 11

He was booked on the next day's morning flight of Indian Airlines to Bangalore.

As usual, there was a delay in the departure, and he felt a tinge of irritation, at coming to the airport so early and having to wait. However, a cup of strong coffee at the airport kiosk got him into a better mood and he settled down into one of the notoriously uncomfortable airport seats.

He was just reaching for the Times of India, tucked in his briefcase pouch, when he happened to glance at the opposite row of seats. He was not one to give more than a casual look at his fellow passengers, but on this occasion, something made him stare in awe. There, sitting opposite him, was the most beautiful woman that he had ever laid eyes on. She must have been looking at him too, because their eyes met. He quickly turned his face away, making a big show of searching for his newspaper, but, like iron filings being drawn to a magnet, his eyes went back to the woman, who, it appeared, had not taken her eyes off him. This time he held his gaze for a moment longer, and felt an immense surge of excitement surge through him. He guessed that she must have been around thirty, taller than the average Indian woman, and built like a super model. Her thick, black hair framed her beautiful face, her dark eyes hypnotic. She had the cutest turned-up nose that he had ever seen and full, sensual lips, which seemed to be permanently set in a mysterious smile.

Vinod forced himself to turn away..feeling utterly self-conscious and stupid. Here he was, forty-five years old, happily married for fourteen years with two grown up children and behaving like a frustrated teenager! He hoped that no one had noticed him and pretended to be immersed in his paper. Further embarrassment was avoided by the announcement of his flight. He got up, assiduously avoiding even the slightest glance towards her, and walked quickly towards the departure gate.

He boarded the plane, automatically acknowledging the plastic smiles and the *namastes* of the near-geriatric air hostesses. Shuffling through the entrance, he put his briefcase in the overhead bin and eased himself into his aisle seat in the Business Section.

As was his habit, he fastened the seat belt immediately, leaned back in his seat and closed his eyes. Already he had put the incident at the lounge out of his mind and was planning his strategy at the meeting that he was to attend in Bangalore at 3:00 pm. Being a frequent guest at the Hotel, he had been able to get his regular 7th floor room at the Oberoi, where the conference was scheduled to be held. He was looking forward to having a nice hot shower, followed by a bite at the Salad Bar, before getting down to business.

His thoughts were abruptly put on hold, when he heard a soft, sensual voice say, "Excuse me."

It was so deep and ethereal that he thought he was dreaming and did not react. But when he felt a light tap on his shoulder followed by a slightly louder "Excuse me," he quickly opened his eyes and looked straight into the same hypnotic eyes that he had seen in the departure lounge.

To say that Vinod got the shock of his life was the understatement of the century. In fact, he was so mesmerized, he just sat there gaping at this fantastic looking woman, who was now smiling at him, and saying, "Excuse me...I have the window seat."

"Oh," he said, "I am sorry," as he tucked in his legs as far as they would go and motioned for her to go through to her seat.

As she slid past him, he caught a whiff of the perfume that she was wearing..it was all at once heady, fragrant and...oh so subtle!

The flight finally got under way, and he settled in. He would have normally slept all through the flight, but for some strange reason, his mind was working overtime on the woman sitting next to him. He just could not help glancing in her direction, while pretending to adjust the air vent on the ceiling. As if on cue, she also half turned and looked directly into his eyes, smiling. He smiled back, and the ice was finally broken.

CHAPTER - 12

She told him her name was Sunaina, and that she was going to Bangalore to attend the same travel conference as him at the Oberoi. She was a free-lance reporter, covering the event for one of the local Delhi papers. She said that she was going to be staying at her cousin's place, as she had not been able to get a room in any of the good hotels.

By the time the flight was nearing Bangalore, he had told her his life story, and she seemed not only fascinated, but genuinely interested. For the first time in all these years, he regretted that this was not a longer flight!

They landed in Bangalore at about 11:30 am, and he went to his hotel in the car that was sent for him. He had offered to give her a drop, hoping that he could spend some more time with her, but she had insisted that she would take a cab.

Once he got to his room, Vinod showered and changed, and read through his presentation for the umpteenth time, making minor corrections here and there. By the time he was satisfied with the final result, it was close to 1:00 pm, and he slowly walked down the seven flights of stairs to the Salad Bar at the ground floor, trying his best to concentrate on what he was going to say. But, try as he did, he just could not help thinking about Sunaina..her voice, her eyes, her lips...

Vinod ate sparingly, as he did not want to feel sleepy at the meeting. He was tempted to have an ice cream but resisted the urge. Having finished his lunch, he moved across to the conference hall.

He looked around the room, hoping that he would see her sitting somewhere, but she was nowhere to be seen. Obviously, she had not arrived as yet. He realized that he was being utterly irrational, but for some unknown reason he was desperate to meet her again.

He looked at his watch and realized that he was clearly early. There were just a few tables that were occupied, and he walked over and sat at a table, from where he had an unobstructed view of the entrance. He must have sat for at least ten minutes, feeling very fidgety and on edge. Other delegates had come in and the hall was quickly filling up, with just a few minutes left for proceedings to begin. With one despondent, last look at the entrance, he forced his mind to concentrate on the business at hand and picked up his briefcase and put it on the table in front of him.

He had just taken out his presentation material, when he sensed – rather than saw – that she was standing beside him. "Hello again," she said, in the same sensuous voice, that sent shivers of excitement through his body. He felt like a clumsy teenager on his first date, the papers dropping from his hands. "Hello," he managed to say, his voice sounding croaky, even as he desperately tried to hold on to the loose sheets of paper, which were now beginning to fly in all directions.

"Oh...I'm really sorry, Vinod...looks like I startled you," she said, as she joined him on the floor, retrieving the papers. Presently they managed to pick up the last of them and straightened up.

He felt very hot and sweaty and hoped that she did not notice his discomfiture. He managed to give her a tenuous smile, wondering if he should invite her to sit at his table, at the same time, fearing her refusal. As if reading his mind, she looked straight into his eyes, pulled up a chair and sat right opposite him.

CHAPTER - 13

The meeting went on for nearly three hours, with delegates presenting their cases. Vinod too did so, when his name was called, and was well received.

All through, he was acutely aware of her close presence and her frequent glances at him. It was obvious that she found him as interesting as he found her. One part of his mind kept telling him that he was being extremely foolish and immature. After all, just what was he expecting to achieve by his irrational longing for her? It was not as though he was footloose and fancy-free, and a person given to flirting. On the contrary, he was a devoted family man, who, in all these years, had never strayed from the straight and narrow path. Yes...there had been women in his life, but all that was before he had met Neelu, and whom he had decided to marry. He was extremely proud of his character, and in fact boasted about it to his close friends, several of whom were given to gallivanting. Neelu too had implicit faith in him, and never had to doubt his single-minded devotion to her.

And now, after all these years, here he was, obviously attracted to another woman, who was also reciprocating his feelings. As much as the sober part of his mind was making him see reason, another part – which he did not even know existed – was goading him on to explore this new surge of emotions...this raw desire for a young, sexy, sensual woman, who was his to have, if he so desired.

His mind was in such turmoil, he did not realize that the meeting had concluded, until she reached across and touched his arm. "Hey, Vinod! Where are you?" she said, playfully tugging at his sleeve.

He came out of his reverie with a start. Looking around, he saw that most of the tables had emptied, and in fact it had become quite dark outside. He looked at his watch and saw that it was close to half past seven. She had not let go of his sleeve, when he turned towards her. He admired her long, sinuous fingers with beautifully shaped nails lightly holding the fabric, and slowly let his gaze travel upwards, over her silky-smooth hands, past her full breasts and her long, slender neck before coming to rest on her stunning face.

At that moment, he knew which part of his mind had won!

CHAPTER - 14

They moved to the bar, where she ordered wine, and he settled for beer.

It was truly amazing how comfortable they were in each other's company, given the fact that they had met barely six or seven hours earlier. She was an extremely interesting conversationalist, and widely read. She also had a subtle sense of humour, which he found delightfully refreshing.

By the time he had had his second beer, it was obvious that there was only one direction that the rest of the evening was going...towards his room! Sitting close to her, he gently put his arm around her and drew her to him.

She did not have to say the words, but her eyes conveyed it all. He slowly got up and she followed him. Hand in hand, they walked unsteadily to the elevator and reached the seventh floor. Once there, they all but ran through the corridor until they reached his room. He opened the room with unsteady hands and they melted into each other's arms as soon as they had stepped inside, tearing away their clothes in a frenzy of desire. Her exotic perfume filled his senses, and his excitement reached fever pitch.

He could not recall the time when his love-making had attained such heights. She was totally amazing and surprisingly strong, giving and demanding at the same time. When it was over, they lay on the bed, totally content, and completely satisfied.

After a while, they ordered some food from Room Service, and some more wine. While their order was arriving, they washed up and got into their clothes, the glow of their recent love-making still fresh on their faces.

The liquor arrived before the food, and they poured themselves a glass of wine each, playfully toasting each other and intertwining their arms while they drank. He could not take his eyes off her and marvelled at her beauty – admiring her flawless face and sculpted body. Several times he thought he would ask her whether she was married (perhaps to lessen the tinge of the guilt that he felt in his subconscious), but he never did so.. afraid that it might upset the relationship.

When the food finally arrived, they went at it with gusto – they had not realized how ravenously hungry they were.

If he was afraid that she would leave as soon as she had eaten, he need not have worried. Once the dishes had been taken away, she came and sat on the sofa, her legs tucked under her, and leaning on him. He tried to concentrate on the news on the TV, but found it impossible, with her head against his face, and the erotic fragrance of her perfume in his nostrils.

If their first time of love-making had been like a tsunami, the second had been tender, loving and unhurried. This time around, Sunaina had slowly taken off her clothes, one piece at a time, gently swaying and gyrating as if to some mysterious, exotic music. Once she was completely naked, she stretched out her arms, beckoning him to come to her. She then proceeded to strip him down, touching and teasing him all the way. Once they got into bed, they had been gentle with each other, exploring and enjoying the warmth of their bodies, before dissolving in an ocean of bliss. Both had fallen asleep almost immediately, her head on his shoulder, and arm across his chest.

It was long past midnight that she had once again kindled his desire. At first, he thought he was dreaming, when he felt soft fingers arousing him. He slowly opened his eyes and looked at her smiling, her lips brushing his cheeks. She kissed him full in the mouth, her tongue inflaming him once again. He reached out and tried encircling her in his arms, but she teasingly moved away from him and sat on the sofa, laughing. She was totally naked, and beckoned to him with her index finger, a look of primeval passion in her eyes.

He was powerless in her gaze, and clumsily dragged himself off the bed.

She had poured two glasses of wine and offered one to him. He shook his head and said "No thanks," as he was not a heavy drinker, and he had already had a couple of beers and two glasses of wine. But when he saw that his refusal to drink had upset her, he accepted the glass, bringing the most beautiful smile to her lips.

He did not remember much after the drink, except that they had made love once again.

EPILOGUE

Vinod tried to look at his watch again. He could not see the time..in fact, he could not even see the watch. He slowly propped himself on his elbows, and shook his head, trying to clear the fog. The movement of his head brought on more throbbing, and he winced in pain. But he still could not see the watch. Had he taken it off last night before going to sleep? He tried remembering but drew a blank on that score. No..he would never have taken off the watch..he never did – not from the time that Neelu had given it to him on their tenth wedding anniversary. He even wore it while bathing..after all it was an Omega, and water-resistant up to 100 metres.

Thinking of the watch being water-resistant again brought into focus the sound of running water in the bathroom. It had now been going on for more than ten minutes. He wondered just how long Sunaina was going to be in the bath.

He swung his legs down from the bed, and sat up, totally naked, trying to orientate himself. His head felt as if it was going to explode, and he held it with both hands. Slowly, very slowly he looked around. He could see light streaming from the bathroom and realized that the door was not shut. He smiled..obviously Sunaina had left the door open for him to join her in the bath! What a woman!

"Hey Sunaina, you naughty girl," he called, as he stumbled to his feet. "Hey..I'm coming to get you!" he called out as he looked for his slippers.

There was no answer from the bathroom: just the sound of water flowing. He felt sudden fear – fear that Sunaina had had an accident..maybe she had slipped and hit her head and was unconscious… "Sunaina," he called again forgetting about his slippers and charging toward the bathroom. He felt unsteady on his feet and had to hold on to the dresser and the wall as he tried to reach the door.

As he entered the bathroom, he immediately looked in the bath tub, and was very relieved to see it empty. He reached across and shut off the water in the shower, bringing on a ghostly quietness. "Sunaina," he called again, but just silence greeted his voice.

Anxiety was rapidly giving way to alarm, as he shuffled out of the bathroom. He stood for a moment, trying to collect his thoughts. His head was pounding, as he looked around and caught a glimpse of himself – stark naked – in the full-length mirror on the dresser. He sat on the dresser stool, and took a deep breath, trying to clear his head and focus his eyes.

He knew that the first thing that he had to do was to get into some clothes. He vaguely remembered that Sunaina had thrown them on the chair next to the television. He looked in the direction of the television but could not see any item of clothing. He got up from the stool and ran to the chair near the television, frantically searching all around. But he could not find his clothes.

By now he was breathing heavily and in a state of total confusion. He went to the small built-in wardrobe, where he had hung his other clothes. Yanking open the sliding door, he looked inside, only to be greeted by empty hangers and bare shelves. Desperately, he opened the drawer beneath the wardrobe, where he had kept his suitcase. It was empty.

He went back to the bed and sat down, fighting the waves of panic that engulfed his mind. The reality of the situation slowly sank in...he had been 'had.' It was now plain to him that Sunaina had spiked his wine with some drug, and once he had passed out, walked away with everything – wristwatch, clothes, wallet, credit cards, suitcase...even his slippers.

He did not know for how long he sat on the bed..his mind had long ceased to think rationally. He only knew that it was all over..his family life...his career..his standing in society...everything was over.

He slowly went to the writing table next to the dresser and took out a single sheet of paper from the hotel stationery. Taking the ball pen from the stand, he wrote just two words on the paper: 'Sorry Neelu.'

With utmost care, he folded the paper and kept it on the table, using the pen stand as a paper weight.

He then walked across to the large French window and opened it. Taking a deep breath, he closed his eyes and stepped out.

ALL IN THE MIND

PROLOGUE

There it was again...that eerie sound, as if someone was walking barefoot on the wooden floor of the upstairs bedroom.

But then, it just could not be...there was no one upstairs.

There had been no one there since the past nine weeks when his wife had committed suicide, unable to bear the anguish. In his mind he could still hear her heart-breaking groans of pain, brought about by the horrors of cancer. She had suffered greatly, and he had suffered with her.

He could see her in his mind, the wasted, depleted shell of her formal self, crying for release from the misery that had been her life for the last thirty months. But she had been strong in her resolve...she would not let the dreadful disease that had turned the once-beautiful, energetic human being into the twisted, terrible, grotesque image (virtually a living corpse), consume her without a fight. He had prayed every single day that she had suffered...prayed that she would die, and finally get relief from her agony.

And then one day, it had indeed happened...the empty bottle of painkillers lying next to her pillow bore mute testimony to her final conscious act of desperation and release.

****

He sat alone in the darkness, holding firmly to the half empty glass in his hand, hoping that the power failure would be short and the lights would come back on soon. He slowly raised the glass to his lips, and in one frenzied movement, tilted his head back and gulped down his fourth drink, instinctively feeling for the bottle of Peter Scot on the table to refill his glass…this was the only way that he could cope with the emptiness that was his life now. It was also the only way that he could cope with the fears that haunted him..fears of the dark and the unknown, fears of spirits and ghosts.

Trying to calm his nerves, he took another long swig of the whisky, grimacing as the raw spirit burned down his throat. "No..it cannot be," he told himself for the millionth time, "there is nothing to be afraid of. Ghosts are what myths are made of..mere stories that, as children, one longs to hear – and at the same time, dread."

He wished that he could build up enough courage to climb the stairs and once and for all convince himself that the weird sounds that seemed to be coming from there were all figments of his own frightened imagination..a creation of his own terrified mind. But he knew that it was no use..he would never be able to do that..it had always been so.

The whisky made his mind wander..to go back in time..to revisit the horrors that had been tormenting him from the time he could remember. It was a drama which was for ever being replayed..a drama without end.

****

He could recall the events of that fateful day thirty-two years ago, as though it had all happened just yesterday. It was a day that would change his personality..for ever.

He and his three friends were playing 'Ghostbusters.' He was the youngest of the lot, and in some ways, the bravest. It was around nine o'clock at night, and the four of them slowly moved towards the dark, desolate house at the corner of the field, where they used to play cricket in the daytime.

There were several stories doing the rounds about this lonely house, which had been nick-named *'Bhoot Bangla'* or Ghost House. It was variously rumoured that many years ago the occupants of the house had been brutally murdered, and that to this day the spirits of one or more of the unfortunate victims were still haunting the house. Another story frequently bandied about was that a woman had committed suicide in the house, and that she would appear as an apparition every night, slowly moving from one room to another. Whatever the truth, it was a fact that no one had ever occupied the house for the past several years. The last occupants – a burly *'Sardar'* doctor from Patiala, his advocate wife and two young children – had stayed there barely two months, until one day they abruptly moved out. It was not known exactly why they left, but it only added to the mysterious tales about the house.

And now...the 'Fearless Four' as they called themselves, were determined to find out the truth about *Bhoot Bangla*.

They had planned their little adventure for several days, huddled together secretly in the tiny room which was their 'headquarters'...their Den. They had not even told their parents about their intent, fearing instant repudiation, and had waited impatiently for several days for the opportunity to put their plan into action, each passing day only increasing their levels of excitement. Finally, such an opportunity did present itself, when their parents had decided to take in a late-night movie at the Liberty Theatre, leaving the four boys together. This was what the Fearless Four had waited for so long, and they were not going to pass it up, although the night was extremely dark, and there was a distinct threat of a thunderstorm breaking out at any time.

As soon as they were alone, all of them ran to the Den, and hurriedly armed themselves with the stuff they had stashed away – two cricket bats, one hockey stick and a torch.

The plan called for entering the house through the unlocked front door, going through each room, and finally emerging from the rear door. They had reconnoitred the area around the house several times during daylight hours, and so were quite familiar with the layout – the latched wooden front door, the tightly shut wooden windows and half broken rear door, hanging by its rusted hinges.

The breeze had picked up in strength as they approached the house and the first drops of rain fell; a streak of lightning flashed, followed by the rumble of thunder. The flash of lightning had briefly illuminated the house, making it look even more ethereal. For a moment all four of them stopped, as if hoping that one of them would say "Let's go back," and they could scramble back to the warmth and sanctuary of the Den. But no one uttered a word..to do so would have been to invite the ridicule of the others and be ignominiously referred to as 'the chicken' for all time to come! The moment passed, and they moved ever closer towards the house. By the time they were close to the house, the rain had increased in intensity, and the wind was gusting wildly.

He was in the lead, holding the torch, its beam making random patterns on the cobbled pathway that led to the door. He was barely able to control his excitement, as he gingerly opened the latch by the light of his torch and pushed at the ancient door. It seemed to be stuck, and would not open. He handed over the torch to his friend behind him and pushed at the door with all his strength, but it would not budge. Just as he was about to give up, it suddenly burst open and he fell head first into the darkness inside, and the door slammed shut behind him!

At that moment, a tremendous peal of thunder rent the air, seeming to shake the very ground where the three boys stood and watched their friend hurtling into the dark chasm and the door slamming shut. That was it! As one, the three of them turned about and ran, screaming in panic, their only thought being to reach the safety of their homes.

He was winded by the fall but did not seem to be injured. It was pitch dark, and for a moment he was totally disoriented. He shouted to his friends to open the door and come in with the torch. There was no response. He shouted again, as loud as he could..only to be met with silence, except for the noise of the rain and the howling of the wind. "Don't panic," he told himself, "there is nothing to be afraid of." He yelled once more, slight desperation creeping into his voice, but could only hear the echo of himself from the darkness all around him.

Slowly, realization dawned on him that his friends had abandoned him and run away..he was now all alone, in this dark, scary house. He felt his way around him, crawling on all fours on the damp and sticky floor, desperately trying to reach for the door. After what seemed an eternity, he managed to touch the wooden door, and heaved a sigh of relief. Knowing that he would soon be getting out, a sudden wave of anger and disgust for his three companions swept over him. Not even in his wildest dreams had he ever expected them to desert him. The great times that they had had in the Den, the vows of brotherhood they had taken, the many times that he had lied for them......vivid memories flashed in his mind, as though an 'instant replay' button had been pressed in his brain. He swore at that moment that he would get even...oh yes, he would surely get even with them, if it was the last thing he ever did!

He slowly ran his hands over the door, trying to find the handle. He did not find anything. Maybe, he thought, he had missed going over the entire door in the all-pervasive darkness. He once again put both his palms flat against the rough wooden surface, and systematically groped for any protuberance that he could use to yank the door open. With growing alarm, he realized that there was no handle or knob...that he would never be able to open the door.

He sat leaning back against the door, trying to calm himself. After all, in a couple of hours, his parents would return from the movie, and then this entire misadventure would be over. Thoughts of his parents made him shudder at what the consequences would be when he returned home...he was surely in for some severe punishment. Perhaps they would even reconsider the idea of getting the new bicycle that they had promised him...oh God...how thrilled he had been that he would soon be riding around and showing off the blue BSA bicycle, with its 3-speed gears and Miller dynamo. And now...now he was sure he could kiss the bike good bye. Once again he heaped curses on his so-called friends and their inexcusable behaviour.

The heavy rain had eased up, and with it was gone the rumble of thunder, and the howling of the wind. The silence seemed to have crept up on him, as he suddenly realized that he could hear his heart thumping. He felt cold in his drenched clothes, and for the first time, very frightened. What if the stories about the haunting were true? What if there was actually a ghost of the dead woman? The rational part of his mind told him that these were just stories and wild gossip..but somewhere inside him, the fear of the unknown pushed him beyond rational thinking, and he trembled. He shut his eyes tightly..not that with his eyes open he could see anything in the total inky blackness that surrounded him. How he wished that he had his faithful torch with him…

How long he sat with his eyes closed, he did not know..time had lost all meaning for him, as he forced his mind to think up excuses that he would give to his parents, and somehow convince them just how remorseful he was. Maybe his father would give him a good belting..but even that would be worth it, if only they would not refuse to get him his bicycle. On the other hand, maybe his parents would just be thankful that he was alright, and not punish him at all..but this possibility was so preposterous, that the very idea brought a smile to his lips…

And then he heard – in fact sensed – the sound that sent a shiver down his spine. Someone (or something) was moving across the room very close to him. It sounded as though someone wearing a loose garment was walking across the room…the unmistakable rustle of the cloth and the supple 'flap-flap' sound of bare feet on the floor. He held his breath until he felt his lungs would burst.

Then, as suddenly as he had heard the sound, all was quiet and the silence once more enveloped him. He let out his breath very slowly, his chest aching from the tension. He was sweating in spite of the cold and could feel the droplets of perspiration flowing down his face, tickling his neck... but he dared not move his hands to wipe them away. He sat absolutely still, slowly getting a grip on himself..he desperately wanted not to believe what he had just experienced and tried to convince himself that it was only his imagination playing tricks.

There was only one way to find out..he just HAD to open his eyes. He mustered up all his courage and willed himself to raise his tightly shut eyelids, when...oh God...there was that sound again..and this time, whatever it was, seemed to move so close to him that he could feel a movement of breeze as it passed by. His eyes remained firmly shut.

Then he distinctly heard the sound of a chair being dragged back.

He fainted.

EPILOGUE

There was that same sound again, only louder this time. He knew that he was not imagining it. He felt himself panicking..he was breathing hard and sweating. He wished he had kept the torch close at hand. The sound was now moving closer..he could perceive it coming near the head of the stairway...

He tried to scream in his horror, but no sound emerged from his throat. He reached out to get the whisky bottle, desperately wanting a drink. He felt a sudden shooting pain engulf his chest. He couldn't breathe..he tried to stand up, but only succeeded in toppling the table, the bottle falling down and shattering into smithereens, the whisky splashing on the floor. He lunged forward in the darkness, trying to hold on to the chair..the wall..anything. The pain was excruciating and his eyes rolled up. He tripped on the fallen table and fell to the floor..his wide-open eyes looking sightlessly up the stairway.

He did not move..he was dead.

A GASEOUS TALE

It all started with a low rumble – and no – I am not talking about the rumble from thunderclouds, or even the rumbling of a freight train as it hurtles across the countryside. The rumble I mention was much closer home, in fact deep within the confines of my abdomen. Yes...you guessed it: it was my beleaguered bowels sending out a strong, low frequency, high intensity signal – an SOS, if you will – that all was not well in the old tummy and attached pipelines.

I must confess that I was totally stumped at this sudden upheaval of the innards, for it came upon me with no forewarning. Since it was so sudden and unexpected, I brushed it aside, and thought no more of it. That is, until a couple of hours later when it recurred, but this time with greater intensity, much like a deep depression strengthening into a cyclonic storm. This time around, I did not think it proper to dismiss it too lightly, and without further ado, swallowed a generous helping of the sweet, pepperminty, pink, antacid syrup, which my wife kept always at hand, swearing that it helped her cope with her arthritis.

Amazingly, the rumbling stopped as suddenly as it had started, and at that moment, a very profound thought crossed my mind, 'God's in Heaven and all's well with the world.'

Alas...the euphoria was to be very short-lived, indeed. In a matter of hours, the 'tempest-in-my tummy' had intensified into a severe cyclonic storm, and I could feel intense pressure building up in my viscera, with the 'eye of the storm' centred below my navel, with tsunami-like waves swirling within my abdominal cavity, causing severe discomfort. Added to that, it seemed that a 'volcano' had formed somewhere beneath my diaphragm, and it was not only spewing large amounts of gas upwards in the form of loud burps, it was also ejecting copious quantities of utterly vile, noxious and foul-smelling vapour via my nether orifice. I believe the medical term for this is 'flatulence.'

Although, I did feel a bit shaken, but not stirred (*a la* J Bond), I could (perhaps) have 'ridden the storm,' so to speak. But my wife would have none of it...mainly because she was convinced that our bedroom smelt like Vijay Mallya's brewery, where the rotting molasses had not been cleared by the striking BBMP workers for a week. And so, with much grinding and gnashing of teeth (and the constant rumble), I was finally forced to seek the services of a doctor.

Having reached the clinic precisely at the appointed time, I was, as usual, subjected to the mandatory thirty-odd minutes wait before I was summoned into the august presence of the guardian of the Hippocratic oath. On entering the room, I immediately realized that the wait was well worth the while, because the good doctor turned out to be petite, pretty and perky. Oh.. and before the reader gets other ideas, I may as well add that it was a 'she' who smiled a welcome, as I entered. Of course, being of the opposite gender, I *post-haste* attempted a young Tom Cruise look!

After the customary preliminary questions on my past life and persistent, intrusive inquiries into my present life-style, we finally got to the rumbling tummy bit. Having ordered me into assuming a supine position on the examination table, she opened my mouth, looked at my tongue, peered into my eyes and poked at my neck and throat. Just when I was beginning to feel like a dead *seer* fish in Russell Market, in one swift move, she lifted my shirt, pulled aside my banian, and got down to the serious business of checking out the recalcitrant part of my anatomy. And to say that she went at it with a vengeance would be a gross understatement – the way she palpated my stomach brought to my mind vivid images of dough being kneaded in a Punjabi *dhaba*!

Mind you, all this time I was (literally) holding my breath, hoping that the aforementioned 'volcano' did not decide to spew gas southwards – which I firmly believe would not only have resulted in the doctor fainting, but in a general evacuation of the clinic! After a final *coup de grâce*, where she practically did a hand-stand on my navel, she was finished, and asked me to disembark from the table.

Sitting across from her, I waited with bated breath to hear her learned diagnosis. Myriad awful thoughts raced through my mind, most of them courtesy

Google. What if I had ulcers? What if it was a tumour? What if..I never got to finish that thought as I was shaken out of my cyber-diagnosis when she announced with great confidence, "You have gas."

Oh my God...did I miss the exclamation of 'EUREKA?' It was at the tip of my tongue to say, "Thank you Doctor Archimedes!" but I wisely held my tongue.

What if she had told me that I was pregnant???

THE TRAIN CALLED LIFE

The single platform at Gummidipundi Station was deserted...except for a few stray dogs lying listlessly in the heat, occasionally chasing away the flies that kept bothering them. The rickety shack (that passed off as a tea stall) which stood next to the Station Master's office had closed within minutes of the departure of the passenger train to Maripur, some four hours ago. Now it would be open for business just before the train to Madras (for which I was waiting) would arrive. Presently, the train was running three hours late, but it was quite possible that it would be delayed even more. The only indication of its progress was the chalk-written notice on the blackboard near the Station Master's office – which also doubled as the ticket counter as well as the Communications Centre with its Morse-code Telegraph machine.

The only Waiting Room in the station was empty. However, the room was unbearably hot and terribly oppressive, since it had an asbestos roof, poor ventilation and no fans. I had, therefore, opted to sit on one of the three benches on the platform, where the occasional breeze brought momentary respite. In any case, there were no other passengers, or even porters to disturb me.

I had come to this God-forsaken town two days ago, having been sent by the District Collector to do a survey of the area. There was talk that the State Government was planning to start a cement factory at Gummidipundi in the next 5-year plan. How far this would become reality was anybody's guess, but my boss, being an ambitious sort, wanted to have all the facts and figures ready at hand, should the State authorities suddenly descend for an 'on-spot' study.

The past two days had been a real test of endurance for me, but thanks to the fact that I knew Tamil (the local language), I had somehow managed to survive. The Head Master of the only school in the town had been kind enough to allow me to sleep in his office, and even sent me meals at the appropriate times. Now, after two days, I had managed to complete what I had come to do and was returning to my Headquarters in Madras. If things did not go terribly wrong, I would be with my wife Mythili and my baby daughter Meghna by lunch tomorrow.

The thought of my family made my mind wander from the present. Memories of what Mythili and I had gone through in the past three years or so came flooding back. They were not pleasant memories, given the fact that we had taken the extreme step of eloping and getting married.

My parents (to whom I was the only child) were rigidly orthodox Brahmins. Although not well off, they considered themselves 'upper middle class,' and with it went the unwritten rules of how and where and whom their son should marry. Moreover, my father had slaved as an Upper Division Clerk for over thirty years, had no savings to speak of, but somehow managed to give me a reasonably good education, and to complete a Degree in Civil Engineering. Naturally, their hopes ran high that I would marry a girl of their choice, from a family of their choosing. In the bargain, they were also 'banking' on the hope that I would bring in substantial dowry, which would be a kind of 'financial insurance' in their old age.

But, true to the old adage 'Man proposes, but God disposes,' all their well-laid plans had gone awry, when I told them that I had found myself someone whom I wanted to marry. It was not so much that they were averse to me finding my soul mate..it was just that Mythili was not from 'our caste!' The fact that she was not a Brahmin, did not matter in the least to me..but to my parents it was totally not acceptable.

This had led to significant problems, and took a very serious turn, when my mother threatened to commit suicide, if I persisted with my intentions. That was when I realised that 'family' as I had known up to that point in time was over, at least as far as I was concerned.

****

At around 3 pm, I must have dozed off, sitting on the platform bench in the sweltering heat. Perhaps it was the weather, or I may have been extremely tired mentally, for I experienced the weirdest dream that I have ever had. It was not a scary dream, but for the life of me, I just could not figure out how I could have become so philosophical in my thinking.

I distinctly remember hearing an announcement on the loudspeaker at the Station, 'Your attention please..28 Down, Life Express is arriving on Platform number seven.' In my dream, I was there, watching the train coming in, the engine spewing out vast quantities of steam. There was a great squealing of brakes, as the train pulled into the platform. With a massive sigh from the engine, it finally came to a stop.

How much like life, I thought..after a long journey, reaching the final destination with a sigh..perhaps a sigh of relief and contentment? Or even a sigh of sadness and despondency...depending on whether it had been a life of happiness and fulfilment or one of sadness and futility.

As in life, most train journeys begin on a high note, with many hopes and aspirations..but before the journey commences, a vast chain of events has to happen, before the train can set off for its destination.

Each bogie corresponds to the various stages in life...childhood, adolescence, adulthood and old age. Even a few hours before the journey begins, the bogies would be standing around aimlessly – without purpose or direction. They would then be moved in sequence and given direction by shunting engines, much like what parents, teachers and mentors do in the life of an individual – until finally, a train is formed, facing in the right direction, and awaiting the 'signal' to move. And once the signal is given, the journey begins. As in life, one never knows if it will be a smooth ride, or one beset with delays, obstacles and unforeseen events.

As the train leaves the station, it moves at a slow pace, as if reluctant to pick up speed and charge into the next stretch of the journey...very much like one is hesitant to shed the comforts of home and family and take a step into independence and adulthood. However, there is no stopping the journey now, and it moves along, passing villages, towns...hills and forests...very much like the journey of youth...learning new things, meeting new people, growing in stature.

After a while, the train settles into a rhythm...the way life settles into a pattern for most people, most of the time.

There are times when the train changes tracks...momentarily swaying and rattling. Then in a short while, it settles on the new track and continues its journey. In life too, changes occur – changes in jobs...changes in location...even changes in life partners. Most of the time, there is some disturbance in the routines, but generally, life settles into the new pattern and moves on.

On rare occasions, the train derails...chaos prevails and the journey comes to a grinding halt. So too in life, sudden and unexpected events occur – sometimes even death – throwing everything out of gear, causing physical, mental and emotional trauma.

****

I don't know how long I had been asleep, but I was harshly jolted awake by the unmistakable din of people scurrying and screaming to each other. Added to this were the trademark sounds of a typical Indian Railway Station...the veritable cacophony of vendors selling snacks, books, toys, tea, hand fans, and a whole plethora of items which the traveller may require. It was as though the once silent, dreary (and almost dead) station had suddenly come alive.

I looked around, and saw that it was dark. The platform lights had come on, and I noticed that the stray dogs too had woken up and gone away and were nowhere to be seen. Fortunately, there was a loudspeaker, just above where I was sitting, and it suddenly came to life, giving me a start. I strained to make out the tinny announcement... 'Your attention please..23 Up Madras Express from Bangalore is arriving on Platform Number 1.'

I was up in a jiffy..stretching myself and picking up my battered suitcase, ready to push my way through the hordes of people scrambling to board the train. My dream was over..now I had to continue with my life's journey!

ALBERT PINTO KO KYUN GHUSSA AATA HAIN -1
(OR WHY ALBERT PINTO GETS ANGRY-1)

Hello there! My name is Albert Pinto. I am 45 years old and am presently employed as a traveling salesman for Freezee Ice Creams. I have never married and live in a tiny house all by myself in Dadar. I make just enough money to live...or should I say, 'exist'? I have no major vices (not because I am a saint – but because I just cannot afford to have any!) other than being short-tempered – or at least that is what my friends tell me.

I have always been interested in Hindi movies..no, not in watching them, but in their names.

Have you ever noticed how names of Bollywood movies are interwoven into a bizarre pattern? I, for one, am absolutely convinced that an uncanny relationship exists between Hindi movie titles and my miserable life.

You probably think that I am nuts. However, I believe that your opinion would change after you read my story.

My fascination with names of Hindi movies goes a long way back...from when I was around twenty. But it was only **Bees Saal Baad**, when I was on **The Train** from **Bombay to Goa** that I decided to seriously explore the common **Dor** that runs through the titles and my life.

My father was a Post master..a **Dak Babu**, and as a child I grew up in Calcutta (now Kolkata). We lived in a small house at **36 China Town**, which was situated just a stone's throw away from the old **Bhoot Bangla**, which was **House No. 44**. The story went that many years ago, a **Major Saab** and his wife used to live there. His name was **Velu Nayakan** and had been a highly decorated **Soldier** who had taken part in the Chinese **Yudh** of 1962. He had even been awarded the **Freaky Chakra** for his bravery against the **Dushman**. Since he and his wife did not have any children, and their house was huge, they had a **Paying Guest** – a strapping young man named **Omkara** – staying with them. He was not only a tenant, but an odd-job man.

Things went well for **Ek Saal** or so, but Omkara was a **Loafer**, and lusted for the Major's wife, who was quite a **Dream Girl**. The Major was a hopeless **Joru Ka Gulam** who loved his wife **Dil Se** and always boasted "**Meri Biwi Ka Jawab Nahin**." So, on that terrible **Black Friday**, when he saw Omkara playing with his wife's **Dupatta**, his **Krodh** was unstoppable. Being a **Sainik** (and a **Commando** to boot), he could see only **Ek Hi Rasta** out of this **Pyar Mein Twist**. Yelling like a **Junglee**, he called Omkara a **Namak Haraam**, and a **Namak Halaal**, and instantly pronounced a sentence of **Mrityudand** on this **Doosra Aadmi**. Taking out his **Pistol** (which he had picked up from the **Border** during **Mission Kashmir**), he quickly loaded six **Kartoos** into it, and shot his **Biwi No.1** and her paramour, before turning the gun on himself. Thus, it was a tragic end for the **Sahib, Biwi Aur Gulam**.

From that day onwards, it was said that **Kabhie-Kabhie** on dark moonless nights, one could hear the **Boom** of a gun and see a **Bhoot** walking around. As a child, I was mortally scared to cross the **Sadak**, and go towards the haunted house, although **Maa** repeatedly told me, "**Darna Mana Hai**." The one time that I did muster up enough courage to go close to that house at night, I mysteriously tripped and fell into a big puddle of **Water**. But that is another story.

Around this time, we had a **Padosan** who had a young **Beti**, who I thought was very **Khoobsurat**. Her name was **Roshni** and we used to spend the hot, humid Calcutta afternoons playing endless games of **Hu Tu Tu**. Sometimes I would pull her around in a small cart, pretending to be a **Rikshawalla**. On other days, we used to go up to **Howrah Bridge.** I still remember that I used to travel on a **Half Ticket** in the tram, because I had not yet turned **Dus**. We would stand on the bridge and watch the **Calcutta Mail**, or the **Bhopal Express** chugging out of **Platform** number six. If we were feeling hungry, we would eat **Kuch Khatti, Kuch Meethi** from the push-cart vendor with the filthy hands, or some sweet **Supari** from the tiny shop next to the **Traffic Signal**. Sometimes I feel that those were the happiest days of my life...no **Page 3**, no **99.9 FM**, and no twenty-nine **Flavors** of ice cream.

****

Growing up brought the painful realization that good things don't last forever. Although Roshni and I became very close over the years, her father, who was a *Professor,* clearly did not approve of me, whom he considered a bit of a *Gambler* and an irresponsible *Khiladi*. No amount of *Boot Polish* on my shoes, or sedate *Black* ties around my neck could change his *Nafrat* for me. After much *Koshish*, I realized that all my *Salaam Namaste* to her *Daddy* was of no avail. In his eyes, I would always be *Shri 420*. Clearly, Roshni and I had reached the *Do Raha* of our lives, and it was highly *Asambhav* that we could ever be *Hamsafar* in our *Zindagi*.

It was then that I decided to move to Delhi in search of a job. But after more than a month of drifting like a *Kati Patang*, I was still *Mr. Bechara* and desperate. I did not have a *Khote Sikkey* in my pocket, having lost my tattered wallet to some *Pocket Maar* near India Gate. It was for the first time that I felt like a *Refugee* in *Mother India*, and would have gladly taken up a job as a *Bawarchi* or even a *Coolie*.

Just when I was thinking of going back to Calcutta, *Achanak* my *Kismat* changed, when I met *Anand*, who was working as a *Guide* at the Delhi Zoo. We literally bumped into each other...he was backing away from a runaway snake named *Nagin*, and I was walking backwards, staring longingly and hungrily at the bananas being fed to a chimp called *Mr. India*. For some strange reason, it was a *Dosti – Friends Forever* relationship between Anand and me from that moment on, and he got me a job as his assistant. We soon became like **Bhai-Bhai**, and I moved in with him, sharing the small house that he lived in, opposite to **Delhi Heights**.

It was while living here, that I saw **Anamika**. She lived on the **Teesri Manzil** of the mansion next to our house and was always dressed in tight **Jeans**. I was intrigued by her beauty, and one day, I heard her saying hello to Anand. Oh...what **Sur**... what **Taal** in her voice! It was as sweet as honey and as mellow as **Chocolate**. I knew at that moment that I had lost my **Dil** to this lovely creature.

I later asked Anand, "**Woh Kaun Thi?**" He told me her name, and that she was the daughter of **Mr. Natwarlal**, who was also the local **Don**. This was quite obvious, since their building had a **Deewar** surrounding it, which was at least ten feet high. The huge gates were always closed and secured with a massive **Zanjeer** and there was a big **No Entry** board in front. There was also this giant of a watchman, dressed in **Khakee** uniform who could have passed off for a **Pahelwan**. In fact, I had nicknamed him **Eklavya – The Royal Guard**.

I was desperate to meet Anamika, thinking about her **Raat Aur Din**. I pleaded with Anand on several occasions to arrange a **Chhotisi Mulakat** with her, but he just would not hear of it. He gave all sorts of excuses – from saying that they were **Oonche Log** – to warning me of the terrible **Risk** involved in such a venture. It slowly became obvious to me that Anand was quite a **Chuppa Rustam**, and also himself very much in love with her. But I was very **Ziddi**, and being a *Baazigar* by nature, made up my mind that this *Ek Phool Do Mali* situation just had to stop. I kept telling myself, "*Jo Jeeta, Woh Sikandar*" and spent all my waking hours making *Chamatkar* plans. *Uff...Yeh Mohabbat*!! Deep inside me, I knew that if I had to have any chance of declaring my *Amar Prem* to my *Guddi*, I would have to become *Hero No.1* in her beautiful *Aankhen*.

After much thought, I hit upon a great plan. If I could rescue her from some *Gunda*, she would definitely say to me, "*Tumsa Nahin Dekha*," and there would certainly be a *Monsoon Wedding* by and by.

Getting an unsavoury character in *Aaj Ka Gunda Raj* was no problem. During my days of pounding the *Footpath* in search of a job, I had met *Munnabhai*, a minor *Gangster* who specialized in petty crime and assorted *Hera Pheri*. Some claimed he was into *Blackmail* also. We still kept in touch once in a while, and I found him to be quite a nice guy, whose only *Paap* was being poor. My plan called for Munnabhai to waylay Anamika on the *Road* and snatch her necklace. I would then appear, and accost the *Jewel Thief*, who would take to his heels. Needless to say, Anamika and I would become *Jodi No.1* shortly thereafter.

I toyed with the idea of acquiring a scooter, on which to carry my future *Dulhan* away, but quickly discarded the plan. No. A two-wheeler just wouldn't do – indeed she might consider it an insult and cast me aside as a *Lafanga Langur*. There was no choice...I just HAD to get a car.

It took me a few days to locate what I needed. It was an old Fiat car, which in its prime had proudly borne the number *Taxi No. 9211*. Now, it was old and decrepit, barely managing to move..its paint peeling off, and springs popping out of the seats. But, since a *Bhikari* cannot afford to be choosy, I bought it and drove it around, shutting my ears to the derisive remarks of *Chalti Ka Naam Gaadi*, from all and sundry.

Finally, THE DAY arrived, when I was to do my 'rescue' act. I parked my car at the corner and sat *Chupke Se*, watching in the rear view *Sheesha* for Anamika to emerge. After what seemed *36 Ghante*, she finally came, swinging her lovely hips. I sat absolutely *Nishabd*, and waited. There was not a sound outside, and things were unusually *Khamosh*. Then, at last I could see Munnabhai coming up behind her, looking like a truly authentic *Dilli Ka Thug*, with his *Kali Topi Aur Lal Rumal*.

As she came abeam my car, Munnabhai caught up with her and lunged across, going for her necklace. *Waqt* seemed to stand still, and then the *Khamoshi* was shattered by Anamika's high-pitched shriek..."*Chor*! *Chor*!" It was my cue to act!

In one fluid motion, I flung open the car door and leapt onto the road. *Oops*!! For some strange reason I was unable to extricate myself from the car. "*I See You*," I shouted, "I am coming!" With superhuman effort I tugged myself from the seat..and that was when I heard the ghastly ripping sound.

The next moment I was next to my beloved..minus my pants, and resplendent in my red and yellow polka-dotted underwear!

Before I could say "***Mein Hoon Na***," Anamika was yelling for the guards from her mansion, "***Amar...Akbar...Anthony***!" even as Munnabhai was hightailing it with her necklace!

In the melee, I had not noticed that Anand had quietly sneaked across, gently comforting Anamika, and helping her onto his scooter. The next moment, he had started his vehicle, and disappeared around the corner with Anamika clinging on to him for dear life. "***Hey Ram***," I said to myself, "***Yeh Kya Ho Raha Hai?***" and walked back, half-naked to the car, avoiding the quizzical glances of the crowd which had gathered. There, hooked on to one of the protruding seat-springs, was my tattered trouser..!

So now you know why, after all these lonely, miserable, forlorn years, every time I see a taxi... ***Albert Pinto Ko Kyun Ghussa Aata Hain?***

ALBERT PINTO KO KYUN GHUSSA AATA HAIN-2
(OR WHY ALBERT PINTO GETS ANGRY-2)

To say that the loss of face (not to mention the loss of Anamika) was a big blow to me, would be a gross under-statement. In fact, I feel that this miserable experience had a profound influence on my *Zindagi* from that point onwards. Every morning while shaving, I would look into the *Aaina* and ask myself, "*Aisa Kyun Hota Hain?*" and every morning, I would get the same stupid answer..*Kyon Ki – It's Fate*.

Lekin, I was not one to be resigned to *Kismat*, and made a *Vaada* to myself that I would not give up so easily..I would try *Ek Baar Phir*. I made up my mind that I would be resolute like *Mangal Panday* and not rest until I made Anamika *Mere Jeevan Saathi*.

I had moved out of Anand's house immediately after the fiasco with Munnabhai and the necklace. After many weeks of searching (during which time I was frequently care of the *Footpath*), I managed to get a tiny room atop a *Ghar* which belonged to one Mr. Khosla – who had aptly named his house *Khosla Ka Ghosla*. He was a businessman, who ran a travel agency called **Honeymoon Travels Pvt. Ltd.** Although Mr.

Khosla appeared to be a perfect **Gentleman**, I had the feeling that he was involved in some **Golmaal** with a girl by the unlikely name of **Julie**. What aroused my suspicion was the fact that Julie always blushed as if she was **Newly Married** whenever Mr. Khosla was around. But then...this was none of my business, and I no intention of playing **Tu Chor Mein Sipahi** with my landlord.

Initially, I had decided to quit my job at the zoo. For obvious reasons, I did not want to be anywhere within Anand's **Duniya**. But by a strange **Ittifaq**, my **Dushman** Anand got a job as an **Officer** in another **Company** dealing with **Mitti Aur Sona**. So, I continued to work at the same place, which was quite easy, and gave me plenty of time to **Plan** my strategy to win back my **Chameli**.

All along I knew that if at all I managed to win over Anamika, ours would be **A Strange Love Story** indeed. One of the ideas that had initially occurred to me was to **Kidnap** Anamika and elope with her. But, deep inside, I knew I was too much of a **Buzdil** and would never have the **Himmat** to carry out such a mission. Perhaps if my parents had named me **Himmatwala** things would have been different. But then, I guess I was stuck with my name, and if I dropped it, I would become anonymous...truly **Benaam**. Actually, that would not have been a bad option, since I had become a **Badnaam** as it is, after my earlier misadventure.

I had to think of something fast, as **Waqt** was running out for me. I knew that it was only a matter of time that Anamika's family would find a filthy-rich, oily-haired, slick-looking **Dulha Raja** for her. It would be **Chat Mangini Pat Shaadi**, which would be over before I could say **Ek Do Teen**. I was deeply troubled by this thought, as also by the fact that if at all I managed to win my lovely Anamika years later, she would probably tell all her friends "**Buddha Mil Gaya**."

While pondering over my next move, I ran into a very interesting character named **Rocket Singh**. This guy was a real colourful character and used to keep saying "**Mera Naam Joker**." But he was a nice guy at heart, and after he heard my **Kahaani**, he came close to shedding **Aansoo**, and promised to help me in my **Zindagi Ka Safar**.

When I asked him what his **Naukri** was, he told me that he was an inventor, and had designed a vehicle, which could travel so fast, that it would take a mere **5 Ghante** to go from **Bombay To Bangkok**! He said that with a little **Jugaad**, he could extend its range to go from **Chandni Chowk To China**. It had space for him and his **Two Brothers**, but he said that he would be happy to fly me and my Anamika over to the Great Wall, aka the **Deewar**. When I heard this idea, I was instantly transported to **Swarg** and started fantasizing about the **Raat Aur Din** that I would be spending with my beloved. I truly believed that meeting Rocket Singh was **Luck By Chance**.

But..first things first. I had to see for myself this marvellous vehicle which would bring me and my **Kashmir Ki Kali** together for **Hamesha**. Also Rocket Singh was insistent that I meet with his personal doctor (one **Munnabhai MBBS**) and get a full medical examination done, especially of my head, because lately I was behaving like an absolute **Pagla Diwana**. I will not digress into the medical examination part – that is another story. However, I must relate what happened when I finally got to see Rocket Singh's invention, which, by the way, he had named **Toofan**.

I clearly remember that day, since this was going to be my **Aakhri Raastha**...or even my **Aakhri Baazi**. Not being a **Great Gambler**, I was very excited, to say the least. It was the day after the heavy **Barsat Ki Raat**, which had flooded most of Delhi. With great difficulty, we managed to reach **Delhi 6**, the farmhouse where Rocket Singh was building his dream machine...which would help me realise my **Khwab**.

I looked around desperately to get **Ek Nazar** of this marvellous machine..but couldn't see anything which vaguely resembled **Airavat**, (which, I had been taught as a child, was the mythical white elephant that carried the Goddess Indira). It was extremely hot there, as a strong **Garam Hawa** was blowing (perhaps this was the reason that he had named his invention Toofan!) Anyway, after another ten minutes of futile **Khoj**, I finally walked up to Rocket Singh and asked him where his Toofan was.

What happened next, could only be described as **Bewafa**...total betrayal! Without batting an eyelid, Rocket Singh unwaveringly pointed to a grotesque assembly of wooden crates, tied together with a blue **Dor** precariously perched on a table which had only three legs. For a moment I thought my brains had been cooked in the intense heat – a kind of **Bheja Fry**. I then noticed that at one end of the pile of junk, there was a round hole, painted red. Curiosity got the better of me and I asked Rocket Singh what it was. He looked at me as though I was some kind of a moron, and simply said "*Aag*," while mimicking lighting a match stick.

It was then that I decided that enough was enough. If this clown expected me and my precious Anamika to sit inside his totally ridiculous contraption while he set fire to its rear end...well, he may as well have been living in his own *Hawa Mahal*.

At this point, I think I totally lost it. The disappointment, the anger and the frustration lit the *Chirag* within me, and I created one hell of a *Hungama*. "*Maa Kasam Badla Loonga*," I screamed at the top of my voice.

There was absolute silence, and I suddenly realized that I was totally *Akela*. In all the melee, Rocket Singh had done a *Choo Mantar* and vanished!

I walked back slowly, all the way to my tiny room atop Khosla Ka Ghosla. All this *Ganchakkar* and *Hera Pheri* had totally fatigued me physically and mentally. For a moment I seriously contemplated suicide, but chickened out. Somewhere, an inner voice kept saying "Leave this *Pagalpan*...forget Anamika...look for *Sita aur Geeta*, *Khushboo* or some other *Dream Girl* who would give you *Amar Prem*."

So now you know why, after all these lonely, miserable, forlorn years, every time someone says the word 'rocket'... *Albert Pinto Ko Kyun Ghussa Aata Hai?*

ALBERT PINTO KO KYUN GHUSSA AATA HAIN-3
(OR WHY ALBERT PINTO GETS ANGRY-3)

Things really went downhill for me after the Rocket Singh episode. I had more or less lost all faith in humans…and indeed my self-confidence. Even as I tried my utmost to get control over myself, I was becoming more and more like **Devdas**. And…I had not stopped pining for my dearest Anamika. My obsession with her was so great that each day my frustrations were getting worse. One day, while listlessly walking around Karol Bagh, I saw a huge hoarding which said **Tanu Weds Manu**. I suddenly got this unstoppable urge to commit suicide, and I took a taxi to Old Delhi station, hoping to put an end to my misery. But, once again, I failed in my attempt to jump in front of **The Train**…I just didn't have the guts. That was when I decided that perhaps **Bhagwan** really didn't want me to die, after all. Perhaps he was challenging me to try one more time.

And so, it was back to the drawing board.

I wracked my brain for ideas, for nearly a month. Finally, on a bright, sunny morning when I had just finished breakfast of one **Roti** and one **Barfi**, I was all ready to set my next plan in motion.

This was fairly simple and straight-forward, and one which I thought was fool-proof. Although, basically it called for kidnapping my beloved Anamika, this time around, I had decided to leave it to professionals to get the job done.

I had read that somewhere in Madhya Pradesh, there were several *goonda* elements, who called themselves the **Gangs Of Wasseypur**, who specialized in this kind of **Gundagardi** for a reasonable price.

I realized that the first thing I had to do was to contact these guys. This was not easy, as they were as elusive as the proverbial **Ghost**. Anyway, since I had no other choice, I approached one **Agent Vinod**, who, I was told, was the best in the business of facilitating **Mulaqat** with these cold-blooded, ruthless kidnappers.

For some strange reason, I had imagined that this Agent Vinod would look like **Paan Singh Tomar**. It came as quite a shock to me that when I finally did meet him, he bore an uncanny resemblance to **Rowdy Rathore**. He also had long hair, which he sported in a ponytail (something which I personally detested). I toyed with the idea of telling him to visit **Billoo Barber**, whose salon I had spotted on my way to this place. However, I held my peace, because I did not want to antagonize him.

His 'office' turned out to be nothing more than a **Sadda Adda** behind the **Dhobhi Ghat**, next to a run-down restaurant called **Madras Café**. He sat on a rickety old chair, behind a table, which had one leg missing. Like **Tere Bin Laden** he was closely surrounded by his three henchmen, who went by the names **Ram, Rahim & Robert**. I also noticed that at all times there was at least one **Bodyguard** next to him. Somewhere in the background I could hear **Dum Maro Dum** playing.

By the time I located this place, it was very late at night. I had not eaten all day, and I must have looked as if I was going to drop dead, for Vinod asked me if I was ill. I just shook my **Sir** and said "**Bhook**"...I was too weak even to talk.

Fortunately for me, Vinod (who, I presumed, was nothing more than an **Anpadh** rowdy) understood what I was trying to say. He immediately called out to Robert, and told him to go to Madras café and get something to eat for "**My Friend Pinto**," along with two cups of **Chai Garam**, but with **Chini Kum**. For a moment I thought of refusing the hospitality, considering the filthy state of the restaurant, but did not say anything, hoping like hell that I would not get **Delhi Belly** after eating the stuff.

Once I had the finished eating the **Aloo Chaat** – which, incidentally, tasted **Khatta-Meetha** – and some watery **Khichdi**, I was beginning to feel like **Toonpur Ka Superhero**, and before you could say '**Dabangg**,' I was relating my **Kahani** to Vinod. He was silent all through my narration, but I thought that his eyes lit up when I told him about my kidnap plans.

"OK," he said, "I get the **Dirty Picture**, but you understand this is not a game of **Teen Patti**. You will have to give me some time to decide whether the plan is ***Right Ya Wrong***. Also, I think that we will have to bring in ***Hanuman***, the one with the ***Japanese Wife***. He is the one who has the ***Acid Factory*** near ***Khandala House*** *and* was the brain behind the ***Shootout At Lokhandwala***."

I was not at all keen that we should involve anyone else in our plans, and my ***Chehraa*** must have betrayed my apprehensions. Vinod was quick to see this, and put his arm around me, and said, "Don't worry, my friend Pinto, ***We Are Family*** now. ***Vaada Raha*** – I promise you, I will get your Anamika for you and fulfil your ***Bloody Isshq***, If I fail, I will change my name from Vinod to ***Singham***."

I thanked him profusely, and said ***Dasvidanya***, hoping that our new-found ***Dostana*** would culminate in ***Ek Vivaah Aisa Bhi***. I could see that Vinod had not understood the Russian I had thrown in to impress him, because he seemed surprised when I said good bye in English. Motioning for me to resume my seat, he said, "***Kabhi Alvida Naa Kehna***," and insisted that I join him for a drink. He seemed even more shocked when I told him that I was not a ***Sharabi***. But he did not insist...offering me a glass of ***Aamras*** instead.

It was while he was handing me the glass of Aamras that I noticed that the second ***Ungli*** was missing from his right hand. I somehow assumed that it had been cut off by the razor-sharp *manja* thread while he was flying ***Kites***. The urge to ask him about it was great, but I managed to suppress it at the time. However, I could not hold back my curiosity after a while, and pointing to his hand, I asked "***Patang?***" He stared at his missing digit for a while, and as though (not) seeing it for the first time and said, "No. Shot off by **Quick Gun Murugan...Once Upon A Time In Mumbai**."

It must have been close to ten, when I finally bid him good bye. By this time, he had had his third or fourth drink (some kind of a heady **Cocktail)** and seemed ready for **Band, Baaja, Baraat**. I certainly was not keen to get involved in any more **Tamaasha**...at least not tonight.

Achanak, I heard Vinod shout, "Hey Pinto...where are you going?"

I was taken aback by such a **Sawaal** and it struck me as downright silly. For a moment I was tempted to say "*Bandh karo* all this **Natak**...after all, **It's My Life**," and find someone else to get me my Anamika. But when I started to voice my feelings, Vinod became aggressive, and said, "*Arrey-o* Pinto *ke bachhey*...you stop this **English-Vinglish**, ok? What you think, *haan*? I am **Bewakoof**? You come *vaapas* right now, and sign on this **Kora Kagaz** that you are appointing me, Agent Vinod as your **Wazir-e-Azam**, with promise not to use **Policegiri** to arrest me."

I was astounded, to put it mildly. This man, whom I had considered a friend and a good **Insaan**, had, in a split second, turned into a **Shaitan**!!

"**Baap Re Baap**," I said to myself, "**Ab Kya Hoga?**" But this was no time to say **Sorry Bhai** or **Wrong Number** and sneak out of the situation.

So, I did what was best under the circumstances...I capitulated. Taking the *kora kagaz* that my erstwhile friend was thrusting in my face, I started to write:

"***Hindustan Ki Kasam***, I, Albert Pinto, son of John Anthony Mario Pinto, solemnly swear not..."

That was as far as I got, because Vinod (who had been lurking behind me and seeing what I was writing), yanked the paper from me and screamed, "***Kaminey***, you making me fool? You thinking I am ***Khiladi 420***? *Bachhoo, yaad rakho*...I am Vinod – Agent Vinod, not your ***Raju Chacha*** or ***Shirdi Sai Baba***. I am a true Indian..and so do not believe in *Hindustan ki kasam*. If you want your life, you eat *kasam* on your mother. OK?"

"***Yes Boss***," I said and began writing again: I, ***Maa Kasam***, solemnly swear that Agent Vinod is totally ***Nirdosh*** of all the ***Golmaal*** that I, Albert Pinto, son of Anthony Gonsolves Mario Pinto am planning to do. He is in this drama only because of some ***Ittifaq.*** He is ***Lakhon Mein Ek*** and like a ***Big Brother*** to me.

Meekly I handed over the paper to him, and he gave it to henchman No.2, Rahim, to read and translate. Finally, he smiled and said, "***You Good Boy Bad Boy.*** But tell me, who is this Anthony Gonsolves? Is he same Anthony Gonsolves Mario Pinto, also known as Anthony Gonsolves, who was *akela* in this world? My father and he had lots of ***Dosti***. *Mere bhai*, if you are his son, your ***Kismat Konnection*** is made!!"

"***Oh My God***," I said to myself. If I say 'yes' I would be called ***Jhootha Kahin Ka***. But if I say 'no,' my only chance of being with my adorable Anamika would be dashed forever. But..I was ***Majboor***..I had been brought up to believe ***Satyamev Jayate*** – truth will prevail. I chose ***Satya***.

And so, that was the end of my association with Agent Vinod, but I considered myself **Lucky** to have got out of there in one piece. Sadly..my dream of embracing my beloved remained just that ..a mere **Khwab**.

So now you know why, after all these lonely, miserable, forlorn years, every time someone says 'Satymev Jayate'... ***Albert Pinto Ko Kyun Ghussa Aata Hain?***

AN EERIE EXPERIENCE

"It is wonderful that five thousand years have now elapsed since the creation of the world, and still it is undecided whether or not there has ever been an instance of the spirit of any person appearing after death. All argument is against it, but all belief is for it."
— *Samuel Johnson*

CHAPTER - 1

The existence (or non-existence) of ghosts, spirits, apparitions and such-like entities has been the subject of articles, books and discussions since times immemorial. Every country, every religion and every belief system has an opinion on such matters. For example, Hinduism propagates the idea of re-incarnation. One of the basic tenets of Christianity is life after death or what is known as the Resurrection. Buddhism maintains that life does not end with death, but merely goes into other forms as a result of accumulated *karma*. And so on.

Great scholars, philosophers and religious thinkers have spent literally all their adult lives trying to find an answer. But at the end of the day, I feel that it is only personal belief which determines whether one subscribes to any of these theories or not.

I, for one, firmly believed (or used to believe) that once a person dies, that is the end of everything. Perhaps this attitude was due to the fact that both my parents too held the same view. Religion played a very small rôle in their life..but that is not to say that they were atheists or agnostics. For them, as Christians, religion was no more than a code of conduct…a set of rules – as it were – which governed what was 'good' and what was 'bad,' what was 'moral' and what was 'immoral' – nothing more, nothing less. Since, from childhood, I was raised under such circumstances, I guess that I too subscribed to such an idea.

Moreover, having joined the Air Force at the tender age of 20, I had come to experience horrific deaths at close quarters, very early in life. My close friend and room-mate died in a mid-air collision right before my eyes. As was the norm in the Air Force, all of us cadets were made to fly that very day, so as not to harbour any fear of flying. What was more unnerving was to be alone in the room at night. However, in a few days, I had gotten used to it, and life became routine once again.

On completion of training and having been awarded the coveted 'wings,' I was posted to various Stations, within the first five or six years of my Service career. During this period, I had got married, fortunately to a girl from a Service family. It was therefore not too difficult for her to rough it out in the wild, inhospitable and desolate places that we were posted to.

One such place was Chabua..located in the extreme North East corner of India, in the state of Assam. To reach there took all of three days from Delhi, and the station where we disembarked (Tinsukhia) was the last one on the Railway map. Being so far to the East, sunrise used to be around 4.30 in the morning, and darkness would set in by 5 o'clock in the evening...the sun having gone down by 4.

Needless to say, that life in Chabua was at best, primitive. Most married personnel lived in grass-thatched bamboo huts (known as *bashas*) within the Air Force Station campus. However, when I got posted there, there were no vacant *bashas* available, and so we had to rent accommodation in Chabua village, which was a good six kilometres from the airfield.

In the early days of my career, my only mode of transport was a Vespa scooter, which I had bought in 1971, for a princely sum of Rs. 2,785. Roads in that part of the country were practically non-existent, and what passed for roads were pock-marked generously with huge potholes, which were more like moon craters! To add to the miserable condition of the roads, the heavy rains (which were a regular feature of the place) made journeys perilous. Riding a scooter under such conditions was extremely dangerous even during day time..at night it was more of a 'death-wish,' because there were no road lights or any other form of illumination.

On both sides of the road were sprawling tea estates, stretching as far as the eye could see. During daylight hours, there used to be quite a lot of activity at the garden itself, as well as on the roads, where trucks and tractor-trailers used to go to and fro, carrying the freshly plucked tea leaves, or ferrying labourers between the gardens.

It was a completely different scene as soon as darkness fell. All activity in the gardens ceased, and the last of the workers would return to their tiny, tin-roofed houses before the last rays of the sun disappeared. The vehicular traffic too would disappear off the roads, and an eerie silence would descend, punctuated only by the screeches of night owls and the occasional croak of frogs.

However, for me, roads or no roads...rain or shine, there was no excuse for not reaching the workplace in time, by day or by night. And so, I used to ride my faithful Vespa every single day from my house to the Air Force Station and back. And when there was night flying, it meant that I would have to do the trip for a second time, and in total darkness. Since there were no mobile phones (or any such luxuries in that era), there was no way one could inform anyone if there were to be any problem or accident en route.

CHAPTER - 2

It was one of those miserable mornings, with buckets of rain falling from the skies, and not even the faintest sign of the Sun breaking through. In fact, the rain had not stopped the entire night, and when I got up in the morning and looked outside through the tiny window of our bedroom, the area resembled a lake. Given half a choice, I would have happily remained at home, for today was the 23rd of March 1970...my wife's 25th birthday.

However, this was well-nigh impossible, as there was no way that I could skip going to work on that particular day. The reason for this was that the dreaded Aircrew Examination Board – or AEB for short – had descended on the Base, and had scheduled the Ground Subjects examination for all pilots for this morning.

If there is anything that most pilots dreaded, it surely would have been a visit by the AEB. At least once every year, pilots had to subject themselves to the most rigorous tests in flying as well as in aviation-related ground subjects, in order to either retain or upgrade their flying proficiency. Failure in these examinations would not only automatically ensure the lowering of one's flying category, but would also deal a mortal blow to one's ego – no pilot likes to be ever told that he was not up to the mark in his profession.

And so it was, that I reluctantly donned my uniform, put on my weather-beaten raincoat and readied myself to ride through the deluge. As always, my wife was at the door to see me leave, with a hug and a peck on the cheek.

Looking at the weather, I was really not sure if I would be able to come home for lunch. To make sure that she did not worry if I did not come home at the normal time, I had told her that should the rain persist, I would grab a bite at the cafeteria, and stay put at the Base. In any case, there was night flying scheduled, which meant that I would have had to ride all the way back after lunch. And that was definitely a no-no, if I could avoid it.

It was a miserable ride from home to the Base, but I made it one piece..and in time for the morning Meteorological (Met) Briefing. If one was to believe the Met Officer, the weather was expected to clear by mid-afternoon, and would be suitable for night flying. But, as everyone in aviation knows, meteorological forecasts can be notoriously incorrect, and from the looks of it, this horrible weather was not likely to clear for the next two days at least. Most of us present at the briefing secretly sniggered at his confidence.

The Ground Subjects examination was scheduled for 1100 hours (11:00 am), and most of us did some last-minute cramming and mutual studies. The Examiners walked into the class room precisely at 1055 hours (10:55 am), and the examination got under way exactly on time.

The question paper was not very difficult, and I felt that I did fairly well.

The rest of the day was terribly boring, as there was no flying due to the bad weather, and we were all cooped up in the Aircrew Room, and passed the time playing Scrabble or Chess. It was still raining heavily at 1330 hours (1:30 pm) – the normal pack-up time –

and so I decided not to go home for lunch, opting for a sandwich and coffee at the cafeteria.

Amazingly, the weather suddenly cleared at about 1500 hours (3:00 pm), exactly as the Met guy had forecast, and we even had a glimpse of the Sun, before it disappeared below the horizon.

Soon the Night Flying Briefing got underway, and by the time that was over, it was completely dark. Those of us who were on the programme changed into flying overalls, and readied ourselves to undergo the Night Flying Test.

Being one of the junior-most pilots in the Squadron, I was scheduled to fly only at 2200 hours (10:00 pm). The flight itself would be approximately of 30 minutes' duration, so by the time I set off for home, it would be close to 2300 hours (11:00 pm).

I knew that in spite of the late hour when I would eventually reach home, my wife would be waiting for me, to warm up my dinner, and ask about my performance in the AEB tests. So, in spite of feeling hungry, I did not have dinner in the Cafeteria, but just had a couple of biscuits and a cup of coffee.

Finally, the hours went past and I got airborne for my sortie, hoping that it would be short. The examiner too must have been quite tired after flying nearly three hours continuously, because he really did not hassle me much with too many in-flight emergencies. Eventually, we landed back after about 25 minutes, and I felt that I had done well. Of course, one could not know, until the results were announced after the final debriefing, which would be on the next day.

By the time I had changed from my overalls into my uniform, and got ready to set off for home, it was about 2315 hours (11:15 pm). As I walked up to my scooter, I felt a few drops of rain fall on my head..and I cursed. This really was too much. All this time the weather had been clear, and now, just as I was leaving for home, the rain seemed to have resumed. However, it appeared to be just a mild drizzle, and I hoped it would stop as abruptly as it had started. I didn't want to take a chance, though, and so I put on my raincoat, started my scooter, and set off for home in the pitch-dark night.

CHAPTER - 3

It was very quiet, except for the usual sounds of the jungle – the croaking of frogs, the chirping of the beetles, and the occasional flutter of wings, as bats or owls sought their dinner. The rain had not stopped, but it was not heavy either..just a steady drizzle, cold and irritable. There was no traffic at all on the road, and the hum of my scooter engine seemed unusually loud.

This was not the first time that I had ridden home at night..every time there was night flying, I would be forced to do so. However, in consideration to the fact that I was living in the town, and that my wife would be alone at home, the flying programme would be made in such a way that I would wind up latest by 2030 hours (8:30 pm) and reach home at a decent hour. But, today was different, because of the AEB test. For the first time, I was riding on this dark, desolate and dangerous road close to midnight.

As I rode on, my mind replayed the happenings of the day…the heavy rain as I left home in the morning, the Ground Subjects examination, the miraculous clearing of the weather in the afternoon, and finally the Night Flying test. As far as the tests were concerned, I thought that on a scale of 1 to 10, I should get at least 8. But then, like I mentioned earlier, one could never be sure until the results were announced.

Lost in my thoughts, I had not noticed that the rain had progressively increased in intensity, and was now beating down hard, making it difficult to see more than about 20 or 30 feet in front, although the scooter headlight was making a valiant effort to illuminate the path ahead. I still had about four kilometres to go, and I cursed my luck, having to ride through this horrible weather.

Having ridden on this road many a time, I knew that somewhere close to where I was presently, there would be a very sharp U-turn. Even during daylight hours, one had to anticipate this turn, and slow down considerably in order to negotiate it successfully. If one were a bit careless, one could easily miss the road, and land up on the narrow, uneven area on either side, beyond which there was a steep drop of at least thirty feet.

I strained my eyes in an attempt to see the road as far ahead as possible and pick up the sharp left turn. However, the rain was so heavy, that it was becoming very difficult to see anything else except the ghostly beam of light from the scooter. I said a prayer of thanks to God that there was no traffic coming from the opposite direction...I surely would have not been able to see it, since most of the trucks and tractors did not have functioning head lamps.

At that very instant, I saw the beginning of the turn, and immediately reduced my speed. The next moment, I was in the turn.

I guess that I must have been about halfway through the turn, staring hard into the dark void, when suddenly I was blinded by a powerful, bright light shining into my eyes from the middle of the road. I stepped hard on the brake, instinctively lifting my left hand to shield my eyes from the bright light. As my hand came up to eye level, I saw the luminous dial of my watch showed 11:59 pm. I could sense the scooter going into a skid, and tilted my body to the right, trying hard to control the skid. By this time, I was nearly abeam the light, and it reflected off my helmet visor, briefly illuminating a figure, holding what appeared to be a huge torch. As I came closer, I must have turned towards the light, for I caught sight of the figure.

It was a sight that I am not likely to forget as long as I live.

The figure holding the torch was that of a young woman, dressed in a white *saree.* The torch was in her right hand, and she appeared to be gesturing with her left hand for me to stop.

By this time, the scooter had slowed down, the skid was under control and I had managed to stop at the extreme right, on the *kutcha* portion of the road.

What happened next could only have happened in a nightmare. I guess that not even a second had elapsed after I came to a halt, when I heard a loud, rumbling noise, which sounded like an earthquake. The next moment, a gigantic tree came crashing down, and fell right across the road, right in front of my eyes! Had I not stopped, I would surely have been instantly crushed to death.

My heart was pounding from the adrenalin rush, and I got off the scooter and managed to put it on its stand, while I tried to get some control of myself. I turned and looked at the woman, who now had kept the torch on the ground, and appeared to be waving good bye to me. I could see her clearly now, her whole body illuminated by the light from the torch..and what I saw made me quake in mortal fear: the woman had no face!

I presume I must have fainted, and fallen to the ground, for I could not remember anything from point in time, until I finally regained my senses.

The rain had stopped, and I stood up on unsteady legs, not daring to look in the direction where I had seen the woman with no face. When I did finally muster enough courage to do so, I did not see anyone there – the figure had vanished as mysteriously as it had appeared. However, I did see something on the road, and walked up to the spot. It was a small torch, barely glowing in the darkness.

I retraced my steps, and came back to my scooter, wondering if it would start. Amazingly, it did so with just one kick, and I rode on, avoiding the tree lying across the road, and managed to somehow reach home. It was 0300 hours (3:00 am) as per my watch.

CHAPTER – 4

The results of the AEB examinations were announced the next day, and I had done much better than I had expected. My harrowing experience of the previous night had quietly slipped into the background..in any case, I had not told anyone of the strange sighting, lest I be the butt of jokes from my colleagues. By the end of the day, I too put the incident behind me, and life came back to somewhat normal once more.

****

Two days later, there was a telegram from my mother. In those days, in the absence of instant phone calls or mobile phones, important news or occurrences (usually alarming) were communicated only by means of the telegram. So, when I got the telegram, my heart skipped a beat, as I hastily opened it and read the contents. It read, 'NIMMI SERIOUS. START IMMEDIATELY.' It had been sent two days ago..and I cursed the system for the delay in delivering the telegram.

Nimmi was my identical twin sister, and we were literally closer than the proverbial peas in a pod. In fact, we were so close that it used to be a joke in our family that our minds were actually one, and only our bodies were separate. I had joined the Air Force, and she had gone on to do her Masters in Chemistry, eventually becoming a research student in the Indian Institute of Science, Bangalore.

The contents of the telegram had shaken me badly. I immediately met my Commanding Officer, and requested him to grant me ten days' leave, so I could go home, which in itself would take me at least three to four days by train. The only way I could reach earlier than that would be if I managed an airlift to Bangalore.

Hoping against hope, I contacted the Command Headquarters in Shillong, which would have the up-to-date movements of all aircraft. Fortunately, there was a Dakota aircraft leaving early next morning from Jorhat on a ferry flight to Bangalore. If I could make it on that, I would be able to reach home by the next afternoon. When I told my Commanding Officer about this, he was kind enough to have a helicopter from my Squadron drop me at Jorhat the same afternoon.

I took the flight out of Jorhat the next morning at 0530 hours (5:30 am). All through the flight, I kept thinking of Nimmi, and praying that she was alright. We made good time, reaching Bangalore at about three in the afternoon.

The moment I reached my parents' home, I knew that something was horribly wrong. There were several cars parked outside, and as I entered, I could sense an all-pervasive pall of gloom inside.

My mother saw me coming, and got up from her bed, reaching out to me. But she never made it. Just a few feet from me, she fell into a swoon, and would have hurt herself badly, had I not managed to break her fall. I managed to put her on her bed, where she was immediately attended to by several of those in the room.

"Where is Nimmi?" I asked my Aunt, who was standing in the room, bleary-eyed.

She did not answer, but simply hugged me, sobs uncontrollably racking her body. I knew instantly that my only sister was no more.

****

It took me quite a while to find out what had happened – everyone was in such a state of shock and disbelief, that it was nearly impossible to get a cohesive answer from any of them.

Eventually, however, I came to know how my sister had died. It was indeed as bizarre as it was tragic, at least as far as I was concerned. From what I could piece together, it seemed that she had been working on a project, which called for synthesis of several volatile chemicals. This meant the use of gas burners in the laboratory.

That fateful morning, Nimmi had gone to the laboratory as usual, and started working on her project. What she was not aware of was that, during the previous night, there had been a leak in one of the pipes that fed the burner. Apparently, the gas had concentrated in the area, since all the windows were closed. The instant Nimmi lit the burner, there was a massive explosion as the gas spontaneously ignited, and she was engulfed in the flames.

Perhaps she would have survived the fire – albeit with severe burns, had it not been for the highly combustible cocktail of chemicals in the retort over the burner. This caught fire, and exploded, resulting in over 90 percent burns to her face.

In other words, there was no face left.

****

The day before I left home to return to Chabua, I sorted out all the paperwork, so that my mother would not have to go through the trauma. Among the various documents that I had to file was the Death Certificate given by the doctor in the hospital, where Nimmi had breathed her last.

I slowly read through the document...

NAME: Nirmala Samuel
SEX: Female
AGE: 26 Years 3 Months
CAUSE OF DEATH: Severe burn injuries
DATE/TIME OF DEATH: 23 March 1970/ 11:59 pm.

AJJI'S CRICKET

I had often wondered why the vast majority of ladies have no interest in the game of cricket – notwithstanding the fact that lately, several countries boast of women's teams. But the fact remains that for most of the fair sex, the game is still a mystery...an enigma, if you would prefer to call it that. Being male, I had convinced myself that this sad state of affairs was entirely on account of the limited mental acuity of the fair sex. However, as I advance in years, I am inclined towards taking a more benevolent attitude..perhaps as a consequence of a very enlightening discussion between my grandson Manish and my wife, which I chanced to overhear recently.

My wife has always been one of the champions in the belief that cricket is totally inane, and those who have even the smattering of interest in it are absolute morons. So, when one of the recent ODI's (One-Day-Internationals..for the uninitiated) was in progress at Ahmedabad, Manish was glued to the 'idiot box,' and in effect thwarting the efforts of his grandmother to hog the tube.

Now this battle for the channels has been going on in our household for long, and I had learned over the years that it is better to relinquish the TV remote than to bicker with the better half over what to watch.

Regrettably, my grandson was a novice, and took it upon himself to enlighten his 'Ajji' on the nuances of the game. Little did he know what he was in for…in fact, little did I know how much my wife had studied the game to develop such an aversion and ridicule for it.

It all started when Manish let out an ear-shattering yelp, as he exulted in Sehwag being dropped. It also resulted in his Ajji dropping three stitches from the cardigan she was knitting for Manish. "What happened Manish?" asked Ajji. "Did something bite you?" There was no response from Manish, who looked catatonic. Ajji repeated her question, a little louder this time.

Manish did not turn from the TV but said, "Oh Ajji…did you see that? Sehwag was dropped by the third man."

"Hmph," chortled my wife, "is he so heavy that it requires three men to carry him?"

"Ajji…" said Manish in a placating, patronizing tone, "third man is a position behind the slips, and…"

"Enough…enough," snapped Ajji. "You know Manish, I think that you should stop watching this stupid and vulgar game. They call cricket a 'Gentleman's Game,' but tell me, which decent gentleman would skulk around behind a slip?"

"But Ajji…" began Manish, now all set to defend his passion, but was sternly cut down by my wife, who was just warming up to the subject.

"Whoever heard of someone with a square leg? And why do they pick players with short legs or long legs? No wonder our fielding is so pathetic!"

Manish was now all worked up. "Ajji," he said, "you just don't know what you are saying. What is the point..."

He never got to finish his sentence. His grandmother was now in full flow. "Yes," she said, "why do captains insist on a silly point..or for that matter on a silly mid-on, when they know it is really silly? Just the other day, I heard this commentator saying that Rahul Dravid played an uncharacteristically agricultural stroke, and that too after doing a bit of gardening on the pitch. Tell me..are these guys cricketers or farmers? Or maybe they are butchers – or even barbers, for that matter. Otherwise how can they be involved in a French cut?"

Manish tried to get a word in edgewise while my wife paused for breath, but he was unsuccessful. "These fellows all belong to the gully," declared Ajji regally. "Only third-rate scum would discuss in public if someone had balls or no balls, and even go to the extent of saying the balls were tampered with, or that someone had handled the ball. *Chee...chee*! Sickening, I tell you..at least I would never in my life talk to someone who bowls a maiden over, let alone applaud that degenerate act. And what is this about a sweeper on the fence? By the way, Manish, don't you know that these days it is wrong to call someone a sweeper? The correct term is *pourikarmika*."

By this time drinks were on the field and Manish was forced to listen to his Ajji's apoplexy. Taking a cue from what was happening on the field, my wife took a sip of water to lubricate her pharynx, and then continued her tirade. "And the terms they have to describe batsmen are absolutely ridiculous..like...huh...why in the name of Heaven is someone called a bunny? Or a night-watchman? Is it because he doubles as a '*chowkidar*' lest the wicket keeper takes away all the wickets away after play is called off for the day?"

"Manish," she carried on, "I tell you, this must be the game with the most ludicrous rules. I can never understand how a batsman is 'in' when he walks out of the pavilion, whereas he is 'out' when he walks back into it. Ridiculous! And I must say that I am appalled when that guy in the coat and hat shows his finger ever so often!"

By this time Manish was all set to pull his (or most likely his Ajji's) hair out. He tried once more to educate his grandmother on the rules and regulations of cricket. "Ajji, if only you will watch the match carefully, you will begin to understand everything. See? Now the drinks are over and..."

He never got to finish the sentence. My wife was aghast – nay – scandalized that right in the middle of the day (and middle of the field too!) people were consuming 'drinks!'

"Manish, this is really too much," she said. "Don't these guys know that there is prohibition in Gujarat?

And here they are merrily guzzling Kingfisher out in the open!"

Before Manish could respond, the match had resumed, and Shoaib Akhtar was getting ready to bowl. "Oh my God!" shrieked my wife, "look at that vulgar, uncouth man. He is rubbing the ball on the most unmentionable part of his body! Manish...please switch this off, I beg of you!"

My poor grandson was absolutely speechless.

But, true to its billing as the game of 'glorious uncertainties,' cricket had the last word..a sudden burst of rain engulfed the stadium, and everyone on the field scampered to the safety of the pavilion.

GHOSTS AND OTHER APPARITIONS

Although ghost stories have been around since times immemorial, no one has been able to prove conclusively the existence (or otherwise) of these so-called spirits. I vividly remember the time when my favourite uncle scared the living daylights out of us children, relating the most grisly and spine-chilling story of a headless man haunting the deserted house on our road, where a ghastly triple murder was supposed to have taken place.

Even more terrifying was the story of an apparition that would silently and suddenly appear beside someone walking home alone at night, past the cemetery up the road on which our house was located.

As a teenager, my first 'authenticated' account of the existence of ghosts was from my own cousin, who was undergoing training at Air Force Station Jalahalli, in Bangalore. He swore that on a particularly dark night, sometime close to midnight, one of the trainees who was on sentry duty at a remote gate saw someone approaching. As was the procedure, he challenged the stranger and asked him to identify himself. However, the 'intruder' just kept walking towards the sentry, who warned him to stop, or that he would shoot. When there was no reaction from the 'intruder,' the sentry opened fire...but the 'ghost' just kept coming closer and closer, whereupon the sentry dropped his weapon and ran for all he was worth until he reached his barracks, delirious and rambling incoherently.

Incidentally, I am told that this particular post still exists, and goes by the name of 'Ghost Post.'

****

At the beginning of my career in the Air Force, I was posted to Chabua – at that time, a god-forsaken Air Base situated in eastern Assam. The Base had been used by the Royal Air Force (RAF) during the Burma campaign, and stories were a-plenty of ghosts and hauntings. Most of us pooh-poohed these tales, ridiculing anyone who even hinted at the existence of such phenomena. All that was until the day that several of us were witnesses to something most inexplicable.

We had all gathered for night flying, and after the briefing, the pilots went off to start up their individual helicopters.

In those days, there were no bright floodlights around the tarmac, where the helicopters were parked, and so, it was pretty dark. One of the pilots – a very sober, normally unflappable individual – climbed into the cockpit of one of the helicopters, and while preparing to start the aircraft, noticed someone in khaki uniform sitting in the co-pilot's seat. Squinting in the semi-darkness, he suddenly realised that the person in the cockpit was wearing the uniform of a RAF corporal! Suffice to say that our customarily imperturbable colleague exited the cockpit with great alacrity and bolted, trembling and screaming on top of his voice.

In the crew room, we managed to calm him down and tell us what the matter was. Later, a small posse of us 'brave' pilots went to check out the same aircraft but did not find anything unusual.

Also, while in Chabua, there was a very tall tree, popularly known as the 'Sergeant's Tree.' This particular tree was very close to one end of the runway and posed a hazard to landing aircraft, especially in bad weather – for which Chabua was notorious. However, the 'Sergeant's Tree' could never be chopped down, for anyone who attempted to do so was duly attended by some misfortune or the other. It was widely believed that a RAF sergeant had committed suicide by hanging himself from that tree, and that his spirit would not allow anyone to harm that tree.

****

This brings me to my personal experience with the mystifying and unexplained. Sometime in 1972, I was driving back to Bangalore from Mysore. The time was just past midnight, and along with me in the car were my driver (sitting on the front passenger seat), and my wife, sitting behind us on the back seat, along with our children. As we passed under the Bangalore Cantonment under-bridge, I saw this very attractive young woman in the car headlights. She was dressed in a white *saree*, standing bang in the middle of the road, and staring directly into the car. I hit the horn, and swore loudly as I swerved, avoiding her by mere inches.

My driver, meanwhile, had gone berserk ...yelling at me to drive faster and get away.

Having passed her, I looked into the rear-view mirror, and what I saw that night makes my skin crawl even to this day. This 'woman' was standing in the same position, but her head had turned completely around, and she was still staring at me while the rest of her was 'facing' the other way! Hearing all the commotion, my wife too looked around and saw exactly what I saw!

I had all but forgotten about the incident, until the time when, many years later, my mother sent me a clipping from a local Bangalore newspaper. It said that another family, also driving back late at night, had had a similar hair-raising experience, although at a different location in Bangalore.

THE TURNING POINT

Do you believe in the super-natural? That events of the future are foretold or are revealed in advance? I, for one, had always considered myself a complete cynic and a pragmatist about 'things mysterious.' For me, ghosts and other such-like entities were mere figments of fertile imaginations, creations of frightened minds. This may have been largely due to the fact, that despite being a girl, I was more 'boy' than most boys, having two older brothers for siblings.

Also, unlike most parents of that era, ours were extremely emancipated, and allowed us kids to sit around with elders and listen to horror stories that were so scary, they used to make our hair stand on end. We were also permitted to go and watch movies rated 'A' for their 'horror' content. Thus, we had seen movies like Dracula and The House of Wax – which were considered the 'ultimate' horror movies of that time.

Both my brothers graduated from the NDA and joined the Army. I was very proud of them and had made up my mind early in life that I too would join the Armed Forces, preferably the Air Force. My parents were not too gung-ho about my plans, since they wanted me to become a doctor. But being very resolute – and in keeping with the universally-accepted dictum that fathers generally 'give in' to their daughters' whims – I eventually got my way and joined the Indian Air Force and was Commissioned as a helicopter pilot.

As with many women Officers in the Service, I met – and fell in love – with a fellow helicopter pilot, and in due course of time, got married to him. By the kind courtesy of a good friend in Air Headquarters, we both got posted to the same Station – Awantipur – way up in the Kashmir Valley.

Life in the Air Force had been exciting, flying being just one part of the thrills. The remote Stations that I had been posted to, the God-forsaken Army posts that I had landed in, the almost 'impossible' tasks that had to be undertaken in the most trying circumstances had, in the past six years, moulded me into (at least what I considered) an absolute unbiased and fearless individual. At the age of twenty-six, having been actively involved in the Kargil conflict, I had seen – and experienced – horrors which most individuals could not have imagined (let alone seen) in their entire lifetime. Gruesome injuries and death had become so commonplace, that they failed to arouse in me the usual emotions and dread, which haunt those who are safely ensconced in the comfort of their homes.

****

You must be wondering why I am at pains to describe my personality in such detail. Let me hasten to assure you that it is not to evoke your praise or admiration. Rather, it is to help you understand what I am today..a miserable wreck of a human being, who is in total dread of sleeping alone in the dark, petrified by even the slightest unexpected sound, hopelessly caught up in superstitions, the occult and the mysterious.

As I recall, it was in the month of August 2000 that my husband and I had planned to come to Bangalore on leave and spend about a fortnight with my parents. I had not seen my parents for over a year and a half and was all excited about the prospect of spending time with them. Thereafter we intended to go to Lucknow and stay with his parents for the rest of the thirty days' leave that we had managed to get together – which, in itself, was a minor miracle, given the fact that there was an acute shortage of pilots in the Unit that we were serving in at the time.

We were very fortunate also, to get our flight bookings on Indian Airlines well in time. I had gone on a shopping binge – picking up the usual goodies from Kashmir..shawls, almonds, walnuts (although they were quite expensive that year), and intricately carved, foldable wooden stools, made from walnut tree wood. Typical of most men, my husband had cribbed about the quantum of stuff that I had bought, but finally, just a day before we were to leave, we had managed to accommodate all the stuff into two suitcases (taking care not to exceed the twenty kilograms free baggage allowance!).

I still remember that day, as if it were just yesterday..it was a Friday, and the 13th day of the month. Not being a superstitious person, I had completed my two sorties for the day, and had come home an hour early to wind up the house and get set to depart the next day.

I cleaned out the refrigerator, taking care to leave the door open for it to dry. Next, I took down the curtains, and used them to cover the sofas. By this time, it was close to 1330 hours (1:30 pm), and I had just finished warming lunch, when my husband reached home. He was looking very stressed, which was quite unusual for a person who normally remained as cool as a cucumber in any situation, and no matter what the crisis. Instinctively, I knew that something was wrong, but before I could ask him, he told me that his leave had been postponed, as the Flight Commander had to suddenly proceed on 'compassionate leave' as his father had suffered a heart attack in Calcutta.

Although I had served in the Air Force long enough to expect – and accept – the unforeseen, I must admit that at that moment, I was very upset. My husband took the situation more stoically and in fact tried to make light of it by joking that I was now free to have a holiday with my ex-boyfriends in Bangalore!

For a moment, I toyed with the idea of cancelling my leave and staying back, but he was insistent that I go ahead, and that he would join me as soon as possible. The decision having been made, practicality took over from remorse, and we got started re-adjusting the contents of the suitcases, now that I would be travelling alone.

The rest of the day went past in a blur of activity, and by the time we went for dinner to the Officers' Mess (our kitchen having been shut down), I was quite tired and feeling strangely distracted, very unlike my normal self. The meal itself was nothing much to write home about and was over within an hour. I felt a twinge of guilt, knowing that my husband would have to put up with this kind of indifferent food every single day, until he joined me in Bangalore.

We slowly walked back home, holding hands, our fingers intertwined. It was a dark, moonless night, and the only light on the narrow road was from a solitary lamp-post, trying unsuccessfully to illuminate the area. In spite of the fact that it was only the middle of August, there was a slight nip in the air, heralding the onset of an early winter. Perhaps this was the reason that the road was deserted, and the only sounds that could be heard were those of the cicadas in the thick foliage on either side of the road.

Just as we were approaching into the circle of light directly beneath the lamp-post, we heard a sudden flurry of sound, as if someone – or something – was running towards us. We froze at the spot, instinctively clinging to each other, staring into the darkness from where we had heard the noise. At that instant, a huge black cat emerged from the bushes, carrying what looked like a fair-sized chicken in its mouth. The chicken seemed to be still alive, flapping its wings and screeching, struggling to get away, and the cat was vigorously shaking it from side to side in an attempt to kill it. Seeing us, the cat abruptly stopped and looked directly at us, its eyes glowing eerily yellow in the light. The next moment, it was rushing past us, in one graceful, fluid motion, vanishing into the shrubs on the other side of the road.

I would not go so far as to say that this encounter un-nerved my husband and me, but I must confess that it gave us quite a start. I remember that he gave a short laugh, and quipped that we had probably disturbed the poor guy about to have his dinner. We resumed walking, and presently reached our house, and went about getting ready for the night. Although I knew it was foolish, the incident of the black cat crossing our tracks just the night before I was leaving somehow made me uneasy, and I was tempted to share my thoughts with my husband. However, once we were in bed, I sensed that he had more amorous ideas on his mind, and so I wisely kept my feelings to myself!

I flew out of Srinagar the next day, reaching Bangalore only late in the evening, as the flight from Delhi had been delayed for over two hours. My father was at the airport to receive me, and we drove home in his old Fiat car, which he swore he would never change. He got a bit of a shock when he saw me coming out of the Airport alone...the shock giving way to disappointment, when I explained what had happened – he had looked forward to getting the better of his son-in-law in chess, a game in which my husband considered himself just a shade lower than Gary Kasperov!

Mother was thrilled to see me, but quite disappointed that her favourite son-in-law could not make it..she just adored the way he flattered her – about her cooking, about her garden, about her beautiful house..just about everything!

There was so much of catching up to do, and over dinner, mother filled me in with the latest news about my friends. It seemed that all of them were doing fairly well, except for Seema, who had been my closest and dearest friend all the three years in College. Mother told me that she was going through a rough time, as her marriage was not working out. I thought of calling her after the meal, but since it was quite late, and as I too was quite tired, I decided that I would call her the next day. Having had two generous helpings of caramel custard for dessert, I went up to my room.

I had been pretty possessive about my room before I left home to join the Air Force, and so my parents had kept it just the way it was. In double-quick time, I brushed my teeth, and snuggled into bed with my favourite *rasai* tucked right up to my chin. I guess that I was more tired than I realised, and I surrendered to the welcoming arms of Morpheus in a jiffy.

Somewhere in the wee hours of the morning, I woke up in cold sweat. My throat was absolutely parched and felt sore. Momentarily, I was disoriented and desperately tried to focus my thoughts. With a great effort, I sat up and looked around. It must have taken me a good five minutes to realise that I was in my old room, in my parents' house in Bangalore. It was pitch dark in the room, and I felt around for the bed-side lamp switch. Finally, my probing fingers located the switch, and I turned on the lamp, the light making me squint. I looked at the alarm clock on the dressing table at the far side of the room – it was showing 2:40 am.

I suddenly felt very cold..as if a draft of freezing-cold air was blowing in from an open window. But I knew that this was not possible, because the only window in the room was behind my bed, securely shut, and with the heavy drapes drawn. My fists were clenched tightly and my nails were nearly piercing my palms. I took a few deep breaths, forcing myself to calm down. But, try as I did, my heart kept thumping so hard, I could actually hear the *lub-dup...lub-dup...lub-dup* quite clearly.

My mind was totally blank. All I could recall at that point in time was what I had vividly seen in my dream – a gigantic black cat with glowing, yellow eyes, holding something horrible in its mouth. At first, I couldn't make out what it was, but slowly it came into focus: it was a mangled human head – with the face of my husband! I had screamed, and screamed and screamed, but no sound came from my throat. And then..I woke up.

My first reaction – after I had regained a modicum of control of myself – was to awaken my parents. But, just as swiftly as I had contemplated that, I dismissed it from my mind..it definitely would not be prudent to do so, especially since my father had had a heart attack just a few years ago and had undergone an open-heart surgery. As far as my mother – who at the best of times, would have asked me to shut up and go to sleep – would not have anything to say, totally dazed as she would be from swallowing so many medicines for her ailments.

By now, being totally awake, and somewhat in control of myself, my rational mind was beginning to kick in. It was obvious that the occurrences of the previous night had had a very intense influence on my sub-conscious than I cared to admit, and thus the ghastly nightmare. Even so, I was disturbed badly, and could not bring myself to go back to sleep.

I got up from my bed and went across to my small book-shelf. After a brief search, I pulled out a book (as I recall, it was 'Coma' by Robin Cook), and returned to my bed. Propping up a pillow against the head-board, and adjusting the reading lamp on the small table next to the bed, I resigned myself to reading something that I had read many years earlier. I guess that I must have finally dropped off to sleep, perhaps an hour or so later. The tiredness of travel, coupled with the interrupted sleep had their combined effect, and I was dead to the world, until I was rudely awoken by my mother, repeatedly calling my name from downstairs. I awoke with a jolt, responding to my mother's insistent voice, telling her that I will be down in a minute.

I could hear unfamiliar voices coming from the living room and wondered who could have come to our house so early in the morning.

Getting out of bed, I shuffled across to the toilet, and after easing my bladder, washed my face in the wash-basin. Catching a glimpse of myself in the mirror, I was quite shocked to see how dishevelled I looked. Quickly, I went to the dressing-table, and tried to make myself look presentable. I had just about finished brushing my hair and anchoring it in a loose pony tail, when I heard my mother call me again – her voice a few decibels higher than the previous time. I felt myself getting irritated, and very nearly shouted back, but controlled myself, recalling that there were others in the living room. Hastily, I wrapped a dressing gown around myself, and went down the stairs, wondering what all the hullabaloo was about.

The living room was L-shaped, and from where I was on the stairs, I could only see my father, who was sitting on the long sofa at the far end. One glance at him, and I knew that something was dreadfully wrong. He looked terribly distraught and appeared at least ten years older than what he had looked the previous night. My first thought was that he had had another heart attack, and that was the reason for my mother's anxiety, and the presence of strangers at this early hour. I took the stairs two at a time, and rushed down into the room, running up to my father.

Although I had not looked to the side, I sensed – rather than saw – what appeared to be an Air Force uniform. I froze, hardly a foot from my father, and slowly turned around.

I was right about the uniform. At that very moment, I knew that my entire world had imploded.

****

What happened in the next few minutes are nothing but a blur in my memory. As I turned around, it was as if everything went into slow-motion. There were two senior Air Force Officers (an Air Marshal and a Wing Commander) there that day. I could see them rising to their feet on seeing me.

Then the Air Marshal uttered the most dreaded words that I would ever hear in my life. "I am very sorry to inform you Ma'am that your husband is no more. His helicopter crashed in Baramulla. We managed to get him to the Hospital in Srinagar. But he had severe head injuries and died at about 2:40 this morning."

FOWL PLAY

Just when most of us in India were praying for a peaceful 2008, there was this story on all TV networks which caused a furore country-wide.

Animal rights activists were up in arms, demanding a CBI inquiry into the matter and Monika Chandy threatened to go on a 'fast-unto-death' unless the Government tendered an unconditional apology to vegetarians.

Shiv Sena supremo Bal Thakore wrote a biting article in Saamna blaming non-Maharashtrian influence for the sordid state of affairs.

Here in Karnataka, Pattal Rangaraj – the firebrand champion of Kannada – sharply decried the use of English in describing the incident. (In fact, several English newspapers bore the brunt of the Kannada Vedike activists' fury, and their offices and vans were torched).

Police had to resort to a *lathi* charge and the use of water cannons in the old city of Hyderabad, where members of two communities came to blows over the issue.

The Army, which was called out in Lucknow, staged a flag march in the disturbed areas. Most of the city was placed under an indefinite curfew, and shoot-at-sight orders issued to deal with miscreants.

While the Home Ministry sought to downplay the reports, a brief statement condemned the incident, and said that the opposition was making a 'mountain out of a molehill.'

Reacting strongly, a BJP spokesman described the incident as 'anti-national' and blamed Muslims for being the root cause, since many of them owned similar businesses.

On their part, Muslim leaders vehemently denied any hand in the violence. In fact, the Imam of Jama Masjid termed as 'baseless' the reports carried by certain sections of the media, alleging that the perpetrators of the crime belonged to a Madrasa.

Not to be left out, the Archbishop of Bengaluru, addressing his flock during New Year's Mass, said that this was certainly the handiwork of Satan, and prayed that God would forgive those responsible.

In a nation-wide television broadcast, the Prime Minister appealed for calm. "The enemies of secularism, socialism and progress should not be allowed to jeopardize our march to prosperity," he said, adding, "let us not forget the great sacrifices made by Mahatma-ji, Sanjay-ji, Rajiv-ji, Sonia-ji, Rahul-ji and Priyanka-ji in promoting *ahimsa*, and showing us the path of peace and tolerance."

Meanwhile, in the sleepy village of Gummadipally, tucked away in a remote corner of Tamilnadu, life has returned to normal.

It may be recalled that this national crisis was sparked off on New Year's night, when three roosters belonging to one Abdul Sattar reportedly ganged up and molested a hen belonging to the local DMK supporter, Maniratnam Pandiyan.

INS AND OUTS

I was at a party in the Club, where I met this guy. We got talking, and he asked me, "What are you in?" – meaning what my occupation was.

I replied him and said, "Inn."

That had him foxed and he said "In what?"

So I replied, "In inn."

At that point, he probably decided that I had just escaped from the nut house, and swiftly moved away, before I could tell him that I worked as an inn-keeper.

This 'inn'cident got me thinking...was I 'out' because I had an inn? Hmm. Interesting thought. Reminded me of the funny rules of cricket. The batsman who is out on the pitch is 'in,' but when he returns into the pavilion, he is 'out!' And why in heaven's name is the sojourn of the team batting called 'innings' when each batsman goes out on the field to bat until declared 'out'...whereupon he comes back in! I would hazard a suggestion here – 'innings' be called 'outings' instead.

These days we read a lot of the P3Ps (for the uninitiated, Page Three People) aka the 'in' crowd. But have you noticed that to make it to P3, these 'in' people have to be 'out' of their homes, and be seen hanging around in Inns or Hotels? Befuddling, to say the least!

Inns have been around for several thousands of years. The Bible mentions that when Mary and Joseph went to Bethlehem, there was no place at the inn. Now, what were the chances that that particular hotel was called Holiday Inn? Quite likely. Eventually, Mary had to settle for giving birth to her Child in the manger..possibly the nickname for another hotel – I hazard a guess – 'The Shepherd's Inn?'

While on the topic, I have a theory why The Holiday Inn in Bangalore went in for a radical change of name a few years ago. A friend of mine told me that he got a call from his friend in the US, asking where he was. He replied, "Holiday Inn Bangalore."

"What?" said the caller, incredulity creeping into his voice. "You are on a HOLIDAY? In Bangalore? You must surely be joking or just plain crazy!" Hmm! That much for our Garden City!

Applying one's mind to 'ins' and 'inns' can be a very interesting and rewarding exercise. Is ordinate the opposite of inordinate? Or solent the opposite of insolent? What about inmate..does one become an 'outmate' once released from wherever one is an inmate? Or take income, if you will. By no stretch of imagination is it related to outcome. Then of course there is 'information.' One knows that aircraft fly in formation..migrating birds fly in formation..but tell me: if aircraft and/or birds fly alone, are they flying 'outformation?'

Why do most wives treat their 'in'-laws as 'out'-laws? Do they have some inalienable right to treat these people as aliens?

These days, several places in our beloved country are burning because of the caste issue. If one is from a lower caste, then one is an 'outcast'...so does that mean those from the so-called 'upper' castes should be called 'in-casts?'

IT'S A WONDERFUL LIFE AFTER 65

I am utterly flabbergasted when I hear folks say 'old age is a curse'... 'better to die, than to live like this'... 'why am I lingering around'...etc., etc.

I, for one, am of the firm opinion that there is a lot of fun in 'going geriatric.' Oh..I agree that most of us may have those odd aches and pains, and a few of us may be afflicted by more dire and sinister ailments – but the vast majority of us 'Senior Citizens' can (and should) see the brighter side of our advancing years. That way, not only can we live happier, but also be less of a 'pain-in-the-posterior' to those around us.

I am presently hovering around at the cusp of the Biblical deadline of three-score-and-ten years, but in my mind, I do not consider myself to be a day older than fifty! Crazy? Maybe. But look how it has helped.

Most folks (including my wife and children) roll their eyes heavenward, and mumble 'second childhood' whenever I go ecstatic over my grandson's new remote-controlled car or have a second helping of the Rich Chocolate Cake, or take the hand of a pretty, twenty-something lass, and pretend to palm-read. Just look at the fun I am having!

Ailments are a bother...I agree. I had a heart attack about six years ago, and fortunately it was sorted out with a simple angioplasty. But just look at the 'mileage'

I accrued...I was (and still am) treated like I would die if someone sneezed. I have had visits from folks whom I had not seen in a zillion years, and...it was fantastic being pampered by young, pretty nurses, who were tickled pink that I was laughing and joking all through my stay at the hospital. Even today, whenever I am pushed into a corner, I evoke – and receive – special consideration by just throwing in the phrase 'I am a heart patient!'

I sincerely believe that one can literally get away with anything short of murder, the moment one crosses the age of sixty-five. All one has to do is say "I don't remember." Now, that can be regarding a telephone number, an appointment with the dentist, the shopping list given by one's wife, how many drinks one has had...even the name of the pretty-young-thing, whose palm one pretended to read! Just about anything. There is absolutely no way that anyone (and I mean ANYONE) can verify if the loss of memory is authentic or just plain 'amnesia of convenience.'

Oh..and before I forget...I must mention that I have been diagnosed with something called Peripheral Neuropathy. Sounds menacing, doesn't it? It is nothing but a loss of sensation in the extremities – especially the feet. Pretty common, I am told, for those who have espoused Bacchus as a bosom pal over the years. It can be pretty 'un-nerving,' especially when getting a pedicure.

But..looking at the positive side, I am totally gaga that I am a victim of this syndrome...I know for a fact that I can kick someone's butt as hard as I want – but..I will not feel the pain!

FATE IS THE HUNTER

THE PARTING

The man stood on the platform, totally oblivious to the mass of humanity swirling around him, clutching his small, wet umbrella, staring unblinkingly at the extremely pretty young woman who sat in the compartment, next to the window. It was difficult to fathom whether his expression was one of pain, or of regret, or of just profound grief. The woman too had her tear-filled eyes firmly locked onto his. The silence that prevailed was prolonged, solid, impenetrable. And yet..a million words seemed to be exchanged between them.

For just a moment, his gaze shifted from her face, as he looked down at his watch. It showed that the train would be leaving in just about two minutes. Somewhere deep inside, he hoped and prayed that the departure would be delayed or even cancelled..but instantly realised the futility of the thought and lifted his eyes to take in her beauty this one last time, reliving what had come to be 'life' for him over the past three years.

His mind went back...way back to the day they had met...to the moments they had experienced...to the daily joy of seeing her youthful energy...to the tinkle of her laughter...to the silence of the days that they just sat together. He sighed, as he recalled in vivid detail every moment that they had shared, loved and lived.

****

The blast of the locomotive's air-horn snapped him rudely out of his reverie, and, as if in a stupor, he stretched out his right hand and gently touched her fingers which were desperately holding on to the window bars. With a slight jolt, the train edged forward. In a frenzy, he sought and clutched her hand through the window. He moved along with the train, his eyes not leaving hers even for a moment. It was getting difficult for him to keep from bumping into people thronging the edge of the platform, but somehow, he managed to keep going...until the train had picked up enough speed and he had to let go of her hand. Now running along with the train, for one last fleeting moment, he looked at her beautiful, sad face, her dark eyes, her upturned nose, and her sensuous, full lips. He thought she said, "I love you..." but the moment was gone in a flash, as he was unable to keep up with the train, and was left staring at the carriages rolling by, the relentless clatter of their wheels drowning out all other sounds.

He had no idea as to how long he stood there...perhaps it was just for a few minutes or it could have been for a few hours. It was only when he suddenly felt heavy drops of rain stinging his face that he seemed to realise that he was still on the now-deserted platform, way beyond where the protective roof ended.

With a deep sigh, he turned and started walking, opening his battered umbrella, and protecting himself from the driving rain. Almost instantly, a vicious gust of wind plucked the small umbrella out of his cold, stiff hands, and it was swiftly carried away, roughly tossed on to the tracks, bumping and turning over and over, as if in a bizarre dance of death.

He stood perhaps for another two minutes, mindlessly staring at the umbrella, which was now a mere black speck in the distance. A wry smile formed on the man's lips, and he sighed again – perhaps not so much at the loss of the umbrella, but more at the utter futility of his existence.

THE MAN

The subdued hum of the air conditioner was reassuring to his troubled mind. He sat on the bed, leaning on the pillow propped up against the headboard. Reaching to his right, his fingers sought out the packet of Gold Flake cigarettes and lighter, which were always on the side-table beside the bed. He slowly extracted a cigarette, automatically tapping the filtered-end on the packet, and putting it between his lips. He lit up, and took a deep puff, inhaling deeply. Warm smoke filled his lungs, the nicotine instantly kicking in and calming his body and mind.

For some strange reason, he held the lighter in front of him and looked at it, as though seeing it for the first time. It was a solid gold Ronson lighter, given to him by his wife, Meena, on their twentieth wedding anniversary. Although she had always been against his smoking habit, she had come to accept that it was something that he just could not do without. He remembered her exact words, as she hugged him, lightly kissed him on his cheek, and gave him the gift, saying, "Here's more gold for your Gold Flake, Willy!" (Since he was a writer, she always addressed him playfully as 'Willy'..short for William, as in William Shakespeare). He smiled, as he recalled the occasion..and for a moment was lost in thought, glimpses of his past life flashing before him, much like watching a jerky video.

It all seemed so very long ago. He had been at his prime then..having made somewhat of a name for himself in the realm of short story writing. In fact, Penguin Books had evinced a lot of interest in his entire collection of short stories, which he planned to name 'Polka Dots on the Canvas of Life.' Yes..had the book been published, Bharat Ramachandran would probably have become a household name..at least in India.

Bharat and Meena had been in their twenties, when they met by sheer chance at the British Council Library. In fact, they had literally bumped into each other, both searching for 'The Complete Works of William Shakespeare'... of which there was only one copy available in the library. Call it luck, coincidence or fate, but both had spied the volume at the same time, and made a beeline for it..reaching the shelf together. The initial shock of nearly bumping into each other gave way to smiles..leading to friendship and eventually, after a very short while, to love. Fortunately, there was no hitch from either family, and they were married in 1968.

Life was blissful for the couple, and they thrived in each other's company. He had always been a romantic and given to flights of fancy. At the time of their marriage, he was working as an Assistant Sub-Editor for a local newspaper but had no ambitions whatsoever of rising to any great heights in that line of work. Rather, he always wanted to be a writer or a poet.

She, on the other hand, was very grounded and practical in her outlook. An accomplished danseuse, she had already become quite well-known amongst the connoisseurs of the classical Indian dance forms. She was also a voracious reader, and a serious critic of literature.

Within a few years of their marriage, he had given up his 9 to 5 job with the newspaper and had started trying his hand at creative writing. Meena supported him wholeheartedly, offering suggestions and constructive criticism, which was gratefully accepted by him. His talent bloomed, and his writing proliferated.

In time, she started a school for teaching classical Indian dance, and it was a huge success. She was sought after by individuals and institutions within the country and abroad and was acknowledged as an authority on the subject. As a result, she used to travel frequently, especially after she stopped giving individual performances.

Bharat's and Meena's life together was all that a happy married life should be. If there was the one regret that left a nagging sadness in their world, it was the fact that they could not have any children...within the first three years of getting married, they had come to know that she would never be able to conceive. It was very painful to accept at the beginning, especially for Meena, who felt that she was something of a freak, and that she had betrayed Bharat. Her disappointment with herself nearly pushed her into a nervous breakdown, and it was only the unflinching and absolute support from Bharat that eventually helped her come to terms with reality. Over time, both of them accepted the fact stoically, and lived life even more fully... even more in love with each other than ever before.

Once they had overcome this trauma, life literally went into top gear in the years ahead. Meena got extremely busy with her dancing, and Bharat tasted the first fruits of success, when he published a few of his short stories with Rupa Publishers...the new Indian start-up publishing house. It seemed that nothing could go wrong in their life, and success brought them even closer in their love for each other.

It is often said that even the Gods become jealous, when they see humans sublimely happy. As if to prove this, Bharat's and Meena's utopia was shattered to smithereens one fateful day in 1990..the fourteenth of February, to be precise.

Meena had gone on a business trip to Bombay two days earlier, where she was planning to set up another school. The meetings had gone well, and she called Bharat and excitedly told him all about it, hoping to be home that very afternoon on Indian Airlines Flight 605, which was scheduled to arrive in Bangalore at 1:30 pm. He promised to pick her up from the airport, looking forward to having a wonderful celebration for Valentine's Day. Wanting to surprise her, and had reserved a table at the Taj West End, where he intended to take her directly from the Airport. He had also ordered a huge bouquet of red roses (her favourite flowers) which was timed to arrive precisely when they reached their table. He just could not wait to see the happiness in her eyes.

Sadly, all this was not to be. The flight from Bombay crashed just minutes away from landing, killing 92 of the 150 passengers and crew on board. Meena was one of those who died.

Even though several years had elapsed from the day his world had shattered, he had still not gotten over the void that her tragic death had left in his life. The terrible event had left him a broken man..his mind totally blank, most of the time. His writing had more or less dried up..as though his muse had disappeared, never to return. Most nights he could not sleep, and he had started drinking quite heavily. When even this did not work, he had sought medical help. His doctor had prescribed the tablet Valium, to relax his body and induce sleep. Practically every night he used to pop one of these pills and manage to drop into a fitful sleep.

Presently, he was so very lost in memories, he had not noticed that the cigarette had practically burnt to a stub in his fingers, the ash balanced grotesquely at the tip. It was only when he suddenly felt the heat on his fingers that he was roused from his reverie, and quickly stubbed out the cigarette in the ash tray.

Instantly lighting another cigarette, he slowly got up from the bed, walked to the open bedroom widow and looked out…putting back the fond memories of Meena. He sighed…a long lonely sigh. It was time to face another miserable, lonely day.

THE WOMAN

Her name was Priya Holla. Born and brought up in Mangalore, she was the only child of Umesh Holla and Malini. She had been a brilliant student, always standing first in class at school and completing her 12th Standard in 2005. Her parents were very keen that she should become a doctor, but since she always had an artistic bent of mind, she chose to join Sandesha Lalithkala Mahavidhyalaya in Mangalore for a three-year degree course in Fine Arts. She excelled at college and graduated with a BFA Degree in 2008. Seeing her excellent performance during the course, she was offered a job as a teacher in the same college, which she gladly accepted. Her parents too were very happy that she would be able to live with them while she worked at a job of her liking.

As with most traditional families, Umesh and Malini began scouting for a suitable groom for their daughter when she turned 23. Since Mangalore had limited scope in finding an ideal match for their only daughter, they checked out eligible bachelors in other major cities. Eventually, after searching for about six months, they narrowed in on a prospective son-in-law.

His name was Manish, and he too was an only child. A graduate of IIT Manipal, he was employed in Wipro as a Senior Engineer at the relatively young age of 26 and lived in Bangalore.

****

Manish and his parents came to Mangalore to 'see the girl,' as soon as the preliminary discussions were over.For Priya, it was love for Manish at first sight. He was all that she (like all girls of her age) had ever fantasised about. Even now she blushed whenever she thought of the moment she had looked at him for the first time, and their eyes had met. Her legs had turned to jelly, and she felt a deep warmth within her..her body tingling and her mind imagining what it would be like to be in his arms. She may have imagined it, but he too seemed excited to see her. Even though both of them modestly avoided direct eye contact, she did notice that he stole furtive glances at her all through the time that he was there.

For some strange, inexplicable reason, she felt as though he wanted to say something to her…

****

The meeting of the parents had been extremely cordial, and in the next few days, the horoscopes and other details were exchanged, and the family priest was contacted for his opinion. This took a few days, and Priya prayed that the result would be positive. She even went to the temple a couple of times, donating generously at the *hundi*, just as an 'insurance-of-sorts' for a favourable report from the priest!

Finally, on the fifth day, the priest came home. As per tradition, Priya was excluded from the discussions, and spent the time in her room, tense and restless.

She needn't have worried…the priest had given a 'clean chit' to the alliance, and in fact had mentioned to her parents that he had not seen a better match. It was as though Priya and Manish were made for each other.

****

The wedding was a grand affair, her parents ensuring that everything was perfect. Priya and Manish took their vows, with both families, relatives and friends looking on and showering their blessings on the young couple. Everyone agreed that this was surely a marriage made in Heaven, as the horoscopes were a perfect match.

As a couple, they were absolutely striking. He was tall, broad shouldered and with the handsome looks of a film star. She too was tall, by Indian standards, coming up to his ears, stunningly good looking with her beautiful dark eyes, slightly upturned nose, a full mouth, long, lustrous black hair and a gorgeous figure. To an observer, they would have seemed the dream couple of romantic novels...the ultimate, sensual twosome.

Their honeymoon destination was Bali, that beautiful island paradise of Indonesia. They had booked a suite at the Four Seasons, and Priya had been happier than she had ever been in her life..never in her wildest dreams had she imagined that she would be married to such a handsome man and begin her wedded life in one of the most exotic places on Earth.

Once they reached the hotel in Bali, and settled into their suite, Priya had expected that Manish would be as impatient as she was to enjoy their privacy. However, he seemed distracted and aloof. When she coyly moved close to him, putting her arms around his waist and drawing him to her, he did not respond in the way she had expected. In fact, he seemed to become stiff, and mumbled something about having lunch. Even before Priya could react, he was already walking away from her, and heading towards the door.

Priya was dismayed, to say the least, but consoled herself..after all, she reasoned, he was probably a shy person, and would take some time to show his emotions...especially given the fact that he was also the only child of his parents, and therefore not used to the close company of another person. Moreover, she recalled that he had hardly touched the meal served on the flight, and so he must have been hungry.

They had lunch at the Riverside Cafe...which offered a fantastic menu. She had toyed with the idea of ordering a large pizza, but changed her mind at the last moment..she did not want to be stuffed and feeling sleepy (for obvious reasons!), once they got back to their suite after lunch.

Eventually, she settled for something light, in the form of a Greek Salad, with cucumber, onion, green bell peppers, Kalamata olives, tomato with Feta cheese and oregano. Manish, on the other hand, opted for a monster-sized Sayan Club Sandwich – whole-wheat bread, chicken breast, turkey bacon, egg, tomato, lettuce and mayonnaise. Seeing the size of the sandwich, Priya smiled...it seemed as though Manish was getting his energy levels up, for what she hoped would be a very exciting afternoon. Just thinking of what lay ahead made her blush, and when she realised that he was looking in her direction, she blushed even more, and shyly turned away, pretending to admire the waterfall, just to the right of where they were sitting.

It was close to three, by the time they had finished eating, and they slowly walked back to their suite. Priya had walked close to Manish, holding his hand, her fingers intertwined in his. Strangely, his fingers felt cold, and this made her look at him. He seemed to be in a world of his own, looking straight ahead, not even acknowledging her presence. "Perhaps he is tired," she told herself, hoping that he would cheer up once they were in the room.

If Priya had hoped for any kind of romantic overtures from Manish after reaching their suite, she was in for a rude shock. Without so much as a glance at her, Manish just took off his shoes and socks, put on the floppies provided by the Hotel and settled down in front of the television.

Priya was disappointed, but she kept telling herself that things would be alright...that romances like those in Mills and Boon were to be found only in mushy novels. But she was a tenacious person, and not one to accept defeat or disappointment easily. She stood looking at Manish for a few minutes, taking in his rugged good looks and his athletic physique, hoping that he would at least cast a glance in her direction...but it seemed that his gaze was riveted to the television screen. With a silent sigh, she turned and walked towards the bathroom, her mind working overtime to find a way to get his attention.

The solution came to her in an instant. She knew that she was pretty and sexy, and now she decided to use her assets to try and get Manish to respond. The word 'seduction' sprang to her mind.. and she smiled. If indeed he wanted to be seduced, so be it. She would give it her best shot.

Priya quickly freshened herself, brushed her long, black hair until it glistened in the light, and tied it in a high pony tail. Changing from her formal clothes, she stepped into a beautiful, delicately embroidered negligee...which was so thin and transparent, it actually revealed more than it concealed. She stood for a moment in front of the full-length mirror and did a little pirouette..puckering her shapely lips, admiring her full breasts, and her slender, hour-glass figure, which seemed to be trembling with excitement within the gossamer fabric. "Beautiful," she said to herself, smiling self-consciously at her narcissism. And then, with a final shake of her head, which made her pony-tail sway naughtily from side to side, she stepped out of the bathroom.

She immediately realised that the television had been turned off. The heavy window drapes had been drawn, and it was quite dark inside. The only faint light which she could see came from the dim lamp over the bed. She felt a surge of excitement, thinking that Manish had made all preparations for a cosy afternoon. "Perhaps," she thought, "perhaps Manish had just wanted to surprise me, and that was why he pretended not to be interested. Yes...that must be it," she convinced herself, as she walked quickly up to the bed, and climbed on to it.

By now her eyes had gotten used to the semi-darkness, and she could see that Manish was lying on the bed, his eyes shut. She noticed that he had changed from his jeans and shirt into a pair of boxer shorts and nothing else. Just looking at him made her all warm deep inside..her mind spinning with excitement. She lay on the bed and edged herself closer to him. Turning to her right, she put her arm around his midriff, feeling his firm muscles.

There was no reaction from him, and his eyes remained shut. "Maybe he is asleep," she said to herself...or maybe he was pretending to sleep...wanting her to take the initiative.

"Ok, my gorgeous hunk," she said to herself, "if that's the way you want to play it..game on!"

Slowly, she let her hand slide down his stomach, moving it lower and lower, until it was where she wanted it to be.

What happened next was so unexpected, that she nearly passed out.

Manish suddenly sat up, his eyes wide open, his face angry and grotesque. "What are you doing?" he screamed. "Just what the hell are you doing? Can't you see that I am sleeping? Can't you see that I am tired? Why the hell can't you go to sleep too, and leave me alone?"

Priya froze, as if struck by a bolt of lightning. She seemed transformed into a lifeless statue...petrified, with her mouth open in a silent scream, eyes wide open and unblinking, her hand still lying where she had so lovingly placed it on his body.

She had no idea how long she sat transfixed. It was only when she felt her hand being roughly lifted and flung towards her, that she roused herself from her catatonic state. Her mind was in turmoil..her brain unable to make sense of what had just happened. Feelings and emotions flooded her entire being, and she thought she was going to pass out. She clenched her fist so hard that her nails dug into her palms drawing drops of blood. She felt herself getting sick, nausea welling up in her throat.

With a great effort, she moved to her edge of the bed, and got down...unsteady on her feet. Holding the dressing table for support, she staggered into the bathroom, and sat down on the small stool there, holding her throbbing, spinning head in her hands. Her nausea worsened to the point that she could not control it any longer. She got up and rushed to the wash basin, barely managing to reach there, before she was racked by an intense spell of vomiting..bringing out whatever she had eaten just a while ago.

After a few minutes, when the retching stopped, she washed her face, and cleaned up the mess in the wash basin. She looked at herself in the mirror. Her face was flushed, eyes wide open. She could not believe that this was the same beautiful face that she had looked at just a few minutes ago. Absently, she dried her face, pushing back a few strands of hair that had fallen on her face while she was throwing up.

Slowly, she went back and sat on the stool once again...her mind unable to think clearly. She just could not comprehend how her moment of bliss could have become such a horror, literally in the blink of an eye. She desperately tried to think of what she may have done wrong...after all, this was the first time that she was alone in the company of a man – not just 'any' man, but 'her' man. Try as she did, she just could not come up with a logical explanation for Manish's vicious and bizarre behaviour.

She cried...cried as she had never done in all her life, chest heaving and tears flowing copiously, as though a dam had burst. And all the while, just one question kept tormenting her...why...why was this happening to her?

She had no idea how long she sat in the bathroom. At some point, there were no more tears left, and only dry sobs racked her slender body, her breath coming in short bursts, her throat sore from the vomiting and the crying.

Wiping her cheeks with a tissue, Priya got up as if in a trance, and slowly made her way out of the bathroom, not knowing what to expect to how to handle matters from thereon.

The lights were on in the bedroom, bright and hurtful, making her squint. At once she noticed that Manish was not lying on the bed..nor was he to be seen anywhere in the room. The shorts that he was wearing a while back were flung casually on the bed, and there was no sign of his jeans, shirt or shoes. Momentarily, Priya panicked..her mind racing. "What if Manish had left her and gone away?" she thought. But then she noticed that the wardrobe was open and his clothes were still neatly hanging within. Calming down somewhat, she walked across to the bedside table on her side of the bed, and picked up her cell phone, desperate to call Manish.

At the last moment, however, she did not call...not wanting to hear him scream at her as he had done a while ago. Instead, she put the phone back on the table, went to the wardrobe and took out a plain nightie, and quickly changed into it. Somehow, in her mind she was sure that there would be no more romance during the rest of the evening.

She lay down on the bed and closed her eyes, her mind replaying the nightmarish events of the afternoon over and over again. Her world seemed to have ended, even before it had begun.

After what seemed a very long time, she opened her eyes and looked at the clock, which showed 8:30 pm. There was no sign of Manish, and once again she felt panic setting in. However, she did not want to embarrass herself by calling the hotel staff and decided to wait for some more time. Briefly, she thought of ordering some food from Room Service, but she really was not hungry, and dismissed the idea.

She must have fallen asleep, because when she next looked at the time, it was 3 in the morning. The room was dark, and only the night light was on. In the dim light, she noticed that Manish had come back and was fast asleep, and in fact snoring softly. For a moment, she considered snuggling up to him, but recalling what had happened earlier in the evening, she did not. Sleep eluded her, and she carefully got out of bed, not wanting to awaken Manish, and went and sat on one of the lounge chairs on the balcony, until the first rays of sunshine broke through the darkness, heralding another day.

If Priya had hoped that the following days would fulfil her dreams of enjoying the bliss of being with the man that she loved, she was totally disappointed. After the disaster of the first day, she had decided to let Manish make the first move..but that never happened. It was not that he was rude to her..in fact, he was quite friendly and attentive whenever they ventured out of the suite. However, if she had hoped for even the faintest spark of love within the confines of the bedroom, it just did not happen. It seemed like a kind of pattern had set in..get up leisurely, have breakfast in bed, go sight-seeing, have lunch, take a short nap, watch TV, have dinner in one of the restaurants and finally go to sleep with not even a cursory 'good night' from him.

After what seemed an eternity, the six days at Bali were finally over, and they flew back to Bangalore..he looking as handsome as always, and she, still the beautiful virgin that she had been before the honeymoon.

THE MAN

As if to add to his loneliness and misery, it had started raining, making it impossible for him to go for his usual walk. He was disappointed, because the five kilometres walk he used to do every morning served to clear his mind – at least for that moment. He also cherished the moments he used to spend with the few stray dogs that had befriended him..mainly because he fed them biscuits every morning. But today, he knew that even the strays would not be at their usual corner, thanks to the rain, which now seemed to have increased in intensity.

The wind had also picked up, and a few drops of rain splattered on him, as he stood by the open window. He shut the window, turned around and slowly walked across to the front door, and proceeded to pick up the newspaper. Absentmindedly, he glanced at the front page, noting that the dateline said Monday, 14 February 2005. And suddenly..his mind went blank.

14 February...the date his world had collapsed. Dear God, he thought to himself, has it really been fifteen years since that fateful day when the love of his life..his soul-mate, his confidante, his inspiration, his harshest critic Meena had been so cruelly snatched by fate, and left him a shell of his former self? He closed his eyes and sat on the sofa..desperately trying not to get into a depression. However, try as he may, he still could not prevent the tears rolling down his cheeks, and the painful tightness in his chest. "I love you Meena," he whispered over and over... "I love you..I love you..and I miss you!"

The ringing of the telephone rudely brought him back to the present. Wiping his moist eyes with the back of his hand, he got up and went to answer the phone. It was his friend Vasu, whom he had become a friend with during his morning walks. Vasu was an excellent amateur photographer and had convinced Bharat to take up photography as a hobby. He had helped him in buying a good camera – a Leica V-Lux 2 – and also introduced Bharat to the basics of photography. Today he was calling to ask if Bharat was interested in going along to a photo exhibition being held at the Karnataka Chitrakala Parishath Art Gallery.

Bharat's initial reaction was to politely decline..he just was not in the mood and only wanted to sit by himself and grieve. But an inner voice kept telling him to get out of the house and go to the exhibition. So, after a moment's hesitation, Bharat agreed to go, and Vasu said he would pick him up after lunch.

The rest of the morning went past in a sort of daze. He had cereal for breakfast, and watched a bit of TV, on which there was nothing interesting, except for the news of a car-bomb explosion in Beirut, which had killed former Lebanese Prime Minister Rafiq Hariri and 22 others.

His domestic help-cum-cook had come at about 10, quickly cleaned the house, done up his bed and cooked his lunch and dinner. She left around noon, and after that he was once again left all alone to ponder over his lonely existence and wonder how much longer it would go on in this fashion.

He had tried resuming his story-writing several times these past years. But somehow, he was just not able to create anything meaningful. His publishers had been very sympathetic and had encouraged him to write. But, after a while, they had given up, and that further deepened his frustration.

These days, he tried his utmost to bring some meaning into his lonely life by pursuing his recent hobby of photography. In fact, he was quite surprised with the results of his amateurish attempts..mostly thanks to the constant encouragement from Vasu. Bharat knew that today also Vasu would want him to try and capture something interesting at the exhibition, and so he took out the camera, and kept it on the centre table, lest he forget to take it on the way out.

It was around 1:45 pm that Vasu arrived to pick him up. Fortunately, the rain had stopped, and the Sun was visible from behind the patches of clouds. The change in the weather seemed to have brightened Bharat's mood, and he even looked forward to clicking some pictures, if it remained clear for the rest of the afternoon.

Traffic was not too heavy at that hour, and they made good time to the art gallery. As usual, there was no parking space available within the premises, and they had to park quite a distance away and walk up to the venue.

Surprisingly, the place was crowded, despite the fact that it was a working day. The organisers had set up the exhibition within the building, but there were dozens of artistes – painters, sculptors, and the like – who thronged the grounds around, seeking suitable points to create their art. Navigating through the crowd was an effort, but finally, Bharat and Vasu were inside the building.

The display was truly excellent...with works of renowned photographers as well as amateurs. Bharat was particularly interested in the black and white images, which he felt had more depth and 'life' than the colour photographs.

It was while they were viewing some photographs by Raghu Rai, that Vasu got a phone call, informing him that one of his close relatives had met with an accident, and was in hospital in a critical condition.

When he told Bharat that they would have to leave, Bharat was disappointed, as he was just getting to learn some of the aspects in the art of composing. He knew fully well that if he stayed back, he would have a tough time getting an auto-rickshaw to return home, and so was in a quandary. However, on an impulse, he decided to stay, and asked Vasu to go back, wishing his relative a speedy recovery.

Over the next hour or so, it seemed that the crowd was only growing larger, and Bharat had a difficult time getting close to some of the exhibits. Typical of most exhibitions in India, there was no order or discipline amongst the viewers, with everyone trying to get vantage spots, totally unmindful of others.

Bharat had his camera out and tried his best to click as many shots as possible...not only of the pictures on the wall, but candid shots of the jostling, milling crowd. Fortunately, he was quite tall, and so had an advantage over several others. He found himself in front of one of the most acclaimed photograph by Raghu Rai...the picture of Mother Teresa with a young child. It was at once a sublime combination of an intense study of the Mother with her boundless love for a destitute child, and a masterpiece in photographic artistry.

Bharat decided that he just had to take a shot of this picture...to depict the contrast between the peaceful, serene and angelic look on Mother Teresa's face...and the almost insane spectre of the mob trying to get as close to the picture as possible. He held his camera high over his head, straining to look into the small viewfinder screen. He had leaned precariously to his side, his right foot on the floor and the left at least six inches in the air. All of a sudden, he felt himself losing balance, and desperately tried to place his left foot on the floor. Trying to find a foothold, he started swaying – gently at first, but soon losing his balance completely. Since both his hands were above his head, holding the camera, he could not hold on to anything to steady himself, and fell backwards, landing on something soft. Fortunately, the strap of the camera was still around his neck, and so it didn't fly off.

His first reaction was one of acute embarrassment..at having made a spectacle of himself, and his only idea was to get on his feet at once. Letting the camera dangle around his neck, he quickly tried to turn over on all fours and get up from the ridiculous predicament that he found himself in. Once he managed to turn around, he realised that there was worse to come..he found himself practically lying on top of a young woman who was clutching on to a monster handbag in one hand, while desperately hanging on to an easel with the other. Embarrassment gave way to shock, when he saw that her face was just inches away from his. He started to apologise..and then he heard her laugh…

THE WOMAN

After the disastrous honeymoon, Priya really did not know what to expect, once she and Manish had settled into married life. They had moved into a brand-new apartment in the heart of Bangalore, and Priya had used all of her artistic skills to do it up extremely tastefully. Manish seemed very proud of her skills, and lost no opportunity to bring friends over, so that they could admire the flat and complement them on their taste. To be fair, Manish never took credit, and would always tell everyone of how Priya had done everything by herself.

After the trauma at Bali, Priya had not risked making any overt gestures in order to kindle some spark of romance in their life. She had hoped that her mere presence, her subtle ways of showing how much she loved Manish, and how much she yearned for his attention and love would someday bear fruit, as it were.

Manish's behaviour was incomprehensible to Priya. He appeared to be an extremely caring, loving and humane person whenever both of them went out or when friends came over. To an outsider, Priya and Manish would have appeared to be the most perfect pair, the ultimate couple. Indeed, they were the envy of most people who came in contact with them.

However, when they were alone together, it was as though Priya did not exist in his world. The only conversations between them was when she spoke...he would reply, mostly in monosyllables, without so much as a glance in her direction. Love and romance just did not exist and sleeping on the same bed became more and more of a torture for Priya. In the beginning of their life together, she had tried her utmost to attract him, with her charm and scanty nightwear and subtle perfumes. When these did not have the desired effect, she had even swallowed her shyness and modesty, and got into bed totally nude, hoping that at least then he would show some inclination to consummate their marriage. Sadly, even that proved to be futile, and night after night she would cry herself to sleep. After a few weeks, there were no more tears to shed, and she would just clutch a pillow, lying awake, listening to her husband's soft snoring. Sometime late into the night, she would drop off into a fitful, dreamless sleep.

Initially, she suspected that Manish had someone else in his life and presumed that was the reason for his aloofness. But, over a period of time, she became sure that this was not the case. It slowly became obvious to Priya that there was something far more serious to his behaviour than met the eye. Many a time she had considered talking to her mother, but each time, she stopped short..as it is, her father was a heart patient, and had had a bypass surgery a few years earlier. Priya was worried that her problems would worsen his condition.

Finally, after about two months, when she could not bear it any longer, she had hesitatingly confided to Sunita, who was her neighbour and with whom she had become good friends ever since moving into the apartment.

Sunita was much older than Priya and had two grown up sons. Her husband, Dr. Sunil Narayanan was a psychiatrist and Head of Department at Manipal

Hospital. Sunita and Sunil had taken an instant liking for their young neighbours, and were especially fond of Priya, treating her like the daughter they never had.

When she heard what Priya had to say, Sunita had been quite sympathetic, but advised her to have patience. Seeing that Priya was at the point of a breakdown, she had tried to calm her down, promising to broach the subject with her husband, and seek his professional guidance. Initially, this did not seem a good idea to Priya, who wanted to keep the matter just between both of them. Sunita, however, reassured her of total confidentiality, and reluctantly Priya agreed. A few days later, Sunita told Priya that she had spoken with her husband, and that he had advised that both Manish and Priya should meet him together one of these days, when he could try to resolve the problem.

Priya knew that getting Manish to accompany her to speak with Sunil Uncle was going to be very difficult. The few times that Priya had hinted about seeing a doctor for his lack of interest in sex, Manish had flatly ignored the suggestions, and on one occasion even told her to see a doctor if she had a problem. She knew that she would have to wait for the perfect opportunity to speak with Manish, otherwise it would probably end up in a fiasco once again.

The opportunity seemed to present itself on that very weekend. Being a Saturday, it was a holiday for Manish and they had gone to watch a movie – *Zindagi Na Milegi Dobara* – in one of the multiplexes. They had enjoyed the film..apparently Katrina Kaif was Manish's favourite actress. He seemed to be in a good mood, especially after they had gone for a meal at Karavalli and enjoyed the excellent seafood at the restaurant.

Priya too was in a very relaxed mood and had fervently hoped that the evening would end on a romantic note. But her hopes were belied once they reached their home, when Manish did not even vaguely hint that he was in any kind of amorous mood. On the contrary, he completely ignored Priya's presence, changed into his night clothes and got into his side of the bed, switched off the lamp on the side table and closed his eyes.

On any other evening, Priya would also have just got into bed and gone to sleep. But on this particular night, the title of the movie kept playing in her head *'Zindagi Na Milegi Dobara'* (You Won't Get Another Life). As much as she tried, it seemed that there was no way that she could stop her mind from replaying this line over and over. It was like she was standing outside her own body and repeating the words…until it became just too much to bear. She closed her eyes tight and put her palms over her ears, as though trying to shut out the voice..but it only became louder.

There was only one way that she could stop this anguish. She just HAD to talk with Manish once again, and try and find a solution to this living death.

She sat up and turned on the light above the bed. Manish seemed fast asleep, snoring gently. Even in her disturbed state, Priya could not fail to admire him…he looked so very handsome, a trace of black stubble on his chiselled face.

Taking a deep breath, Priya moved closer to Manish, and gently touched his forehead with the tips of her fingers, moving her face close to his and softly calling his name, "Manish...Manish..."

Initially there was no response from him, but she was not going to give up. She bent even lower and kissed him tenderly on his lips, breathing in the faint fragrance of his cologne.

This time his eyes opened a wee bit, and then went wide open, when he saw her face just next to his. "What is it?" he said sleepily, turning to his right, swinging his legs down and getting up to a sitting position. Half turning, he again repeated, "What is it? What do you want?"

Priya knew in her mind that it was now or never...if she passed up this opportunity of speaking to him now, she knew that she would never be able to muster up courage to do so again.

"Manish," she started, "Manish, there is something that I want to tell you."

This time, he turned and faced her. "What is it? Are you not well?" he asked.

"No...no, nothing like that...I am quite well," she stammered, desperately trying to form the words she wanted to say. "It's just that I was chatting with Sunita Aunty the other day, and she was teasing me about when we are going to have a baby, and..."

She did not finish her sentence. Manish abruptly got up and walked menacingly around the bed towards her. He had instantly become like a man possessed...his eyes were wide open...his nostrils flared and quivering, his lips drawn back into a horrible snarl. "What? What did you say?" he shouted. The veins in his neck stood out and his face had turned a deep shade of red. "What did you say?" he repeated, his voice rising by several decibels, raising his hands, and moving closer to Priya.

She cringed in fear, her eyes wide, her body trembling, as she tried to get down from the bed. Although she had expected some sort of reaction from him, she had not anticipated anything like this. "I..I..I..." she stuttered, trying desperately to talk. "I..I..I was only saying..." but that was as far as she got.

He was standing over her, breathing heavily, drops of saliva dripping from the edges of his mouth...his outstretched hands inches away from her face. Priya fought back her panic, thinking that he was going to strangle her. He reached out and caught her by her shoulders, shaking her violently, screaming at the top of his voice, "You bloody slut! How dare you talk to anyone about me? How dare you? How DARE you!!"

Priya's head bobbed back and forth as he shook her, and she feared that her neck would snap from the ferocity of his shaking. She tried to scream for help, but no sound emerged from her lips.

Finally, after what seemed like eternity, he let go of her...pushing her away so hard, that she fell back on the bed. "I want you to get out," he yelled. "I want you out of my life!" Having said that, he stomped out of the bedroom, slamming the door behind him.

Priya sat on the bed, stunned, unable to move or even think coherently. In just a matter of a few minutes, her world had violently imploded. For a moment, she thought that this was just a horrible nightmare, and that everything would be normal, once she awoke from her sleep. She desperately wanted to cry, but somehow the tears refused to come.

With a great effort, she got down from the bed, and looked around her...orientating her confused mind...taking in the empty bed and the closed door. It slowly dawned on her that she was not dreaming, and that this situation was indeed real. All the time, Manish's final words kept screaming into her ears: "I want you to get out...I want you out of my life!"

Priya did not know what to do...where to go, whom to turn to. Her first thought was to call her parents, and pour her heart out. But she held herself back...it was late, and they would have probably gone to bed. Calling them with this news at this time would surely have a detrimental effect on her father's frail health.

She went to the bathroom, and washed her face, feeling the soothing comfort of the cold water. She dried her face with a towel, looking at her reflection in the mirror over the wash-basin. Her nightie had dropped from her left shoulder as she wiped her face, and she caught a glimpse of the red welt that had formed at the spot where Manish had so brutally held her. Dropping the towel, she checked her other shoulder...which was also badly bruised.

All at once, her mind seemed to have calmed down, and she was beginning to think coherently again. The sight of her discoloured shoulders had suddenly yanked her into the present, grief giving way to anger. No..it was not just anger, but hatred – a deep hatred for the man whom she had married, loved and literally worshipped until today.

At that moment, she knew that her marriage was over.

Priya had spent the rest of the night packing her belongings. In between, Manish had come into the bedroom, but had not uttered a word..indeed, he had not even looked in Priya's direction. She was done by four in the morning.

She had decided to go back to Mangalore that very day. The first train out of Bangalore was from Yeshwanthpur, and departed at 6:30 am. She felt guilty at not being able to say goodbye to Sunita Aunty, but it could not be helped. She did not look back, when she rolled her suitcases out, caught a passing auto-rickshaw at about 5:00 am, and made her way to the Station.

She reached her parents' home late in the evening, hoping that her sudden arrival would not be too much of a shock to them. Surprisingly, they were very calm when she told them that she had come back to stay, and even sounded happy to have her back. Her father looked in reasonably good health, and that was a big relief for her.

As the days turned to weeks, and weeks to months, her parents had hoped that there would be some kind of reconciliation in the marriage. But Priya had made up her mind that she would never ever go back to

Manish and wanted to get formal divorce proceedings going as soon as possible. When she told them gently, but firmly, about her resolve, they accepted it, knowing full well that their daughter would not do anything frivolous...especially in such a serious matter.

Within a few days, they had met Mr. Kamath, an advocate-friend of her father, and legal proceedings commenced soon thereafter. Surprisingly, Manish responded almost immediately, and conveyed his intention to grant the divorce on mutually agreeable terms. It was apparent that he did not want a protracted legal action, where his impotence would have been exposed.

Barring the mandatory legal period of separation, Priya and Manish were formally divorced in nine months.

All this time, Priya had kept in touch with Sunita Aunty, who sympathised with her, and supported her decision totally. When the divorce was complete, she even invited Priya to go and spend a few days with them, but Priya politely declined...the raw wounds had yet to heal completely.

About six months later, Priya chanced to see an advertisement in the local newspaper, announcing a vacancy for an art teacher in Karnataka Chitrakala Parishath in Bangalore. Although it was very tempting, her first instinct was to disregard it, as it would mean going to Bangalore once again. However, when she mentioned it to Sunita Aunty, she was very enthusiastic, and told Priya that she must not give up her vocation. She even promised to find her suitable accommodation for her to stay independently. After all, she and Sunil were always there to help her should the need arise.

When Priya sent in her application along with her qualifications and employment records, little did she know what a dramatic turn her life would take from that point onwards. She was called for an interview, and the Selection Panel was clearly impressed with her resume. Soon after, she got her appointment letter, and Priya once again bid farewell to her parents and came to Bangalore. She was met at the station by Sunita and Sunil, who took her to the one-bedroom studio apartment that they had found for her.

From day one, Priya loved her new job, and her new home. When she was not at the Academy teaching art, she would spend all her spare time decorating her flat. Much as she would have liked to visit Sunita Aunty and Sunil Uncle, she could not bring herself to go to the building which held such unpleasant memories for her. More importantly, she definitely did not want to risk the embarrassment of running into Manish.

Her fears, however, turned out to be unwarranted. Sunita Aunty told her that Manish had got another job in Mumbai, and had moved out, just about two weeks after Priya had moved to Bangalore. After that, Priya would spend most weekends and holidays with the Narayanans, and they too welcomed her visits.

It was just after six months since Priya had taken up the job that Karnataka Chitrakala Parishath that she was involved in a major event organised by the

Academy. The event was an exhibition of photographs by India's best lens-men, and she welcomed the opportunity to coach her students in creating sketches of some of the photographs. She had not expected such a massive turnout for the event, and it was quite a herculean task for her to get her team into the best positions to capture the images on to canvas.

After reviewing the exhibits, she decided to have her students sketch a masterpiece by Raghu Rai, one of the most celebrated photographers in the country. The photograph itself was the famous one of Mother Teresa with a destitute child, captured in black and white. Unfortunately, it seemed that most spectators also had the same idea, and there were at least twenty or thirty people crowding around this particular exhibit. Not surprisingly, Priya's entreaties for allowing them some leeway to get a clear view fell on deaf ears, and she and her students had to make do with the available conditions.

Priya herself wanted to sketch the photograph and was about to set up her easel practically at the outer fringe of the crowd. In front of her was an oldish-looking man, holding a camera with both his hands over his head, precariously balanced on one leg, trying to get a shot of the exhibit. He seemed so totally absorbed in his attempt, that he did not realise that he was losing his balance, and tilting to his right, until it was too late. Desperately, he tried balancing himself, letting go of his camera and trying to get a handhold. Unfortunately for him, he was so unbalanced, that he toppled heavily backwards. Although Priya saw him falling onto her and her half-set-up easel, she just did not have time to move way. The next moment she found herself flat on the ground, the man practically lying on top of her!

She felt her breath being forced out of her because of his weight, as she struggled to extricate herself. The man, in the meantime, had turned on his stomach, and was on all fours, trying to get up. His face was just a couple of inches from Priya's face, totally red. It was obvious that he was terribly embarrassed, and was trying to say something...probably apologising, but although his lips were moving, no sound emerged. He somehow reminded Priya of Donald Duck, and she couldn't help laughing out loud.

THE MAN AND THE WOMAN

It was probably one of the most awkward moments in Bharat's entire life, though not as bad as the time when, after a drink too many at the Bangalore Club, he had strayed into the ladies toilet by mistake, and was nonchalantly undoing his zipper, when a high-pitched shriek from a couple of ladies had left him red-faced, and feeling like a pervert. On that occasion at least, he had the excuse of being drunk..but here he was, stone sober, lying on a strange, beautiful, young woman, faintly smelling of Chanel No.5. To add to his discomfiture, she was laughing out so loudly, that several persons in the crowd turned around and were staring at him.

Finally, after what seemed like ages, he managed to extricate himself, repeating over and over, "I am sorry Madam..I am really sorry Madam," which made her laugh even more!

He was now in a standing position, but the young woman was still flat on the floor, her easel lying by her side. Out of sheer instinct, he reached out and offered his hand for her to hold and get up. She appeared to hesitate for a moment, but eventually grasped his outstretched hand, and hauled herself off the floor, mumbling her thanks. Her hand felt soft and warm, and as she stood up, he once again got a faint whiff of her perfume.

It is said that smells evoke the strongest memories in humans, and obviously that was true. The moment he got the faint whiff of the fragrance, Bharat's mind was transported back in time, and he recalled that this was the very perfume that had been Meena's favourite. He stood mesmerised..his mouth open and literally gawking at this young woman, absolutely speechless. He did not realise that he was still holding her hand, until he felt her trying to take it back.

He pulled his hand away, as though he had touched a live wire. He must have blushed, because the young woman was looking at him, with a trace of a smile on her lips. "I..I..I'm really sorry," he managed to mumble. "I didn't see that you were behind me...I should have been more careful."

Her smile seemed to have widened, and she shook her head and said, "Oh, no...no. It is I who should have been more careful. I should not have set up my easel right behind you. Anyway, I am ok, and I hope that you too have not injured yourself."

"Oh, I am fine," he replied, "I only hope that your easel is not broken. Here, let me set it up for you."

"No..no..it's ok," she said, "I cannot get a proper view in any case. Guess I will return later when the crowd has gone. Oh, by the way, I am Priya..I teach art here," and she held her hand out.

All this while, Bharat's gaze had not left her face. It was one of the most beautiful that he had seen..perfectly heart-shaped, with large, expressive dark eyes, accentuated by long, tapering eyebrows, a slightly upturned nose, shapely lips with just a trace of light pink lipstick. Her hair was long, shiny and black...worn in a high pony-tail, which swayed from side to side when she moved her head.

So engrossed was he with admiring her face, that he did not notice either her outstretched hand, or hear her words...until she repeated herself, a little louder this time, "Hello..I am Priya. I teach art here."

This time around, he was jolted out of his reverie. "Oh..so sorry," he stuttered, stretching out his hand and lightly taking hers in his palm. "Hello..I am Bharat..I was trying to take a photo of Mother Teresa," as if that explained his embarrassed look. He once again felt the soft, warm fingers..and a strange excitement coursed through his body.

In all the years since Meena had died, Bharat had never ever been physically so close to anyone..especially another woman. It was not that he did not have opportunities to do so..but he had consciously avoided becoming friendly or close to anyone...totally content and satisfied with his fond memories of his beloved Meena. In his mind, he felt it would have been a betrayal of the love he and Meena had shared, and he certainly did not feel the need for someone else in his life..lonely though it was.

And yet..here he was today, all wobbly and as shy as a schoolboy on his first date, feeling an inexplicable attraction towards this woman...who could have been even younger that the daughter he never had. His mind was a blur, his thoughts confused and muddled. He didn't know what to say..if at all he wanted to say something. He didn't know whether to stay or just go away.

His confusion was abruptly settled when the woman smiled and said, "Would you like to join me for a cup of coffee at the cafeteria? I am nearly done here for now and would like some caffeine to calm my nerves after all the recent excitement."

Bharat hesitated for a moment...words not coming from his throat. It seemed to him that he was dreaming..in a world away from the real world. When he did not reply, the young woman repeated her question, thinking that he had not heard her. This time, he did reply. "Sure," he said. "Sure. That would be nice." He waited for a few minutes, while Priya gathered her students and gave them instructions. From where he stood, Bharat could see her, and followed her every move, his eyes riveted on her lovely face, her slender arms as she gestured animatedly, her beautiful black pony tail, which seemed to have a life of its own.

All of a sudden, she turned and looked straight in his direction. If she had been surprised that he was staring at her, she did not show it, but smiled as she walked up to join him. "Ready?" she asked, leading the way to the cafeteria, which was a short distance away from the main hall, where they were.

He walked a step behind her, feeling strangely excited as well as awkward. He kept glancing around, as if to make sure that he was not being watched by anyone he knew. One part of his mind kept thinking that he should have declined the offer to have coffee, and gone his way, when he had the chance. Strangely, the other part of his mind kept urging him onwards, compelling him to enjoy the company of this beautiful young woman.

Presently, they reached the cafeteria, and ordered coffee and some snacks to go with it. The place was quite crowded, mainly by students. Priya seemed to be very popular amongst the students, and several of them came over to chat with her. Bharat could not help observing that she hardly looked older than many of the students, chatting and laughing with them freely. Her laugh was throaty and spontaneous, and he felt it very hard to take his eyes away from her. "Come on Bharat," he said to himself, "take control of yourself..here you are, over 60 years old, and behaving like a love-struck teenager."

As if reading his thoughts, Priya turned to face him, smiling. "Do you come here often?" she asked, delicately nibbling on a potato wedge.

He was tempted to say that he was crazy about art, and that he came there often..just to impress her. But as quickly as that thought came to his mind, he pushed it aside, and said truthfully, "No. Actually this is the first exhibition that I am attending..and if today is anything to go by, it will probably be the last!" he added, laughing.

She joined in his laughter, agreeing with him that it was indeed a surprise that there was such a crowd. She asked him about his photography, and his camera, and seemed genuinely interested when he explained his preference for black and white compositions.

Bharat had never felt so much at ease in a long time, and her youthful, lively disposition seemed to rub off onto him. The coffee got over, and it just seemed natural for them to order another round, and enjoy each other's new-found company.

Priya too was very surprised with herself. She had never considered herself an extrovert, especially with members of the opposite gender, preferring to be by herself, or at the most, share some time with her female students. But, somehow, she felt very comfortable in Bharat's company, inwardly laughing at his shyness and discomfiture at being with her.

In the nearly two hours that they had spent together, they had quickly become comfortable in each other's company, and had briefly touched upon their individual lives. She told him that she was divorced, but not the reason for it...and he had been too much of a gentleman to ask. He had also touched upon Meena's tragic death, not with the idea of seeking sympathy, but in a matter of fact way. It was as though two friends were meeting after a long time and sharing events that had happened in their lives during the period.

It was nearly 4 o'clock in the evening when they left the cafeteria and it seemed as though the time had literally flown by. As they were saying goodbye, he was sorely tempted to ask her if they could meet again...but could not bring himself to say it. As though sensing his thoughts, she turned, looked him straight in the eye and said, "If you are not busy on Saturday, maybe we can meet over coffee," adding with a mischievous smile, "it will be my treat this time."

For a moment, Bharat was taken aback, although he felt immensely happy that she had voiced what he could not. "Sure," he replied, "I would really like to get out of the house..but, let's not come to this place. There is a nice Coffee Day outlet near my place, and I can pick you up, if it's ok with you." "That will be just great," she said. "Will you call me on Saturday morning?"

It was then that they realised that they had not exchanged telephone numbers and did so without the slightest hesitation. With a final goodbye, they parted, promising to meet on Saturday.

****

Much to his surprise, Bharat's kept frequently thinking of Priya all through the week. The temptation to call her was strong, but he managed to hold himself back. He just could not understand himself, and several times he wondered if he was losing his mind. Here he was, 62 years old and literally gushing over a young woman who was less than half his age. Much as he tried to keep her out of his thoughts, it seemed that this was just not possible.

Finally, Saturday arrived, and Bharat was up early. For the first time in several years, he was in a cheerful mood, and not in dread of facing another day..in fact, he was wishing the hours would pass soon, so he could be with Priya again.

Priya too was keenly looking forward to a nice evening with Bharat. There was something about him that had made her extremely happy..but she just could not put her finger on it. She realised that he was much older than her, and initially had felt very embarrassed for laughing when he had toppled over on top of her. However, over coffee, she realised that he too saw humour in the situation, and it was only his shyness that made him reticent in the beginning.

The evening at Coffee Day went off exceedingly well. Both Bharat and Priya had shed whatever hesitation that they had felt at their first meeting and were chatting as though they had known each other for a long time. For the first time in years, both felt unburdened by their past, and enjoyed the moment to its fullest.

It was close to 6 o'clock and they had finished a second round of coffee. The sun had set as they sat, intently looking at each other in the semi-darkness of the fast-falling dusk. The chatter and laughter that they had shared for the past two hours had given way to a kind of mellow stillness, in which silent, unspoken thoughts seemed to flow between them.

"Priya," he started to say, but stopped when she said "Bharat," at that very moment – and both of them suddenly realised that it was the first time that they had actually called each other by their names. It somehow seemed very funny, and they burst into spontaneous, uncontrollable laughter..laughing till their eyes filled with tears. It was to be the start of an amazing relationship between Bharat and Priya... a relationship which would bring back happiness, cheer, and the zest for living into both their lonely lives.

From that day onwards, not a day passed without them meeting and spending time together. The vast difference in their ages did not seem to matter, as each became closer to the other as if they had always been this way.

As far as Bharat was concerned, it was as though the dormant muse had suddenly awoken and, much to his delight, he started writing again. He had completely stopped drinking and had given up the daily Valium to fall asleep. If he had felt self-conscious to be seen with Priya, it soon became a thing if the past, and he revelled in taking her out to movies, restaurants and shopping...all he wanted was to see her happy.

Priya too had become absolutely uninhibited and free with Bharat. She was amazed at his intelligence, and his capacity to create stories out of literally nothing. When he had wanted her to pose for his camera, she had initially been shy. But over time, all shyness had disappeared and he had been able to capture her beauty in all its splendour...much to the admiration of his friend Vasu. In fact, Vasu kept encouraging him to exhibit some of his images whenever the opportunity presented itself, but Bharat was not inclined to do so.

During the years that they had become close, there were several occasions when Priya's parents would cajole her to get married again, since they were also growing old, and her father's health was not all that good. Priya, however, felt that she was not ready for the commitment, and managed to stall her parents' wishes.

Early into their friendship, Bharat too had advised her to find someone and settle down, but she had made it amply clear that she did not want to do so – at least not yet. She was perfectly content in her work and to be in the company of Bharat. Although he had not broached the subject in the recent past, in his heart of hearts, Bharat knew that one day or the other, her marriage was inevitable, but he did not want to think of that day. He was sublimely happy just to see her every single day and spend time together in their own world.

However, for the second time in his life, it seemed that the Gods had decided that too much happiness was not good for Bharat.

****

It happened on the day that he and Priya had gone to watch a Russell Peters show at the Chowdaiah, and had thoroughly enjoyed the performance. As they were walking back to the car, still laughing at some of the jokes, there was a phone call from Priya's mother, sounding extremely distraught. Apparently, she had called earlier in the evening, but since the phone had been on silent mode, Priya had not been aware of the call. She told Priya that her father – who had recently been going into occasional bouts of depression – had suddenly taken a turn for the worse. It was not as though his physical condition had deteriorated, but his mind seemed to be regressing at an alarming rate. It was obvious that he was getting more and more agitated by the fact that Priya did not heed his advice to get married..so much so that Priya's mother feared that he would attempt suicide.

What her mother had said had come as a terrible shock to Priya, and she had sobbed, desperately clinging to Bharat. He had tried to comfort her, but she seemed inconsolable, and kept blaming herself for all that was happening.

Bharat's mind too was in a state of turmoil. On the one hand, he could empathise with Priya, and feel the anguish that she was experiencing. On the other, he was mortally scared that his life was falling apart, all over again.

When they finally reached her home, she seemed to be in a daze. She sat on the sofa, silent, her eyes closed, her head in her hands. He had tried speaking with her, but she did not respond. Eventually, he too went and sat down, not knowing what to say or do.

After about an hour, she seemed to get a hold of herself. Getting up from the sofa, she went and washed her face in the bathroom. When she came out, she walked slowly, directly up to where Bharat sat, and in a calm, quiet voice said, "Bharat, I want to go home."

Bharat did not answer. He felt as though he was in a nightmare, tumbling uncontrollably into a black, bottomless pit.

Somewhere, deep in the recesses of his mind, he knew that this was the end...that she would not come back...ever.

FATE IS THE HUNTER

The man slowly walked the length of the empty platform, his thoughts confused, his mind incapable of thinking coherently. For a moment, he seemed lost in time and space, unable to figure out where he was.

He didn't know for how long he paced up and down the platform. It had become dark, and the lights had come on. In his mind he could only see Priya, hear her voice and her tinkling laughter. He stopped and looked around, as if he would see her, standing behind him, a bright smile on her beautiful face. He seemed surprised when he didn't, and rubbed his tired, bloodshot eyes.

He continued to walk aimlessly, as though in a daze, until a sudden, loud blast of the air horn from a passing engine brought him into the present with a jolt. He stopped once again and wiped his sweaty face with his handkerchief. He squared his shoulders and took a deep breath. He seemed transformed, as though he had suddenly found a purpose in life. Without a backward glance, he walked out of the station, got into his car and drove back slowly and carefully to his flat.

Once he reached home, Bharat sat down on the sofa and closed his eyes. Meticulously, he recalled his life until now, much like replaying a video tape...pausing at certain points, reviewing the highs and lows that had left lasting impressions on his mind.

He dwelt long on recent events, trying to analyse and put into perspective all that had happened in the past few years. There had been many occasions during this period that he had experienced feelings of guilt...questioning himself if he was betraying the sacred bond that he had shared with Meena...and for which he had never been able to find suitable answers. For some strange reason he kept recalling the title of a book that he had read decades ago... 'Fate is the Hunter.'

Finally, after nearly two hours, he finished his journey into the past...his mind clear...his conscience unclouded. He got up and went into his bedroom, walking directly to the dressing table.

He took one final look at himself in the mirror, as he opened the last drawer and took out a small metal box…one that he had not touched since the day that he had met Priya. With steady hands, he opened the box and took out a brown bottle, labelled 'VALIUM 10mg.'

Calmly and deliberately he unscrewed the cap, emptying the entire contents of the bottle into the palm of his right hand. He reached out with his left hand and picked up the glass of water from the bedside table. With one swift motion, he lifted his hand and put the contents of his palm into his mouth. He tilted his head, took a large swig of water, swallowing the tiny tablets in one gulp.

LUNGI DANCE

I have often been asked why I am always in jeans and Ts, or in pants and shirts during the day, and in pyjama night suits at bedtime. I guess that it is a valid doubt, considering the fact that I hail from the South of India..and am considered a 'Madrasi' by all those of my compatriots who happen to belong to the regions North of Nagpur. I guess that in their mind, I should be attired in garments more appropriate to my land of origin..just like they are for ever clad in *kurta*-pyjamas, or similar outfits.

In the past, I had always held the opinion that there was absolutely no necessity for me to explain to anyone about my sartorial preferences. In fact, I was perfectly at ease to let them infer whatsoever they wanted, and/or derive any vicarious pleasure from such inferences. However, as I advance in years, and Father Time marches on relentlessly, I now think I owe it to my friends and acquaintances to know why I am forever seen in clothes which seem to be a throwback of this nation's colonial past or (indeed) I have a fetish for Cowboy outfits from the American Wild West.

This thought is also compounded by the fact that my memory is not as good as it once was, and – even more alarmingly – diminishing faster than the tree-cover in Bengaluru! And so, before I myself forget why I started wearing these so-called 'Western' outfits, I have decided to reveal the reasons, and put these queries to rest.

Let me start by stating that I have not been always wearing Js and Ts, Ps and Ss or PNSs. In my younger days, I used to dress very much like most men do in South India (i.e. in *dhotis* or *lungis*).

Incidentally, these garments were – and still are – the most comfortable and practical items of clothing ever designed. Please allow me to elaborate. Does anyone know of any other dress that can be left draping to the ankles one moment, and folded up in half the next, should there be a need to flee in the face of imminent danger? Or – begging the reader's pardon – if one has to ease oneself at short notice, should such an unfortunate occasion arise? Clearly the answer is an emphatic 'NO!'

Yes, my dear friends...the *dhoti* and the *lungi* are clear winners when it comes to versatility, affordability and ease of wearing.

If I have such high praise for these clothes, you may well ask why I chose to discard them and opt for the aforementioned complicated style of dressing. Let me assure you that it was not with the desire to ape Western styles that I decided to switch from the ubiquitous dress of the South, and don the Js and Ts, Ps and Ss and pyjama night suits.

No. It was as a result of an extremely severe traumatic experience that I had about forty years ago, and one which I am not likely to forget until my very last breath on Earth.

****

Those of you who have known me for a while would recall that I served in the Indian Air Force for over two decades, before retiring and settling down in Bengaluru. During my years in Service, I had the opportunity to travel the length and breadth of this great country, and experience at first hand, things that most folks would not have even read about.

Life in the Services was not easy in those days..in fact it was very tough, not only for those in uniform, but for the families as well. There were frequent transfers – or postings as they were referred to – and these were pretty disturbing experiences, given the fact that most of the time, there would be no proper accommodation at the new place of posting, especially when one got posted to the North-East of the country. In fact, there were several places where *pucca* houses were non-existent and everyone lived in tents or in structures known as *bashas.*

For the uninitiated, let me explain what a *basha* was. It was nothing but a bamboo hut, erected on a cement plinth, with a thatched grass roof. *Bashas* came in various sizes..depending on the dimensions of the plinth, and could have one or two bedrooms, a living-dining room, a kitchen and a very rudimentary bath-cum-toilet.

It was not easy getting used to living in a *basha*. Given the fact that perennial heavy rains were commonplace in the North-East, one quickly accepted the leaky roofs, and flooded toilets. What took more courage and grit, was getting used to the assorted animals, insects and reptiles which would be unconcernedly milling about all around.

It was quite common to come across massive monitor lizards, casually ambling along in front of the *basha*...or giant rhinoceros beetles which would suddenly fly in, scaring the living daylights out of us...or even various species of snakes which would nonchalantly slither down the bamboo poles inside the *basha*, stare at us with cold, beady, unblinking eyes, and slither away without a second glance.

The *bashas* were all located in an area called the '*basha* colony.' Here there were rows of *bashas*, all facing each other with a clear area of land in between...with a width of some twenty feet or so. Needless to say, one could clearly see across this 'no-man's-land' and have a clear view of happenings in the *basha* opposite. Why I mention this apparently trivial fact will become clear, as my tale progresses.

The traumatic incident that I had mentioned a short while ago had occurred whilst we were living in one of these *bashas* in a God-forsaken corner of North Eastern India. The name of the exact location was Chabua, and it was one of the most isolated and forlorn places to be posted in. It was also one of the wettest places in the country, and heavy overnight rains were almost a daily phenomenon. It really was a miracle that the flimsy bamboo-and-grass *bashas* were able to weather the daily storms and provide a roof over our heads.

The *basha* we stayed in was relatively new, and had a compound of sorts all around, with several trees randomly growing here and there. Incidentally, the combination of fertile soil in the area and the copious amounts of rainfall made ideal conditions for flora to flourish. One of the popular stories that did the rounds was how a wooden stool left in the open overnight had sprouted leaves by the next morning! Frankly, I have not been able to authenticate the veracity of this story, but I mention it, only to highlight the conditions prevalent at the place.

Anyway..let me come back to my traumatic incident.

I remember clearly the date that it happened..Sunday the 21st of May, 1972. Even if it was not for the traumatic incident that I will shortly relate, I would have probably remembered this particular day..as it was a day after my birthday, which, having fallen on a weekend, had resulted in the most boisterous party that I have ever had. And, when I say boisterous, I mean that it was really wild. It had also been one of the rainiest nights of the month.

All the guys and ladies from Air Force Station Chabua had landed up in our *basha*, and booze had flowed like the mighty Brahmaputra! The last of the guests had departed close to 2:00 am and I guess that by the time my wife and I retired to bed, it must have been nearly 3 o'clock in the morning..and I distinctly remember that it was still raining heavily. In fact, the roof of our 'living room' had sprung a leak, and I had to put a bucket beneath it, hoping it would suffice to collect the water dripping down.

I guess that I must have been quite tired and – aided by copious quantity of Hercules Rum in my belly – I dropped off into deep sleep.

The next thing I remember was being loudly awakened by my wife. When I managed to pry open my heavy eyelids a wee bit, I could see that it was very bright, and the sun was actually shining. In spite of the fine weather, I would have gladly shut my eyes and gone back to sleep..as I had a hangover of monumental proportions. However, this was not to be, because my wife kept yelling something about a fallen tree, and for me to get out of bed.

Now, if ever there was any calamity more disastrous than the *basha* catching fire, it was a tree getting uprooted and falling on the roof. Therefore, it was no surprise that I was out of bed instantly, and heading for the door, while hastily knotting my *lungi* around my waist. In my sleepy, confused and panic-stricken state of mind, I had totally overlooked the fact that I was wearing only my *lungi*..no *kurta*, no banian, no underwear.

As soon as I stepped out of the *basha*, two facts struck me, more or less simultaneously: one...that there were several neighbours (including ladies) standing in front of their respective *bashas* and enjoying the rare sunshine; two...that I was utterly and embarrassingly under-dressed to be wandering outside, especially with mixed company all around. My instant thought was to retreat into the safety of my *basha*, but realised that I must already have been spotted, and it was futile to try and undo the damage.

Alas! At that time, little did I know what greater catastrophe was about to occur.

Anyway...I looked around to see what my wife had been in a panic about, and almost immediately noticed that a rather hefty papaya tree had tilted over and looked as though it would fall to the ground at any time. I also realised that this tree was an anchoring point for a plastic chord tied between it and a bamboo pole at the other end of the yard for hanging clothes to dry. Now...just having a papaya tree falling off would never have brought upon a panic attack in my wife, who was made of much sterner stuff. However, the prospect of not being able to dry the clothes on one of those rare, bright, sunny days was undoubtedly a legitimate reason for pushing the panic button.

Having successfully established the reason for my wife losing her normal cool, I realised that now it was up to me to try and remedy the situation...and that is just what I did. After a final glance around (and satisfied that there was no one even vaguely glancing in my direction), I marched off towards the precariously-poised papaya tree.

Now, if there was anything that I was totally confident of doing (other than flying, of course), was restoring tilting papaya trees to their original and pristine, vertical state. So, on reaching the stricken tree, I quickly assessed the situation, and came to the conclusion that it was definitely far from hopeless. In my expert opinion, all that was required to set things right was to gently push the tree back into an erect position and stomp the mud around its base with my feet, and anchor it firmly back into the *terra-firma*. Moreover, since I was wearing a robust pair of slippers, this should be an absolute piece of cake.

Without further ado, I positioned myself perfectly in front of the tree, grabbed it with both my hands, and started pushing it back into position. As I started pushing, I realised that it was not as easy as I had expected it to be, and the silly tree was offering quite a bit of resistance to revert to its normal position.

Considering my situation in retrospect, perhaps I should have gracefully conceded failure, and requisitioned help. However, at that point in time, I quickly dismissed that option. After all, there was my ego which was at stake, and (not forgetting) the wrath of my wife!

Well..as it happened, I decided to go ahead and put in more effort. This was my first big mistake of the day.

Taking a deep breath, and slowly spreading my feet apart to obtain more purchase, I proceeded to use all my strength to nudge the stupid tree back to its position. I think that about 15 or 20 seconds must have gone by, and just when I thought that I was succeeding in my efforts, I suddenly felt a draft of cold air blowing on my body, just south of my navel. For a moment, I was inclined to ignore the feeling and get on with the task at hand. However, curiosity got the better of me, and I looked down my bare chest..and what I saw sends shivers down my spine even today.

For a moment, I thought I was hallucinating. However, in a flash I realised that this was no illusion, and that my *lungi* had come off and was lying in an untidy heap around my ankles!

My first thought was to let go of the wretched tree and retrieve the fallen garment. But I instantly realised that if I did that, the tree would fall on my head, and probably cause severe cranial injury.

That was when I made the second mistake of the day..I yelled for my wife at the top of my voice.

It is widely believed that one is always wise after the disaster, and I completely agree with that theory. I really feel now that if I had not shouted for my wife, and had gently allowed the tree to fall down, I could have managed to get away and slunk back into the *basha*. However, my loud scream not only alerted my wife (who came charging out of the *basha,* perhaps thinking that I had been attacked by a snake or some such lethal creature), it also made all our neighbours – gents, ladies and kids – turn as one and stare in the direction of the noise.

And there I was..standing totally and absolutely nude (much like Michaelangelo's David) hanging on desperately to a *papaya* tree!

I will not go into the agonising trauma that I have suffered after that unforgettable incident, for it is very painful to recollect, even after so many years.

However, it was on that day that I decided that never, EVER would I wear a *lungi* for the rest of my life!

NO-FRILLS AIRLINES

With the opening up of the Indian skies, several new airlines have sprung up on to the aviation scene. Their logos are different, their planes are different, but their philosophy is the same: they don't sell tickets...they sell 'chances' – your 'last chance' to fly from Bangalore to Xanadu at 93% off by booking your flight 793 days in advance...your 'last chance' to beat the fuel price hike...your 'last chance' to be a part of aviation history...just call the toll-free number, and you can fly at Re.1, which – incidentally – you have the option to pay before boarding.

So, you take the 'chance of a lifetime' and book the flight. You manage to get the ticket and tell all your friends what a smart aleck you are. The small print on the ticket says "This is a one-way ticket and refunds are not permissible under any circumstances."

You start the countdown to D-day...793...792...791...

Finally, after what seems a millennium, THE DAY arrives when you will be able to fly to Xanadu for Re.1!

You reach the airport six hours in advance, beating the traffic, and pat yourself on your back for being so clever. You enter the airport after much shoving and jostling, and the first thing you notice is that the 'check-in counter' for your flight is nothing more than a dilapidated table, behind which sits a bored-looking, dishevelled girl, wearing a crumpled uniform. You stand in the serpentine queue, and after what seems an eternity, you finally get hold of the boarding pass...your lifeline to join the jet-set.

The security check is a nightmare...even the plastic tooth-pick you had surreptitiously appropriated from the restaurant the previous night is confiscated. The X-ray machine is on the blink, so your bag is turned inside out, and the contents scrutinized. You are frisked, patted down and (just short of undergoing an endoscopy) body-searched. Your blood pressure reaches an all-time high, and your head feels like it has been pulverized by an earthquake measuring 7.2 on the Richter scale. But you grin and bear it..after all one Rupee is...one Rupee!

And at last...you are inside the plane!

Since there are no seat numbers allotted, you push and shove through the melee to get to a window seat. You somehow manage to thrust your small bag into the overhead bin which is already stuffed with two gunny sacks containing potatoes. Having achieved this minor miracle, you squeeze yourself past the obese, pot-bellied passenger in the aisle seat, who is clutching a huge plastic 'airbag' as if his very life depended on it.

The atmosphere is homely...your neighbour opens his 'airbag' and takes out an oily packet of *puri* and lime pickle and proceeds to eat it with great relish. The smell is over-powering, and you feel like throwing up even before getting airborne. You hold your nose and close your eyes. Just as you feel that you are going to pass out, the stewardess yells from the back "All passengers fasten your Velcros."

At last the Captain arrives, moving slowly through the aisle, smiling at the passengers. You have this sudden urge to speak to him, and you wave your arms to attract his attention. Your happiness is complete when he stops and says "Hi!"

You are dumb-struck. Just imagine...talking to the PILOT!!! You pluck up enough courage to ask him what you consider to be a very intelligent question... "How often do your planes crash?" And he says, "Only once," and moves on into the cockpit.

While you ponder whether this is good news or bad, you hear the doors shut, and an absolute, ethereal silence prevails. That is, until you hear the Captain yelling to one of the ground-crew outside on the apron, "Hey Shekar...which direction did you say that I should fly to reach Xanadu?"

Your entire life flashes before your eyes.

"What the hell," you say to yourself, "when you've got to go, you've got to go. Perhaps that is why every single one of these new super-jets comes equipped with both – a bathroom and a Chapel!"

THE CROSSWORD PUZZLE

PROLOGUE

13th November, 2007

I was sitting out on the balcony, trying to complete the crossword puzzle in the Times of India, which had become somewhat of an addiction with me, right from my Air Force days. Presently I was stuck with 4 Down, and I was getting increasingly frustrated. I had tried all the permutations and combinations, but the solution to the 5-letter word eluded me. Perhaps the frustration had to do more with my feeling of dissatisfaction with life, which it seemed, threw up unsolvable clues now and then. Or maybe it was due to the lack of proper sleep all of last week, thanks to the enthusiastic Diwali celebrations in the area.

It was really ironic. Here I was at 64, a pensioner (in the true sense of the word), having retired and come back to the place of my birth and my youth, hoping to find peace in the quiet environs, salubrious climate and laid-back culture. I soon realised that things had changed, and Bangalore, far from being the much-envied Pensioners' Paradise, had become an overcrowded, polluted, horrible concrete jungle. I suppose this was the price that all cities paid for 'progress.'

I felt a sudden chill, as a gust of wind rustled the newspaper. For a change, the monsoon had been quite active this year, and it felt a bit like the Bangalore of old. There was a sudden flash of lightning and the ear-shattering peal of thunder, which appeared pretty close.

Momentarily, I was transported back in time..back..back...many years back...

10th July, 1972

It was just one of those typical monsoon days in the North East – dark, low clouds and intermittent rain, reducing the visibility even more. I was tired and sat beneath the main rotor blades of my helicopter on the wet tarmac of Jorhat Air Base, waiting for the fuel bowser to arrive. It had been a long day, and except for a couple of slices of bread and a soggy omelette (which passed off for breakfast), I had not had anything to eat the entire day, and it was now close to 1500 hours, i.e. 3:00 pm. I knew that if I was going to make it to Chabua by last landing time, I would have to be airborne in the next half an hour or so. I looked at my watch for the umpteenth time and cursed everyone – from my Flight Commander to the re-fuelling section – for having to be in this situation. Here I was, on a Saturday afternoon, away from my wife and little son, not even sure if I would reach my destination.

My mind drifted back to the events of the past four days..it seemed more like four months since I had left my home base at Bagdogra and gone to Chakabama, in Nagaland. I had recently been posted to the Unit, and being the junior-most among the pilots, it was hardly surprising that I was detailed to go and ferry this helicopter to its home base in Chabua.

There used to be a permanent helicopter detachment at Chakabama, with one Allouette helicopter, two pilots and a set of ground crew, all belonging to the Helicopter Unit in Chabua. Crews and helicopters were changed every month or so. On this occasion, both the pilots had got injured when their jeep driver lost control, and the vehicle had fallen into a twenty-foot-deep pit just close to the old helipad. Fortunately, the pilots had escaped with a few injuries, but were presently admitted in the Army Field Hospital at Kohima. As luck would have it, the helicopter was due for major servicing and it was mandatory that it reached its base before the last date, after which it would have been grounded, and could not have been flown.

It was for this reason that I had been sent from Bagdogra, with special permission to fly 'single-pilot' (i.e. without a co-pilot) from Chakabama to Chabua. Unfortunately, the past four days had seen some very foul weather, and it was just not possible to take off. Today was the last day that the helicopter could be flown, before its 'calendar life' was over.

Having managed to get airborne from Chakabama in extremely marginal weather, and flying by the seat of my pants, I had somehow made it to Jorhat. In good weather, it would have been possible to fly directly from Chakabama to Chabua, but with the weather being what it was, re-fuelling en-route was inescapable. And so here I was, hungry, tired, trying to make my destination in minimal weather conditions, and with sunlight fast running out. Adding to my anxiety was the fact that I was an absolute rookie in this area, and not at all familiar with the route. The only navigational aid that was available was the Radio Compass in my helicopter, which even at the best of times, was not to be relied upon.

I took out the map from my overalls and studied the route once more, trying to memorise the ground features and navigational pin-points. This was vital, since I was flying alone: reading the map and flying the helicopter at the same time (especially in bad weather) was definitely a 'no-no' as far as safety of my butt was concerned!

I carefully folded the map and was putting it back in my overall, when I sensed – rather than saw – someone peering over my shoulder. Turning around, I found myself looking up at a tall, well built, handsome officer wearing dark grey overalls. He must have been around 28 or 30 years of age and had one of those beautiful drooping 'wings' over the left pocket and a gold-coloured metal name plate which read 'Paddy,' over the right. I noticed that he had light brown eyes and the hint of a smile on his lips.

"Hi..good afternoon," he said, breaking into a wide grin.

It was then that I observed that he was also sporting the pips of a Squadron Leader. This made him senior to me, and as customs of the Service dictate, I was bound to pay him appropriate complements. Slowly unwinding myself, I stood up and bracing myself to attention, said "Good afternoon, Sir," at the same time wondering why he was here at this particular time.

I was in no mood for small talk, what with the tension building up in me, thinking of the flight ahead. Perhaps he was the Duty Officer and was checking up to see when I would get the hell out of his base and avoid sending a report to Command Headquarters on a 'Visiting' aircraft, as was required by regulations.

I did not have to keep up the guess-work for long as to the purpose of his presence. He took a step closer and said "I am Padmanabhan. Heard you were going to Chabua." It was more of a statement than a question.

"Yes Sir," I replied, "I am just waiting for the refueler."

What he said next took me totally off-guard. "Can I take a lift with you?"

This was the last thing that I had expected, for I could just not believe that anyone would want to go to Chabua...most people were trying their darnest to get out of that God-forsaken place!

My surprise must have showed, for he immediately added, "Of course, if you have any problems, don't bother."

It was my turn to smile. "Oh no Sir," I said, "no problem at all. You are welcome to come along." And I couldn't help taking a dig at the poor logistics at his Station. "That is, if at all we are able to take off, which is looking more and more unlikely, as the refueler has not turned up as yet."

"Point taken," he laughed, "but I am not from Jorhat…"

It was at this point that the refueler did finally arrive, with much groaning and meshing of gears. I was so relieved, that once the fuelling was over, I completely forgot to ask my new-found companion where he was from. I was now running against time, and quickly ran to the telephone in the Duty Crew hut and informed the ATC (Air Traffic Control) of my revised ETD (Estimated Time of Departure). I then called the Met Section for the latest weather reports, which, to my dismay, were quite grim. Heavy rain and very low clouds were forecast for Jorhat after about an hour, but the route for my flight seemed to be OK. What was causing me concern was that although as of now Chabua was reporting just cloudy weather, they were expecting thundershowers later in the evening.

It was now up to me whether I should get airborne or play safe and stay the night at Jorhat. There were two reasons why I was loath to choose the second option – the first was that the helicopter would have to be grounded permanently at Jorhat if I did not make it to Chabua this day itself. The second reason was ego…what would my passenger (a pilot himself) think of me if I should scrub the mission? The word 'chicken' kept popping into my head, and I could just imagine the good laugh my colleagues back in Bagdogra would have when they came to know of this!

I kept running the options in my mind as I walked back to the helicopter, hoping that I was about to make the right decision. My hitch-hiker companion must have noticed the look of uncertainty in my face, for he came up to me and put a hand on my shoulder and said "Don't worry..I am with you." For a moment I was tempted to ask him if he was a helicopter pilot, and whether he was familiar with this area and the route. But once again, I dithered, not wanting him to think that I was scared. I tried to flash a smile of thanks..but it was actually a smile to reassure myself.

By the time I had reached the helicopter, I had made my decision – I would go to Chabua. Little did I know at the time, standing on the wet and windy tarmac in Jorhat, what a profound effect my decision would have on me for the rest of my life.

Having made the decision to fly, I hurried with the preparations for starting the helicopter. Removing the chocks from the wheels and all the engine blankings and other covers, I motioned to my passenger to board. After a quick 'walk-around,' I got into the pilot's seat, noticing that my companion had settled into the passenger seat at the rear, and not occupied the co-pilot's seat. Briefly I toyed with the idea of asking him to come into the cockpit, but dismissed it. If he wanted to be a 'passenger'...so be it. I also could not help observing that he did not have any baggage at all – not even a briefcase. This, I thought was odd, but did not pursue the thought further, as I got busy with the cockpit checks before starting the engine.

Having obtained the necessary flight clearances, I started up and taxied on to the helipad for take-off. Just before asking the ATC for clearance to take off, I realized that I had not extended the courtesy of offering my passenger the spare head-set – if not for anything else – just to protect his ears from the awful whine of the Turbomeca Artouste engine. I picked up the headset from the co-pilot's seat and turned around to hand it to him but got the surprise of my life…Squadron Leader Padmanabhan was already fast asleep, stretched out across the seats! Well…that was that.

"Jorhat Tower, Helicopter 2-6-5 ready for take-off," I called on R/T.

"2-6-5, you are cleared for take-off, winds Easterly 8 knots. After take-off, turn right and climb on track to 2000 feet AGL (Above Ground Level)," responded the voice of the Air Traffic Controller.

I acknowledged the instructions from the Tower, and taking a deep breath, came up on the collective lever, increasing power on the engine and hearing its typical banshee scream. Being very light, the helicopter leapt into the air, and after a moment to steady the machine, I eased forward on the cyclic stick and we were away, the ground falling swiftly beneath the wheels. Once I got climb speed, I turned right and set course, climbing in the process.

"Jorhat, 2-6-5 on course, climbing to 2000 feet AGL. Estimate arrival Chabua at 1-6-4-5 Echo Fox (Indian Standard Time)," I reported.

"Roger 2-6-5, call one-zero miles out," said the Controller, in his monotonous drone.

With a routine 'Roger' to Jorhat ATC, I fished out the map from my overall, and laid it on my lap, orienting it in the direction of flight. I knew that I would have to do some pretty accurate map-reading, if I were to navigate in these reduced visibility conditions. But somewhere in the back of my mind, I knew that if the worse came to the worst, and I became unsure of my position, I could always hit river Brahmaputra, and follow it all the way to Chabua. Even as these thoughts went through my mind, I glanced outside to my left, and was rewarded with the awesome sight of the mighty Brahmaputra. The river was broad even in the dry season, but during the monsoons (like the present), it looked more like an ocean, and it was nearly impossible to see the other bank.

The weather did not look too bad, after all, and I congratulated myself for not playing over-safe and cancelling the flight. I looked at the map, and going by the features on the ground, reckoned I was 10 miles out. I called up Jorhat, and informed them of my distance and altitude, as instructed.

The Controller seemed very relieved that I had finally moved out of his airspace.

"Roger 2-6-5," he responded, "you are clear to change over to Route Frequency. Good night and happy landing!"

I said, "Good night," to Jorhat ATC and was sure that they would be winding up, since it was highly unlikely that there would be any more flights in or out of the airfield. We were on track as per the map, and I was glad to see that the Radio Compass on my instrument panel was steady and pointing to Jorhat NDB (Non-directional Beacon). Using the bearing indicated by the Radio Compass, I did a quick mental DR (Dead Reckoning) and was very pleased to know that I was indeed absolutely on track to Chabua.

After a while, I turned around and glanced back at the passenger cabin and was rather amused to see that my companion was still fast asleep – and actually looked as if he was snoring! "Amazing," I said to myself, for sleeping in an Allouette was next to impossible, what with the infernal engine noise.

****

It would not have been more than thirty seconds that I had diverted my attention from looking ahead. But in those thirty seconds, there had been a mysterious change in the scenario. Where there had been bright sunlight ahead of us, it had become quite dark and the clouds appeared to have become lower. I looked out to the left, and was startled to see that the visibility had dropped abruptly, and I could barely see the nearer bank of the Brahmaputra. But I did not have to worry, as long as I had visual contact with the ground below me – I could always descend lower and keep below the clouds. I was quite sure was only a local phenomenon, and I would have clear weather beyond this particular patch of low clouds.

I started descending straight ahead, maintaining the course and at the same time concentrating on the map. I must have descended about 500 feet but could see that the base of the clouds ahead was getting even lower. I had no choice but to descend further.

At the same time, I realized that it was becoming more and more difficult to read the map – it had grown progressively darker, and mild jolts of turbulence rocked the helicopter. I shifted in my seat, reducing the speed by a couple of knots and trimming the controls to maintain steady flight. By now I had come down to 1000 feet, but even this did not seem low enough to remain below clouds. I glanced at the Radio Compass and was aghast to see that the needle was slowly going around the dial, indicating that the instrument had lost the Jorhat radio beacon to which it had locked on so steadily just a few minutes ago.

I was now beginning to get a bit apprehensive, since the cloud base was getting extremely low. The turbulence had also increased in intensity. For the first time, the thought crossed my mind that I may have to return to Jorhat, after all. But even as I considered that option, I realized that Jorhat may be shutting down at any moment – in fact may have already closed for the day. There was no time to lose, and I immediately gave a call on the radio, hoping that Jorhat ATC would respond. I waited for a response from Jorhat ATC but heard only static on my headset.

I could feel my heart pounding in my chest, as I tried calling again "Jorhat..Jorhat, this is helicopter 2-6-5, do you read me?"

Once again there was only silence, punctuated with bursts of static, coming through my ear-phones. Either Jorhat ATC had gone of the air, or my transmission was not getting through because of my low altitude.

I looked around outside, desperately seeking some landmark or feature by which I could orientate myself. It was no use..it had become very dark and streaks of lightning flashed to my right.

I had always considered myself an above-the-average pilot, and not given to alarm easily. In fact, I had flown in pretty harsh weather conditions, and been quite comfortable at that. But today, I felt real fear. Here I was, flying alone, in extremely poor visibility and completely unsure of my position.

At that moment, I took the decision to return to Jorhat..at least I would have better visibility going back than going ahead. Concentrating as much as possible on the wildly gyrating instruments, I turned hard to my left, trying to get on to the course back to Jorhat.

The helicopter was getting tossed about quite severely, and I had to struggle with the controls. I had barely managed to turn a quarter of the way when I felt a tremendous jolt which shook the helicopter so intensely, I thought that it was going to break up. The engine was screaming crazily and I could feel the forces of gravity pinning me to my seat as the helicopter was plucked upwards, as if yanked up by some mysterious force. Instinctively, I lowered the collective lever, reducing power and hoping to arrest the climb, but it had absolutely no effect. The altimeter was winding up wildly, and in next to no time we were going past 7000 feet!

I could see absolutely nothing outside the cockpit as we became enveloped inside thick dark clouds. It was obvious that we had gotten into a Cumulonimbus cloud – the most ferocious of all clouds. As fast as we were gaining height in the up-draft, I knew that it was only a matter of time when we would hit a down-draft and would plummet with equal (if not more) severity towards the earth!

At that moment I was gripped by intense panic, knowing that this was probably the end. For some strange reason my mind kept playing back an old nursery rhyme, over and over...Humpty Dumpty sat on a wall...Humpty Dumpty had a great fall...All the King's horses and all the King's men couldn't put Humpty Dumpty together again! It was so turbulent and chaotic that I had totally lost orientation and had no clue as to which way was up and which way was down. I prayed...prayed hard that this would end soon, and without pain...

At that precise moment I felt something on my shoulder..just a brief touch, but a touch all the same. I turned and looked and what I saw was the most unexpected sight. There, sitting on the co-pilot's seat was my passenger – whom I had totally forgotten in the ongoing mayhem. For the life of me, I could not figure out how he could have crossed over from the rear seat and settled himself down in the cockpit...but there he was, as real as real could get. I stared at him in total disbelief and noticed that he was absolutely calm and (I imagined) even had the trace of a smile on his lips. He turned and looked straight in my eyes and said in the most matter-of-fact manner, "I have the controls," meaning that he was flying the helicopter.

On any other occasion, I would have probably not allowed anyone to handle the controls..but at this moment, I knew I had no chance of getting out of this disastrous situation. I just nodded and let go of the controls, which I had been clutching with all my strength.

What happened in the next few minutes is all a blur. I can only recall that just as I relinquished the controls, the helicopter slammed down into a terrifying dive, obviously caught in the unavoidable down-draft. I closed my eyes tightly shut, not wanting to see the inevitable. I cannot be sure, but I think that I may have passed out momentarily.

I don't know for how long I had my eyes closed, but a sudden change in the noise level and vibration in the cockpit made me open them. It had suddenly become very bright and absolutely calm. For a moment I thought that I was dead and had reached the state of tranquillity that one reads about.

I shook my head to clear it, and slowly looked around. I could not believe my eyes...the helicopter was in absolute stable flight at about 800 feet, and we were in clear weather. What was even more amazing was that the Radio Compass was locked on to Chabua beacon. Even as I was coming to terms with the situation, I heard Chabua ATC calling me, and asking about my position. I glanced outside and saw that we were bang-on on track, and just abeam Moranhat, clearly identifiable by the ever-present flame from the oil refinery.

I responded to the call from Chabua ATC, and informed that we were about 25 nautical miles from them and gave them my ETA (Estimated Time of Arrival).

All this time, my erstwhile 'passenger' was calmly flying the helicopter, not even glancing in my direction. Just as I finished my R/T transmission to Chabua, he looked at me, smiled, and said, "You have the controls."

The rest of the flight was absolutely uneventful, and we landed in Chabua precisely as per the estimate. I had requested for Aircrew Transport, which – surprisingly – was already on the tarmac, by the time I taxied in and parked. I got out of the helicopter and made a bee-line to the toilet near the hangar...my bladder was bursting, after all the excitement of the past 90 minutes!

After relieving myself and splashing some water on my face, I returned to the helicopter, retrieved my small overnight bag, told the Duty Crew personnel to lash (tie down) and cover the helicopter, and got into the Aircrew van. Except for the driver, it was totally empty, and there was no sign of my passenger. Perhaps he too has 'gone around the corner,' I thought to myself, and settled down into the seat.

After about ten minutes of waiting, I began to wonder what had happened to him. I asked the driver of the van if he had seen the officer, but he replied in the negative. I got out of the van and looked around and in the hangar, but there was no sight of him. It seemed as though he had walked off on his own, without saying a word.

I was a bit miffed..here was a guy who had hitched a ride, in my helicopter, and not even had the basic courtesy of saying 'thanks.' On the other hand, perhaps it was I who should have been eternally grateful to him for bailing me out of potential disaster.

I got back into the van, and after waiting another ten minutes, asked the driver to take me to the Transit Rooms in the Officers' Mess.

On reaching the Officers' Mess, I found to my dismay that all the Transit Rooms appeared to be occupied and cursed under my breath. I desperately needed to rest..I suddenly felt very tired and exhausted – perhaps the stress of the previous few hours was finally catching up.

As I was contemplating the next course of action, the Transit Bearer appeared on the scene, and when I asked him about accommodation, he shook his head and confirmed my earlier suspicion that there were indeed no rooms available in the Transit Block. However, he said that I could put up for the night in the Single Officers' area, where there was a room available. This meant walking another half a kilometer, but there was no other choice. I wearily followed the Bearer, and finally reached the room.

After fumbling with a huge bunch of keys, he finally managed to open the door, and I walked in, followed by the Bearer. It had become quite dark, and he switched on the light, parking my suitcase at the foot of the bed. I looked around, and saw that it was a typical bachelor's room, but very neat and tidy. The bed was made and looked very inviting indeed.

The Bearer had in the meanwhile switched on the hot water geyser and told me that was going to get me some tea from the Officers' Mess.

I sat down on the bed and yanked off my boots and socks, and – still in my overalls – stretched out on the bed, propping up the pillow and leaning on it. I could feel the weariness permeate my entire body. I knew that if I closed my eyes even for a moment, I would probably drop off to sleep. This I did not want to happen, as I would be woken up shortly by the Bearer.

In an attempt to stay awake, I looked around the room a little more closely, and noticed that it had the normal odds and ends that most bachelor officers possess: an alarm clock...a tennis racquet dangling from the wall next to a poster of Alfred E. Neuman (of Mad comics fame, with his signature phrase, 'What? Me worry?'), a small money plant, growing out of an empty Chivas Regal bottle...

I concluded that the original occupant had perhaps gone on leave or on Temporary Duty, and that was how the room was available for me.

Just as I was completing the visual tour of the room, something on the dressing table, which looked oddly familiar, caught my eye. It looked like a flat bit of yellow metal, glinting in the light. I was about to get up and examine it at closer range, but at that precise moment, the overhead light flickered, and went off completely, plunging the room into total darkness. This was probably one of the frequent power failures that Chabua was (in)famous for.

I lay back on to the pillow, once again cursing everyone under the sun for my predicament. After perhaps ten or twelve minutes, I was getting fed up lying in the darkness, and decided to get up and stand outside the room. However, just as I swung my legs down from the bed, the power came back on, the sudden glare from the light making me squint. For some strange reason, my eyes went back to the dressing table, and the shiny metal plate which continued to glint.

Curiosity got the better of me, and I got up from the bed and went across the room to the dresser. As I got closer, I could make out that it was a name plate..similar to the one that I had noticed on my erstwhile passenger's overall. I reached out and picked it up, trying to read the name. When I did manage to..it was as though I had been subjected to a high-voltage shock: the name-plate said simply 'Paddy'!

At that moment, the Bearer walked in with my tea. Seeing me holding the name plate, he said, "Yes Sir, this used to be Padmanabhan Sir's room."

For a moment I felt very irritated as I realised that now I would have to shift out to some other room, since I knew that the rightful occupant of this room was back in Chabua.

Taking the cup of tea that the Bearer was holding out to me, I asked him, "Was he on leave?"

"Leave? Oh no, Sir," he replied. "Padmanabhan Sir died last week in a motorcycle accident near Jorhat."

EPILOGUE

13 November, 2007

The wind-speed had really picked up, and the clouds had become darker. In fact, the first drops of rain splattered on the balcony, dropping on the crossword, and nearly obliterating the solutions that I had filled in. I quickly got up and entered the house, glancing one last time at 4 Down, the clue for which was 'Golden harvest, mostly of the Far East.'

The solution came to me that instant... 'Golden harvest'...of course...paddy! What else but paddy!!!

THE GHOST IN THE GRANDFATHER CLOCK

Right from my childhood, I have had a fascination for clocks...no, not the ordinary, mundane table clocks, but the stately, ornate grandfather clocks. And the more ornate, the better.

Perhaps this trait had something to do with the fact that there was this beautiful and ancient grandfather clock at my home. It had belonged to my great grandfather, from whom it had passed on to my grandfather and then to my mother (she being the only child to my grandparents). It was really big..at least 6 feet tall, with a massive pendulum which slowly swung back and forth, with the regular tick-tock sound of seconds slipping by.

Ever since I could remember, I had this great desire to open out the clock, just to see how the insides looked, with the great many wheels, cogs and levers. I was also curious to know exactly how, unfailingly, day after day, the clock sounded the passage of time through its rich, brassy gong.

Alas...this was not to be. Although I had the freedom to meddle with just about anything in the house, I was expressly forbidden to so much as touch the clock. My plaintive and repeated entreaties to have just a teeny-weeny peek at the innards of the clock fell on totally deaf ears, especially those of my grandmother, who guarded the clock as though her very life depended on it.

This unfulfilled desire of mine had a profound influence on me, and I swore to myself that when I grew up, I would get myself one of these clocks and explore its innards, come what may. Whereas other kids of my age longed to get a swanky sports car or an air rifle once they could afford to get one on their own, every passing moment of mine was focussed on acquiring one such metronomic marvel. My desire was so intense, that my friends were convinced that I was absolutely (pardon the pun) cuckoo. This, however, did not bother me, and my resolve only became stronger by the day.

It is said that time flies.. and I feel that the saying is true, at least in my case. In what seemed an amazingly quick period, the years had gone by, I had completed my studies and managed to secure a decent job. I found myself a small apartment, furnished it well and acquired the latest gadgets. I was 26, a bachelor, and with not a care in the world.

Although my life seemed complete, and I should have been content the way things had turned out, I felt as though something was still missing. Needless to say, I was still yearning for the grandfather clock that I had sworn to get for myself, many years ago.

If it had been difficult to lay hands on a genuine grandfather clock when I was young, it was even more difficult – in fact, well-nigh impossible – to do so after so many years. After all, these mechanical masterpieces were no longer manufactured, and those that were in circulation were firmly entrenched in the antique collections of the rich and famous. The one-odd piece that surfaced at auctions once in a blue moon would have cost an arm and a leg to acquire – and most definitely beyond the realms of my moderate financial situation. And so, I had more or less reconciled myself to the fact that I was not going to ever fulfil my dreams.. at least in this lifetime.

That was until one bright Sunday morning, when I was relaxing after a leisurely breakfast of buttered toast, fried eggs and bacon. I remember that I was half sitting and half lying down on my bed, with my pillows propped up against the wall. I was casually browsing through the morning papers, which contained not much news other that of some murder here, a robbery somewhere else, an accident at a third place. The rest of the paper was filled with advertisements, and I was getting rather irritated...in fact I was contemplating stopping the newspaper altogether.

In total disgust and boredom, I folded the newspaper and was about to throw it away into the waste-paper basket, when a small item on the page caught my eye.

For some strange reason, I was drawn to this six-line advertisement. I squinted my eyes to get a better look, and what I saw made me spring out of my bed, totally thrilled and excited. What I read is still vividly etched in my memory:

FOR SALE
ANTIQUE GRANDFATHER CLOCK
IN WORKING CONDITION
IMMACULATELY MAINTAINED
CONTACT: MATHEW 98665 43267

For a moment, I couldn't believe my eyes, and I re-read the advertisement a couple of times. Having convinced myself that I was not dreaming, I quickly made a note of the contact details on my mobile phone.

As it was just going on to 9:00 am, I presumed that this Mathew guy would also be relaxing on a Sunday, and it would be best if I were to call him after 10 o'clock.

Time seemed to be crawl by from that moment, and I kept looking at my watch repeatedly. After what seemed half a day, it was finally ten, and I hastily dialled the number given in the ad. I could hear it ring at the other end, and it just kept ringing. Just as I was about to disconnect, I heard a deep, gravelly voice at the other end say "Hello."

I quickly explained who I was and why I had called.

The deep, gravelly voice responded, "Meet me at 42 Cline Road in Cox Town, before 11," and the line went dead.

For a moment, my irritation flared up, as I stared at my silent mobile phone, and I was about to forget the whole incident as a bad joke. However, the thought of actually seeing – let alone possessing – a grandfather clock made me reconsider my hasty decision, and I quickly changed my clothes and set off to the address that had been mentioned.

Fortunately, I did not live too far away, and being a Sunday, traffic was not as dense as it normally would be, and I made good time to Cline Road..thanks mainly to the GPS in my phone. Another couple of minutes, and I was standing in front of a massive, ornate, gate, with '42' written in black on the huge pillar on the left.

There was a bell-push just below the number, and I jabbed at it tentatively. Almost instantaneously, the massive black gates swung open inwards, and a speaker came to life from the pillar on the right. The same, deep gravelly voice that I had heard on the phone intoned, "Drive up the path and come to the house. You may park under the porch."

The path was long, winding and narrow, lined with trees on either side. I drove gingerly, not knowing what to expect ahead. All of a sudden, the house came – or rather, burst into view. It was huge..more of a mansion, than a house.

I proceeded under the porch and killed the engine.

I opened the door and stepped out of the car, taking in the magnificent building that stood like a citadel before me. I guessed that it must have been at least 150 to 200 years old, but maintained spotlessly.

As I approached the tall mahogany doors of the house, they slowly opened with an eerie, creaking sound that made my hairs stand on end. It appeared to be dark inside, but it well may have been due to the bright sunshine outside, where I was standing.

At first, I did not see anyone, although I was squinting my eyes to look into the house. Then, suddenly, as if by magic, there was a man standing right in the middle of the doors. He must have been barely five feet tall, wearing black trousers and a thick black coat. He seemed to be old, his hair was like silver, shining from the reflected sunlight. But it was his eyes that held me mesmerised. They were huge and bulging, with specks of red all over the whites of the eyeballs...evil and menacing.

My eyes had gotten used to the darkness within the room, and it was then that I noticed that the figure in front of me had a massive hunch on his back...so much so, that he looked doubled-up. Absolutely gruesome and ghastly..and scary!

I was about to turn and run to my car and beat a hasty retreat, when I heard the same deep, gravelly voice say, "Come," waving his right hand towards the rear of the room. As if by magic, a bright light came on and shone directly on the most magnificent grandfather clock that I had ever seen in my life! I stared, as though mesmerised. Then, as if in a trance, I stepped in through the door and slowly moved towards the clock.

I was at a loss to describe the sheer beauty of the clock. The entire frame was made of wood..probably oak, polished to a high gloss. The pendulum was like burnished gold, moving as if in slow motion, catching the light with each oscillation. The dial was at least a foot across, off-white, and most probably made of ivory. The hands were black..perfectly symmetrical and dainty. The clock must have easily been well over a hundred years old.

For a moment, my mind went absolutely and totally blank. Here I was, within touching distance of one of the most exquisite creations that I had ever seen and hoping to make it my own! All of a sudden, I realised the futility of my thoughts..this clock would cost more than a fortune..in fact more than what I could muster, if I worked my entire life!

"So...you want to buy this clock?" Said the deep gravelly voice, jolting me out of my thoughts.

"I..I..actually..I was going to..I mean I was..." I stammered.

"You can have it," continued the deep gravelly voice, as if I had not spoken at all. "You can have it for one thousand Rupees."

"What?" I said, sure that I had not heard him right. Perhaps he meant one hundred thousand Rupees. "What did you just say?"

"I said that you can have it for one thousand Rupees. I would have given it to you for free, but you see, I am a businessman, and never part with something for nothing."

This time, I nearly fainted...I had indeed heard him right...one thousand bucks? "Oh my God," I thought. "I must be dreaming!"

"Sir," I said, "are you serious...or are you just teasing me?"

"My dear boy..I have never been more serious in my life. If you are willing to pay me the amount right now, and give me your address, I shall make sure it is delivered to you by mid-day tomorrow."

To say that I was dumbfounded would have been the understatement of this millennium. I just reached for my wallet, extracted two 500 Rupee notes and extended it to him, along with my business card. He accepted it, without so much as a thank you, turned around and walked off.

I stood there for a moment, admiring 'my' grandfather clock, and then started back to my car.

I would have probably taken a couple of steps, when I heard him say from the darkness of the inner room, "Wait. I hope that you are not afraid of ghosts. You see, this clock is haunted. Or maybe, it is just the imagination of an old man."

And with that, he was gone.

****

I returned home in great spirits..just could not believe that I was finally going to get a grandfather clock of my own! Oh, how I would love to strip it open and see for myself the wheels, the gears, the levers and the springs that made it tick!

In all this excitement I had all but forgotten the old man's parting statement about the clock being haunted. Now it suddenly came to my mind, and I thought over it for a while. I knew that I was one who never believed in any such weird stuff. But even so, the old man's words kept going through my mind. However, by the time I got home and went about finalising a place for the clock, all thoughts of ghosts and hauntings vanished from my mind. I was barely able to sleep that night and kept waking up and checking the time. In fact, I kept thinking that had the clock been there, I would not have to check the time, as it would sound every passing hour without fail.

Finally dawn broke, and a new day began. I had already decided to bunk office and stay at home, and so I called in sick at about 9:30 am. I did feel bad that I was telling a total lie, but the feeling of guilt quickly vanished when I thought of the clock which would be arriving in a short while.

Time seemed to crawl. But finally, it was 11 o'clock, and I went and stationed myself at the gate to welcome my 'treasure.' Minutes ticked by, and a thought briefly crossed my mind "What if the old man had cheated me?" But I banished such negative thoughts immediately, and once again went back to daydreaming about the clock.

At precisely 11:15 am, a mini lorry pulled up near my gate, and four burly men hauled out my most prized possession! I could have swooned with the excitement. However, I knew what had to be done. Motioning the men to follow me, I went ahead into my house, and guided them to the precise location where I wanted the clock to be placed. They were professionals and did a fine job. I paid a hefty tip to the supervisor of the gang, which he accepted gratefully...it was obvious that not many would tip so lavishly for such a simple job. But then, little did he know how much the clock meant to me!

Having let the labourers out, I shut the door and proceeded straight to the clock – MY clock – to admire it to my heart's content, and at very close quarters. It was beautiful…in fact, even more beautiful than when I had first seen it in the old man's house. The dark wooden grains were perfectly straight…the edges and corners smoothed immaculately. As I had suspected, the dial was indeed made of ivory, with the words 'Smiths 1865' embossed in black. The back of the clock was covered with a single plank of wood…not any cheap plywood, but a smooth, textured board, which I guessed was fine quality teak. There were two round openings about a foot from the bottom of the clock, each about three inches in diameter, obviously provided for ventilation. The body of the clock rested on an ornately carved base…with elephant heads at the ends. Oh…it was so lovely, and I was so happy!

I had toyed with the idea of opening up the clock on the day it came, but something made me change my mind. I just wanted to see it and admire its grandeur, hear the deep, resonating chime when it sounded the hours. With great reluctance, I finally left the clock at about 11:00 pm, and moved away from the dining room (where the clock was positioned) to my adjoining bedroom. I guess that I must have been dog tired, because I dropped off to sleep almost at once.

Sometime around midnight, I woke up with a start. I thought that I heard some weird noises coming from the dining room. I lay absolutely still for a moment but could hear only the gentle 'tick-tock' of the clock. I stayed awake for a few minutes more, but there were no other sounds.

I must have fallen back asleep, when I was once again roused by the same, strange sound..as if someone was tip-toeing around in the dining room, accompanied by the rustling of paper.

This time I knew that I was not imagining things, and slowly got out of bed, and went quietly into the dining room, switching on the light at the door. But there seemed nothing amiss..everything was in its place, the pendulum of the clock systematically swinging and the 'tick-tock' monotonously going on. After another minute or so, I returned to bed and soon went back to sleep.

The next morning, I woke up to the chiming of the clock at six, and immediately went about my routine activities. Much as I would have liked to stay home and admire my new possession, I knew that I just had to go to work..and any more requests for sick leave would be frowned upon by the management.

Having completed my morning ablutions, I dressed, and went to the dining table to make myself two toasts from the loaf of bread that I had left on the table the previous evening. It was then that I noticed something strange. I distinctly remembered having kept the bread in the middle of the table, but now it was sitting at the right edge..in fact nearly falling off. "Very strange," I thought to myself, but surmised that I may have moved it accidentally in my drowsy state when I was checking up on the strange sounds in the dining room.

Anyway, there was no time to bother about such trivia, and so I hastened to make the toast, applied some butter and washed it down with a cup of hot coffee that I brewed from the coffee maker. Soon after, I left for the Office, and got immersed in my work, returning home only around 9:30 pm.

I had had a bite in the Office cafeteria, and so did not have to eat dinner at home. However, I had picked up a loaf of bread for the next morning's breakfast (as I usually did) and left it on the empty table (the remains of the previous night's dinner and that morning's breakfast having been cleared by my domestic help, who would come every day around 10:00 am to tidy up the place). I stood for a few minutes admiring the clock, and then changed into my night clothes and dropped off to instant sleep on my bed.

As on the previous night, I was once again awoken by strange sounds emanating from the dining room...faint pitter-patter (like a baby's footsteps) followed by what sounded like the rustling of paper. I lay quietly, listening. The sounds were repeated after a gap of about a minute. I was wide awake by now, and so couldn't have imagined it.

I was out of bed in an instant, nearly knocking over the small wooden stool near the headboard, in my attempt to pick up the torch kept on it. I was determined to find the source of the noise and had no intentions of turning on the light in the dining room. The next moment I was at the door leading into the dining room, torch switched on and waving the beam of light like a sword around the room.

Nothing seemed to be amiss, and so I turned back and switched on the light. It was then I noticed that the loaf of bread that I had left in the middle of the table had shifted to the right. I froze. The hairs on my neck bristled and sweat drenched my pyjamas. Suddenly the deep gravelly voice of the old man started playing in my head... "I hope that you are not afraid of ghosts. You see, this clock is haunted..I hope that you are not afraid of ghosts. You see, this clock is haunted..I hope that you are not afraid of ghosts. You see, this clock is haunted..."

I don't know what exactly happened thereafter. I may have screamed..maybe, even passed out. All I know is that when I got some kind of control over myself, it was bright daylight outside my flat, and I was sitting on my bed, with all lights on. I slowly got up and opened the front door wide, letting in the light and a draft of fresh, cool air.

The fact that it was day set my mind at rest, and the panic of the previous night subsided. In fact, I felt a bit foolish, thinking back at my fear. The rational and reasonable side of me took over, and I was able to stand up, and in fact go into the dining room. Everything was calm and quiet, except for the tick-tock of the grandfather clock. For a moment, I toyed with the idea of calling the old man and telling him to take back the clock..even if he did not want to return my money.

But then another thought struck me. If I was actually going to get rid of the clock, why not I open it up, satisfy my childish desire of inspecting its innards, and then give it away? The more I thought of this, the more I was convinced that it was the right thing to do.

I rang my office, and informed them that my 'flu had relapsed' and that I wouldn't be coming in. I thought I heard my Manager starting to grumble, but I hung up at once...office could wait. I just HAD to look inside the clock.

Like a man possessed, I got out my tool kit and proceeded to the clock. I roughly turned it around, the pendulum clanging on the side walls. With growing impatience, I unscrewed the old brass screws that held the board at the back of the clock...there were twelve in all, and it took me about a quarter of an hour to unfasten all the screws. At last, I was ready to take away the board, and look at the mechanism.

It suddenly dawned on me that it would be dark inside the clock, and I would not be able to see anything clearly. So I went to the bedroom, and fetched the torch, which I switched on and kept next to me while I gently shook the board, trying to remove it from the body of the clock. It did not budge...possibly it was stuck in that position since the day the clock was made. But I was not going to give up. Using all my strength and taking a grip from the two air holes on the board, I shook it violently, until I felt it shift. Sensing victory, I have one final tug, and with a cracking sound, the board came right off all of a sudden, making me lose my balance and fall down flat on my back. The impact seemed to have winded me, and I just lay there, trying to get my breath back.

Suddenly, I felt something warm and soft touch my feet.

I froze, reaching for my torch, and turning it on.

What I saw at that instant made me want to laugh and cry at the same time.

There, in the bright beam of my torch, scampering out of the clock were two large rats...running for their lives...out of the dining room, via the bedroom and out through the open door!

THE EVIL EYE

I am sure that at least some of you would have read my earlier narrative 'The Gaseous Tale.' It was the one which dealt with my experience of visiting a doctor when my alimentary system decided to play truant, and the gases within my abdomen came closer to exploding than the time when President John Kennedy threatened to nuke the USSR during the Cuban missile crisis.

At that time, the good doctor had prodded, probed and even did a hand-stand on my stomach, before reaching her conclusion that the deep rumbling within my innards was nothing more serious than the result of excess gas. Her diagnosis had been spot-on, and I had been so impressed with her professionalism, that I decided to make her my regular physician, visiting her every time I needed the services of a member of the medical fraternity.

Her name was Doctor Mrinalini K. The first couple of occasions that I tried pronouncing this tongue-twister of a name, my tonsils nearly got dislocated. I therefore, refer to her as just 'Dr. M' these days.

The reason why I presently mention Dr. M will become apparent as my narration progresses, and I beg your indulgence and patience in this matter.

About two weeks ago, I was suddenly afflicted by a mysterious malady, which came upon me with absolutely no advance warning signs...no sneezing, coughing, wheezing, itching or even flatulence. Here I was one moment, feeling fit as the proverbial fiddle, and the very next moment I was being wracked with acute pains in my joints – both major and minor. These pains were accompanied by a mild fever, which, as is commonly known, causes the severity of the pains to escalate to a higher level – acting as a kind of 'force multiplier,' if you will.

Now, those of you who have known me for any length of time, would appreciate the fact that I am not the type of person to cringe and grovel at the slightest manifestation of pain. I even have the dubious distinction of having undergone a root canal treatment without local anaesthesia! Incidentally, among those present at the Dental Clinic on that occasion, opinion was divided as to whether I was very brave or whether I was a lunatic. I suspect that most tended to subscribe to the latter point of view.

But I digress, and humbly solicit your patience.

Coming back to my mysterious ailment, it seemed to be getting even more mysterious with the passage of time and brought with it intermittent chills. My body went into severe bouts of shivering – at times so severe that I worried my teeth would fall off, or that my brain would become like scrambled eggs! To try and control the pain and the violent convulsions of my body, I swallowed some half a dozen paracetamol tablets, turned on the room heater to full and hugged a scalding-hot hot-water-bottle as if my very life depended on it. However, the chills continued, unabated.

I soon realised that these measures were woefully inadequate to counter whatever was causing the symptoms that I have described. In fact, my condition seemed to be worsening, causing extreme anxiety among those around me. It was then that I took the decision to pay a visit to my friend and keeper of the Hippocratic Oath: Dr. M.

After the 20-minute wait that seems to be mandatory at every physician's clinic, I was ushered into the presence of Dr. M, who – I felt – gave me a kind of a very wry smile. Perhaps her mind went back to the time that I had nearly demolished her clinic with the spontaneous explosion of acrid, vile-smelling and potentially inflammable abdominal gas. Or perhaps it was due to the fact that I was in the middle of one of my shivering bouts and would have resembled a pulsating jelly fish. Anyway, whatever the reason, she immediately donned a face mask and slipped on a pair of gloves...as if I was an alien life-form and suffering from acute Martian Flu!

What followed next were the standard investigative procedures: check of pulse, blood pressure and temperature. By the way, have I mentioned earlier that I am particularly worried whenever my temperature has to be taken? No? Well...it's because I am petrified that someday, someone would use a rectal thermometer! Ah well...this time too I got away, when a small, digital thermometer was tucked into my armpit for the purpose.

Having recorded my 'vitals,' she asked me to lie down on to the examination table and proceeded to poke and prod all over my body, occasionally asking me to breathe, or to stop breathing or to hold my breath. As a grand finale to her explorations, she did her signature handstand on my stomach, and then asked me to dismount from the table and settle down on the stool next to her chair. Thereupon, she asked me to stick out my tongue, say 'aaaaaah,' and proceeded to stare inquisitively into my nostrils. She then picked up a mini mallet-shaped gadget (I came to know later that its medical name is 'reflex hammer), which had been lying on the table, and without any warning whatsoever, administered a sharp blow just below my right knee cap.

What happened next, could only have happened in a Laurel and Hardy movie. The instant she whacked me below my knee cap, my leg jerked forward, hitting the revolving chair that she was sitting on. Since this chair was one equipped with wheels, the impact of my leg striking it made it move backwards, propelling it at a fair rate of knots. In an attempt to stop the runaway chair, Dr. M had stretched out her right hand, trying to hold on to her table. Unfortunately, she missed the table, but only managed to grab the BP instrument which was on a stand, right next to the table. The stand instantly tilted forward, and the BP apparatus fell to the ground with a loud crash and shattered...the mercury dribbling around like tiny silver balls.

Mind you, the chair was still moving backwards with Dr. M perched on it, dragging the BP apparatus stand along with her. As the stand went past the table, it snagged with the telephone cable which ran from the wall-socket up to the instrument. The wire, in turn, yanked the telephone, and it tumbled from the table, the handset separating from the base, and the dial-tone going 'brrrrrrrrrrrrrrrr!'

Realising what was happening, Dr. M let go of the stand. At once, it fell completely over and landed heavily on her left foot, whereupon she let off a piercingly loud banshee scream, which brought her staff scurrying into the room to see what all the commotion was about.

The chair, in the meanwhile, had reached the end of its wild run, and came to an abrupt halt when it hit the wall at the back of the room.

Through this entire chaos, which must have lasted all of three seconds, I was still sitting on the stool...perhaps with my mouth hanging open, so shocked was I.

I think Dr. M was the first to recover, and I was amazed to see how quickly she once again became the true medical professional. Dragging her chair back to its original position, she proceeded to sit on it. Then she looked me straight in the eye, and said in clear, unequivocal words, "Sir, I do not find anything medically wrong with you. You have most likely been affected by Maleficentiasis Occulus...commonly referred to as The Evil Eye."

ONE BRIGHT SUNDAY MORNING

The man stood still on MG Road and admired the impressive Cathedral. It was truly an awesome structure. The saying on the board at the corner held his attention for a while… "Ye are the salt of the Earth." How apt, he thought to himself. Those who worshipped here must truly be the salt of the earth.

He hesitated for a moment before he decided to enter the gates, wondering what people would think of his attire. He looked down at his faded trousers, his sweat-stained shirt and the patched shoes that he wore. He very nearly turned and walked away, but the urge to worship in this magnificent edifice made him enter the gates. Slowly, haltingly he made his way in, staying to one side. He had never felt so self-conscious in his life.

Around him, other worshippers arrived – most in swanky cars, dressed in immaculate clothes, ladies adorned with jewels that sparkled in the morning sunlight. He took a deep breath, and moved on towards the entrance, remembering the words of the Psalm that he had learnt as a child…'The Lord is my Shepherd…I shall not want.' It gave him strength and courage, and he immediately knew he had made the right decision to worship here today.

If he had been impressed with the external beauty of the building, he was absolutely and totally overwhelmed by the awesome grandeur that greeted his eyes once he entered the building. The magnificent pillars that lined the main aisle, the stunning stained-glass windows, the splendid pipe organ, the ornate pulpit, the elaborate flower arrangements...all these were like a dream to him, and he felt that the congregation of this Cathedral were truly blest.

As he made his way to one of the pews, he looked around and noticed how happy the people were...greeting each other and smiling the smiles of the contented. As he settled down in the seat, he could hear snatches of conversation from behind him. "Oh yes," a lady was saying, "we are definitely going to Chowdaiah Hall today...and you know something? The tickets are 2,000 Rupees each...but then it will be worth it to hear Jagjit Singh live, no?" A male voice responded, "Oh yes...unfortunately Esther and I won't be able to make it, as we are entertaining tonight. Oh, by the way, did I tell you that Darius, the famous Radio Jockey, is coming?"

By this time, the Cathedral was nearly full, except for the row in which he sat. Just then a gentleman in a pin-striped suit and his wife in a shimmering turquoise blue saree made their way to the row where the scruffy man was sitting. Their two children preceded them, competing with each other as to who would get to the seat first.

The pretty little girl beat her brother to it...but her happiness was short-lived. The pin-stripe suited gentleman sternly ordered the child "Come this side Mona...come and sit near your mother."

Having said that, he moved in next to the man who was still looking around in awe.

If the man had hoped for a smile of friendship from his new neighbour, he was disappointed. Not only did the pin-stripe suited gentleman not smile at him, it appeared as though he assiduously avoided him. The man was disappointed..he had hoped that he could have struck up a conversation and got to know more of the Cathedral. However, he dismissed the regret, and tried to concentrate on the Service which had just begun.

As the Service progressed, the man was greatly awed by its dignity. The words and the music took him away, as it were, to another world..he could not have hoped for anything more than being able to worship in this Cathedral...one among those who recited the prayers, begged for forgiveness, sang the hymns and praised the Lord for all His wondrous gifts.

Presently, the Presbyter introduced the speaker for the Service, who slowly ascended the pulpit steps, and began his sermon by saying "May the words of my mouth and the meditations of all our hearts be wholly acceptable in thy sight oh Lord, our Rock and our Redeemer."

It was an excellent sermon, on the ever-popular (and oft-repeated theme), 'Do unto others as you would have others do unto you.' The speaker was very gifted and was able to evoke the emotions of the entire congregation. The man watched from the corner of his eye, as his pin-stripe suited neighbour jotted down notes on a small pad with his gold Cross pen, nodding in appreciation and agreement at the words that were flowing from the pulpit.

The sermon ended and the congregation sang the 'Creed'...which the man could hardly follow, even with the help of the prayer book...where he came from, they had never sung the 'Creed.'

As he was mulling over this, he realized that the 'Peace' was being passed around, which again was something that he was not familiar with. However, he was exceedingly pleased, as he would finally be able to shake his neighbour's hand..and may be even exchange a smile. He could see the people in the rows ahead of him turning to each other, smile and grasp each other's palms. He could hardly wait for his turn. Now there was only one row left..and then it had reached his row.

Barely able to hide his excitement, the man turned to his right, holding his hands out...palms together and with a smile of great joy on his lips. His mind was a-flutter, desperately thinking of what he would say when he held his neighbour's hand. Should he say 'Hello'...should he say 'Nice to meet you'...should he say 'I have found peace...' or should he just hold the hand and smile as he had never done before? He decided to flash his brightest smile.

The pin-stripe suited man did not turn. He simply stared straight ahead and merely made a cursory gesture of holding out his hands to his left, and barely touched the very tips of the man's fingers, which were waiting, quivering with eager anticipation. Having done that, he hastily withdrew his hands, and proceeded to wipe his fingers with his silken hand kerchief, as though he had touched something repulsive.

The man just stood there – numb, his smile grotesque, his hands beginning to tire.

After what seemed a lifetime, he slowly turned away, drawing his calloused palms into the comfort and solace of his worn out trouser pockets. He was bewildered, perplexed and – more than anything else – saddened. He closed his eyes, and desperately tried to keep the tears from flowing down his hollow cheeks.

Somehow, he managed to sit down.

What happened around him from that point onwards did not register. He had been shattered by the experience, crushed by the humiliation. He was vaguely aware of people proceeding to the Altar. He could not get himself to move...to convince himself to be part of the Holy Communion...indeed to partake of the body and the blood of Christ with the kind of people he had just come into contact with.

With a heavy heart, the man got up, and slowly walked out of the Cathedral. At the door, he turned around and stood for one last fleeting moment...taking in the spectacle before him...marvelling at the look of piety on the faces of the men and women returning from the Lord's Table...the look that seemed to convey 'I am now without sin...I am enriched...I am blest.'

The man finally stepped out into the bright sunlight and moved away. He took out a grimy piece of cloth from his tattered trouser pocket and wiped the tears from his eyes.

He walked out of the gate, never once looking back.

THE SHIRT-TALE

If there is one thing I absolutely detest, it would surely have to be wedding receptions. I find the activity boring and totally unnecessary. The very idea that the bride and groom, already tired from the long day and the rigours of the wedding ceremonies, having to display themselves like some sort of exhibits to all and sundry, strikes me not only as downright dumb but genuinely torturous.

Now, factor in the trauma that the young couple has to endure when they are confronted by some toothless, hearing-aid toting, geriatric individual, who claims to have known the groom's great grand uncle, when they were studying at the Kumbakonam Government High School! I mean..in such a situation what the Dickens is one supposed to say? Or how does one introduce the ancient geyser to the blushing bride? And don't forget, the couple has to smile all through this harrowing ordeal.

It is nearly as bad too, for the invitees. From picking an appropriate gift, to deciding on how to spend at least two hours in a totally alien environment, to standing in an interminable queue in the dining room..it is sheer agony.

Having carefully considered all this, I had been completely against having a reception for my own wedding but had to reluctantly acquiesce to the wishes of my immediate family...who regarded not having a reception as a 'loss of face' for them.

I distinctly remember that when I had broached the idea of dispensing with (what to my mind), was a useless enterprise, there was a major upheaval in the normally placid Nayaham household – my father had tried talking logic to me, my mother had shed tears and my 86-year-old grandmother (who was a great admirer of the Father of the Nation, Mahatma G) had threatened to go on an indefinite hunger-strike.

I knew that I could counter my father's arguments, and probably get him to agree with me. As far as my mother's crying was concerned, I was sure that her histrionics would cease in a few days, and she would relent. What disturbed me greatly was my grandmother's threat. I was mortally scared that the adamant old girl (whom I loved greatly) would indeed shun all manner of food and drink and embark upon a *satyagraha*. I was extremely concerned that such a decision could well result in her being summoned by her Maker, well ahead of the scheduled (and hitherto unknown) date and time of departure to her Heavenly Abode.

Although I knew that I would be totally grief-stricken if this were to happen, my more immediate and serious concern was about what would happen to my wedding – which would definitely have been postponed, until the mandatory mourning period was over. Wanting to avoid such a calamity at all cost, I had no choice but to grudgingly comply with their demands and found myself in the thick of it, with my newly-acquired *ardhangini* standing stoically by my side.

How we endured the two-odd hours of trauma is another story, which I will relate at a later date.

The reason why my mind suddenly recalled my distinct distaste of wedding receptions was due to the fact that I had been unexpectedly saddled with the prospect of having to attend one if these ghastly functions, and just could not come up with a plausible escape route. It was not as though I hadn't tried..but all my efforts had been effectively stymied by my wife, who was hell-bent on attending the function...perhaps (I suspect) to show off her newly-acquired diamond necklace and ear-ring set. Be that as it may, the point is that, here I was, getting ready to endure the tedium...much like the proverbial sacrificial lamb.

I had chosen a black trouser and a striped, pale blue, light weight, half-sleeved shirt for the occasion. Despite the fact that the clothes had returned from the dry cleaners just a day ago, I still ironed them again..lest there be the minutest wrinkle on any of them – you see, I have a slight trace of OCD, which my mother used to say I had acquired from her side of the family, who were always 'perfect' in whatever they did.

A good half an hour before we had decided to set off for the venue, I had worn the selected clothes. Looking into the mirror, I had been quite pleased that they matched well.

It was at this point, that I made my first big mistake of the evening, when I asked my wife if my combination was okay. She was in the middle of donning the new jewellery that I had mentioned earlier, and reluctantly turned and looked in my direction. I had expected her to respond as always with a "Hmph," but was in for a surprise. Even before she opened her mouth, her contemptuous look told me that she did not approve.

"Are you wearing 'that' today?" she asked incredulously..as if I was standing there clad only in yellow polka-dotted jocks and nothing else.

I took a quick glance at myself, just to make sure that I was indeed wearing trousers and shirt. "Yes," I replied, "Quite nice, no?"

"Nice? Nice?" She sneered. "You call that 'nice?' How can you come for a wedding reception dressed like that..in a half-sleeved shirt?"

I think it was then that I may have made my second big mistake of the evening. I said, "Why? What's wrong with this?"

Her instant reaction was what I would have expected if I had been caught having my third drink on the quiet. "How many times have I told you not to keep buying half-sleeved shirts? But, will you listen? No. You will do just what you want." Having said that, she lapsed into silence and went back to admiring her ear-rings from various angles in the mirror that she held in her hand.

I took the silence to mean that her tirade was over. But, as always, I was wrong. In a clear and sombre voice, she declared, "From now on, you will buy only full-sleeved shirts," much in the manner of Ayatollah

Khomeini issuing a *fatwa*. "And," she continued, "If you are going to the Reception like this, I am not coming with you."

To say that I was dumbstruck would have been the understatement of the millennium! My mind reeled, much like a spacecraft gone out of control. Questions flashed, desperately seeking answers. "How can I go alone? What will I tell my friends? Should I also not go?"

There were no easy answers. Slowly it dawned on me that I had once again lost the battle. There was only one way out of this mess..I just had to eat humble pie, wear a full-sleeved shirt and go to the function.

"Ok," I said as nonchalantly as possible, "perhaps I should wear a full-sleeved shirt after all..it does seem a bit cold this evening."

My wife had the look of the cat which got the cream..but I ignored that, as time was of the essence.

A quick search of my wardrobe unearthed a full-sleeved shirt, which I had not seen for at least a year. When I put it on, it seemed to fit, and secretly I was happy that I had not put on weight.

To me the shirt appeared to be a bit crumpled, but when I sought my better half's opinion, she barely glanced in my direction and said, "Its fine." However, when I looked in the mirror, I got a shock – the shirt was so crumpled that I looked as if I had just been through the washing machine and the clothes dryer!

I hastily took it off, plugged in the steam iron, spread the ironing board, and proceeded to iron the shirt. My speed of ironing would certainly have come close to making it to the Limca Book of Records!

As soon as I had finished, I put on the shirt again...completely forgetting that it had just gone under the steam iron. I instantly felt as if I was in a sauna with a busted thermostat. "Owwwww!" I yelled, pulling out the shirt once again. I hung it on a chair and turned the fan to full speed, to cool the garment.

After about ten minutes, (during which time my wife kept grumbling like an idling tractor engine) the shirt finally reached wearable temperature. I proceeded to put it on for the third time in twenty minutes, and we finally set off.

The drive was sheer murder owing to the traffic, and we took more than an hour to cover the three kilometres to the venue. During the entire period, my wife kept up a constant litany of how stupid I was to wear a short-sleeved shirt in the first place. Although I was still smarting from the recent blow to my ego, I managed to maintain a phlegmatic silence, pretending to concentrate on negotiating the horrendous traffic.

We eventually managed to reach the Reception Hall, just as the last of the guests were moving out of the Dining Room. Despite a thorough search, the bride and the groom were nowhere to be seen. Luckily, we found the bride's parents, to whom we handed over the gift we had got. Hastily, we bid them goodbye, making up some inane excuse why we had to depart immediately, and drove back home through the mad traffic.

What had started off as a perfect day had ended miserably.. and all because of a totally avoidable, completely unnecessary and patently abhorrent function!

I guess now you know why I absolutely detest wedding receptions!!

WHO'S THERE?

It had been a long day at work, and I was dog tired. Having reached home about an hour ago, I had a hot shower and had just poured myself two fingers of Jack Daniels and had settled into my favourite chair, when there was a knock on the door. Being too lazy to get up and see, I let off a loud yell, "Who's there?"

There was a moment of silence, and just as I was getting ready to bellow again, a high-pitched voice drifted in through the door, "Who."

For an instant, I was speechless. But I quickly got myself together and shouted, "Who?"

Promptly came the reply, "Who."

Now I was beginning to get irritated. I was clearly in no mood to play games and decided to put the matter to rest at once and go back to my attempt at unwinding. I parked Jack Daniels on a side stool, extricated myself from the chair, and went to the door, which I opened with increasing impatience.

I had to squint my eyes to focus on the stranger who was standing on the step, but even so, I could barely see his face, as the porch light was behind him. "Who are you?" I asked, with a trace of edginess in my voice.

"I am Who," said the figure...but the way he said it, it was not a question, but more of a statement.

This was getting very frustrating, and I could barely restrain myself from throttling the guy. However, I tried again...this time in Pidgin English.

Pointing directly at his chest, I asked "You who?" I thought I noticed his mouth forming a smile.

"Ya...Who," he replied, nodding his head and tapping himself on his chest with his right hand.

And I was now very sure that he was smiling, as if he was expecting me to shake his hand or something. This was really too much!

"Look here buddy," I sneered, "I am not interested in Yahoo or Google..I just want to know who you are!"

"Ah," he replied, "me Who...you who?"

I have always considered myself a calm individual, not given to losing my cool or to yelling. But at that moment, I just lost it. The cumulative effects of slogging all day, the agony of driving through murderous traffic, getting disturbed from my Nirvana with JD..and now, this ridiculous exchange with a perfect stranger precisely matched the weight of the straw that caused severe and permanent damage to the camel's back.

In a flash, I lunged at this scrawny guy and grabbed him by his collar. Being a couple of heads taller than him, and at least twenty kilograms heavier, I lifted him off his feet and shook him from side to side, much in the same way a dog would shake a stuffed toy. And all the while, I kept yelling, "Who are you? Who are you?"

And he kept squealing, "Who...Who...Who."

I guess this must have gone on for a while, because my arms were beginning to ache. Eventually, in a final fit of rage, I flung the guy all the way across the porch, and he landed in a heap on a row of flower-pots, breaking at least three of them.

Momentarily, my uncontrollable anger turned to utter panic, knowing my wife would kill me when she discovered the loss of her prized petunias. To an independent observer, the scene would indeed have seemed absolutely bizarre – here was the master of the house, standing immobile and frozen in fear, a formless figure lying askew on the ground, and petunias, strewn all over the porch!

Considering the scene that I have just described, I can totally understand the reaction of my wife, who had come out to investigate the hullabaloo. With a banshee scream (that sent at least a dozen bats fleeing to safer environs, and our dog Rufus yelping in mortal fear from his kennel), the lady of the house charged across the porch, only to come to an abrupt, screeching halt a few inches from the guy who had started it all. Utterly unmindful of the shattered flower-pots and scattered petunias, my better half just yelled, "Who, Who!!"

I stared, amazed, as the despicable heap of humanity, (whom I had so recently dispatched unceremoniously into the flower-pots), actually smiled..slowly got up, and – believe it or not – bowed a perfect bow in front of my wife!

The memories of the next few moments are still totally hazy to me. As I recall, in what seemed like watching a movie in ultra-slow motion, my wife turned to me and said, "Honey, meet Mr. Hu, my Chinese chiropractor."

A HAIRY TALE

Several years ago, while I was still a happy-go-lucky bachelor, Saturday evenings were occasions for unbridled fun and uncontrolled inebriation. As a consequence of which, it was well-nigh impossible to wake up on Sundays, and face the world before midday. Even then, it would take super-human effort just to open my eyes, muster enough courage and eventually stagger out of bed.

If you are wondering just why I was so masochistic, well, the answer lay in the fact that not doing so would have led to even more radical situations. You see, although I was just a few months shy of turning twenty eight, my mother (God bless her soul) still considered me her 'little boy,' and I was expected to go and look her up every Sunday, so that – firstly – she would be satisfied that I was still alive and in one piece, and, secondly – she could continue her one-point agenda of trying to convince me to get married and 'settle down,' before (as she put it), "I am too old to carry my grandchildren." This particular scheme, of course, did not even remotely fit into my next three five-year plans, and so every Sunday evening was a challenge in warding off the unthinkable.

One particular Sunday, unable to conjure up any new excuse as to why the term 'matrimony' was not to be found in my lexicon, and also labouring under a monumental hangover, I had committed the grave error of not visiting her. At the time of making this decision, I had not foreseen how foolhardy it was. Having decided not to go, I had drifted off blissfully into the welcoming arms of Morpheus and continued to slumber way beyond the customary hour of my visit. I don't rightly remember right now what exactly (or about whom) I was dreaming about at that point in time, but I do recall with absolute accuracy the events that followed thereafter.

It started with me hearing (or, rather, feeling) some sort of pounding – so violent, that it literally shook my room, and, as I recollect, I was convinced that it was an earthquake.

Now, if there is anything that gives me the heebie-jeebies (other than spiders, of course) is an earthquake.

This has been a phobia, or paranoia (if you prefer to call it that) from the time I could remember. It all started when, as a child of eight, I had been trapped in my upstairs bedroom as the result of an earthquake which struck just past midnight. The power had failed, but somehow, I managed to find my way to the door, only to find that the stairway to the ground floor had collapsed. I could hear my mother screaming my name, and I screamed back, but we could not see each other in the total darkness. By this time my father had located his (ever handy) torch, the tremors had ceased, and I was able to slide down the bannister (which, amazingly, had not collapsed, and join my parents, unhurt, but shaking like a leaf. I mention this incident, because it had left me permanently mortified of earthquakes..however minor.

But, I digress.

Ah...where was I? Oh yes...I heard – nay – felt this massive pounding, and not wanting a repeat of events long past, I was instantly wide awake, and sitting bolt upright on the bed, quivering in fear. I could hear my mother screaming my name, and I screamed back that I was alright. Then, abruptly, the pounding stopped. It was then that I realised (rather foolishly, I must confess) that this was no earthquake..it was just my mother pounding on the door trying to wake me up!

Eventually, after maybe like three more cycles of pounding, screaming and counter-screaming, my quivering finally stopped, and I was able to get off the bed. Knees wobbling, I managed to walk to the door and open it.

My mother must have been leaning against the door, because the instant I had it unbolted, it swung in with a mighty 'WHOOSH' and all three hundred pounds of my dear 'life-giver' tumbled in, totally devoid of balance and floundering on the floor, much like the over-stuffed bedrolls (or holdalls, as they were commonly called) which we carried while setting off on the frequent postings that my father had during his Air Force career.

To the uninitiated, and for the benefit of those readers who have not even heard of holdalls, much less seen one (since these contraptions have more or less totally disappeared), they were broad strips of canvas, designed to accommodate a thin mattress, a sheet, possibly a light blanket and a pillow...the entire collection being rolled snugly into a roughly cylindrical shape, and secured all around with two leather (or canvas) straps. The idea was to have a portable bedroll, which could be effortlessly carried in through the narrow doors of train carriages, and be easily opened and spread over berths, as and when one decided to lie down, or had the opportunity to stretch out in the perpetually over-crowded compartments.

The original designers of the holdall had clearly not catered for the likes of my dear mother – who took the name 'holdall' quite literally. For her, anything was fair game to go into the holdall. Besides the aforementioned items (mattress, sheet, etc.), shoes, cricket bats, roller skates, woven plastic baskets, etc. regularly fitted into the holdall which my mother packed. On one occasion, even a long, pointed Samurai sword (which had at one time belonged to my grandfather, who – the story went – had snatched it from a Japanese soldier somewhere in the Pacific Theatre during the Second World War) had found its way into one of our holdalls! While the story of how the Samurai sword came into my grandfather's possession could not be authenticated, one thing I could vouch for was that the Japanese steel had not lost its sharpness even after several decades. I say this with a certain degree of confidence, because of a traumatic incident that I was involved in, at Gauhati Railway Station.

I vividly remember the scene, as if it all happened just yesterday. We were on our way from Chandigarh to Tinsukhia (the eastern-most station on the Indian Railways map), and we had to change trains at Gauhati. As usual, there were no reservations available on the train, and (again, as usual) my father had gone in search of the 'Agent' – who, incidentally was a Mallu – to get at least two berths in exchange for a bottle of good old Hercules Rum (specifically procured and carried for this very purpose).

Our entire luggage (some 32 pieces) had been unceremoniously dumped on the platform, and my mother had ordered me to sit on the holdall, and keep a sharp eye on our worldly possessions, while she scouted around for some oily *puri* and *sabzee* – the staple meal during all such journeys. Whatever else I was (or was not), I certainly was extremely attentive of my mother's orders, as even a minor infringement would have attracted immediate and severe corporal punishment from her, with whatever 'weapon' was readily available at hand.

So, there I was on Platform No.6 at Gauhati Station, perched precariously on a holdall, and keeping an eye on the rest of the items. However, being all of twelve years of age, the reader would agree that it would have been well-nigh impossible for me to assume a totally rigid posture and sit absolutely still, especially when mosquitoes (the size of underfed dragon-flies), were desperately trying to get a taste of my (rare) AB-ve blood. I don't recall exactly the precise manoeuvre that I executed to avoid a particularly persistent blood-sucker but, suffice to say, that the very next instant I felt a terrible jab in my posterior, and I took off vertically, screaming like a crazed banshee. My spontaneous acrobatics brought most people in my vicinity to a screeching halt, and in no time at all, a sizeable crowd had gathered, with everyone speculating as to how on earth the rear of my khaki shorts was spotted with blood.

In spite of the cacophony that is part of all Railway Stations, my high-pitched scream had reached the ears of my mother, and her maternal instincts had unerringly analysed the sound to be that of her offspring.

Clutching the three newspaper-wrapped packets of *puri-sabzee*, which she had just bought, she instantly took off in the general direction of the sound. Unfortunately, in her state of panic, she had completely overlooked the fact that she had not paid for the victuals that she had so recently acquired from the Bihari *puri-wallah*, who, in all fairness, was justifiably indignant at what he must have perceived as blatant daylight robbery.

The change in his demeanour was amazing. One moment, he was a smiling, indolent individual, and the next, he had metamorphosed into a snarling, foul-mouthed monster who had been conned of his rightful dues. (Incidentally, this is a common trait that I have noticed in Biharis during the course of my extensive travels in that part of India: the speed at which they switch identities from being passive *puri-wallahs* or placid *paan-wallahs* to vicious, merciless monsters is truly astounding!).

Anyway...the point I am trying to make here is that at that moment in time, my mother was galloping down Platform No.6, *puri-sabzee* packets in hand, feverishly tailed by a Bihari, wielding a huge colander and shouting, "*Chor...Chor!*"

I suppose that instinct told my mother that the scene of action was at the spot where the jobless crowd had gathered, and she headed directly there and at a fair rate of knots (at that time, she weighed-in at around 175 pounds, and was thus able to accelerate and sustain quite high speeds).

All the while, the Bihari kept yelling, "*Chor*! *Chor*!" and this had a remarkable effect on the crowd – from gawking at a twelve-year-old kid with a bleeding backside, it spontaneously changed direction to watch the on-going action of a portly *puri*-pincher being pursued by a bare-chested, *lungi*-clad, colander-wielding Bihari!

My mother immediately spotted me, and charged right in, screaming, "What happened...what happened?"

For once, I was speechless, and all I could do was bend over and display my blood-speckled posterior to her, pointing to the holdall at the same time.

By this time, the *puri-wallah* had reached panting and puffing, and took in the scene with admirable serenity. Perhaps the sight of a skinny twelve-year-old, with bloodied shorts, pointing to an over-stuffed holdall had the salutary effect of calming him down. Following the direction of my quivering finger, both my mother and the Bihari set off towards the blood-thirsty bedroll. I think they reached the holdall together, for they let out a collective gasp. There, sticking out of the faded canvas was the razor-sharp, blood-smeared point of the Samurai sword, which my mother had packed inside our 'bedroll!'

As the popular saying goes, 'All's well that ends well,' and matters soon returned to normal, with the mystery of the bleeding bottom having been solved. Needless to say, things were sorted out amicably between my mother and the Bihari as soon as the *puri-sabzee* had been paid for, and the erstwhile monster instantly – and miraculously – transformed back into the smiling *puri-wallah.*

At precisely that moment, in true Hindi movie fashion, my father arrived, gleefully clutching reservation slips for three berths.

****

Shucks...I seem to have meandered off into something totally unconnected to what I started off with. If my memory serves me right, I was in the middle of narrating the incident wherein my mother had literally 'dropped in' unannounced, because I had not paid her my weekly visit.

Well...to continue the tale, it was indeed something that absolutely shocked me..first the panic about the earthquake, and then the 'holdall act' by my mother. I am certain that, had such an incident happened to someone else, or even under different circumstances, I would have exploded into uncontrollable laughter and unmitigated mirth. But...this was happening to me, and the person presently wallowing on the floor like a beached blue whale, was none other than my dear mother!

I would also like to mention here that although I was extremely distressed at the indignity of the situation, I was actually more concerned and flustered by the mortal fear that my mother would discover on the floor, traces of my amorous activities of the previous night with a certain pretty lass!

At this point, let me enlighten the reader that although I clearly did not qualify to be a certified Lothario, I must confess that abstinence was not my *forte*. This, I think, was but natural, when one was in the prime of youth, reasonably well-heeled, living alone and (in all modesty) not too abhorrent to the opposite sex. Consequently, I had the good fortune of striking acquaintances with several charming, young ladies at bars and pubs, and who (I liked to convince myself), were totally gaga over my brilliant sense of humour. And (as all budding Casanovas would confirm), most times the humour did not end at the bar or pub-closing time but would invariably find its way into my humble lodgings..along with the 'awestruck' admirer!

The particular weekend that I alluded to at the beginning of this narration, was one such. If my memory serves me right, I was at my favourite bar and having had three large whisky and soda, was feeling very humorous indeed.

I was about to order my fourth w&s, when in walks this amazingly beautiful woman. I guess that I nearly fell off the bar-stool, for the barman gave me one of those patronising looks that barmen generally reserve for sozzled customers. I managed to recover my composure, just as this ravishing angel on two legs sidled up to the bar-stool next to mine. Now that she was in my proximity, I was able to admire her beauty from close quarters.

The first thing that struck me was her long, lustrous, shiny black hair, which she had left loose, and which reached down to her slim waist. I must confess that I have (and always had) a strong fetish for long, lustrous, shiny black hair. In fact, the only advertisements on TV that I have ever paid any attention to were the ones for hair oils, shampoos and conditioners, where pretty models showed off their magnificent tresses.

Anyway..so much for the ads. Suffice to say that one thing led to another, and before you could say 'Johnnie Walker,' I had this demure damsel of my dreams in splits, regaling her with the choicest jokes and stories that I could conjure up. I was also absolutely amazed to see how much she could drink. Incidentally, my fondness for women who can guzzle large amounts of whisky comes a close second to my fondness for women with long, lustrous, shiny black hair, and by the time the barman had rung the bell announcing that there would be no more booze, I was convinced that the night was going to be a long one indeed.

As it happened, I was dead right! We reached my abode in high spirits (if you will pardon the pun), and it was one of the most frenzied nights that I'd ever had.

It must have been around three in the morning, when I dropped her to her home (for some unfathomable reason, she insisted on going home) and made my way back to my bed and instantly passed out.

I think I woke up sometime when the sun had already ascended high in the sky, but decided that my regular Sunday visit to my mother was just not going to happen. Then I drifted off back into sweet oblivion.

****

I beg the reader's indulgence for my frequent forays into nostalgia, and I hope that I will be pardoned for my prevarications.
To recap, here was my mother on all fours on the floor, struggling to get vertical. Then there was me, bleary-eyed and fuzzy-headed, desperately looking around, hoping like hell that no itinerant item of lingerie was lying around, which – to say the least – would have most likely led to my mother having a cardiac arrest. Not seeing any incriminating evidence of the night before, I breathed a sigh of relief, and mustering up all my strength, managed to haul my mother off the floor, and sat her down on my dishevelled bed.

Although I was still reeling under the cumulative effects of a massive hangover, and the obscene levels of physical activity of the previous night, I knew that I had to pre-empt my mother, before she started her tirade regarding my failure to visit her. For the life of me, I just cannot remember what excuse I proffered, but it seemed to have worked.

Not only did it work, it also seemed to have brought out the milk of maternal kindness in my mother, who was convinced that I was too ill, even to straighten out my bed! Her recent misfortune was a thing of the past, and in spite of my vociferous protests, she set upon restoring a modicum of neatness and order in the room.

She started the restoration process with getting the bed in order..but did not progress very far. For there, on my spotless white pillow, resplendent in all its splendour, was a strand of long, lustrous, shiny black hair!

THE CHALLENGE

I have always been a person who liked challenges. Right from my childhood days, I constantly looked forward to doing things, which others may have ignored, or even avoided if possible. It was not that I was foolhardy or had any intentions of showing off to my friends...it was just that I felt a great deal of joy, and a sense of accomplishment if I were to achieve something which was not normal or mundane...especially should someone dare me to do it.

If I recall correctly, the first time that I consciously undertook a challenge was when I was around seven or eight years old. My father having been in the Railways, we were living in quarters that had been allotted close to the Railway yard, with plenty of trees and shrubs all around. The house itself was a massive stone building, with a sloping, red-tiled roof, typical of all Railway buildings of that era. The front and rear verandas were enclosed with wooden trellises, (always painted green for some unknown reason), which allowed for very effective cross-ventilation, keeping the house cool, even on the warmest Summer day.

As children, my friends and I would spend hours together, climbing these trellises, and going up all the way to the rafters which held up the roof. In fact, one of the most popular games we used to play was 'Hide and Seek,' and what better place to hide than on top of the rafters in some corner of the verandah? Of course, at times one would get the fright of one's life, if one spotted a huge black spider, or a lizard next to where one was hiding. The screams which accompanied such unexpected encounters would be a dead giveaway, and the one 'hiding' would be 'caught' by those 'seeking' and sent to the 'jail' for the rest of the game.

On one such day, we kids were taking a break from our games, and just lazing around, eating the crunchy rusks that my mother had got for us. Suddenly, we heard a buzzing sound followed by three or four bees flying in through the trellis. They seemed to be on some kind of mission and flew right past us and around the corner of the verandah. Instantly, we were all up, and following the bees to see where they were headed. To our surprise, they abruptly zoomed upwards and disappeared into the rafters at the far end. We all ran behind them and peered intently into the dark space between the roof and the rafters. It was then that we noticed a huge hive, teeming with hundreds – perhaps thousands – of bees. The hive must have come up just in the past three days, since I remembered hiding at that very spot just the previous Sunday.

Our first thought was to run as far away from there as possible, knowing that if the hive were to be disturbed, we would all be certainly stung by the bees. But, for some strange reason, my closest friend in the group – Arvind – turned to me and said, "Hey Dilip, I bet you that you will not be able to climb up and get some honey for all of us to enjoy."

This was a crazy bet, and we all knew it. I had more or less decided to ignore it, but somewhere within me, I felt that I could not turn away from this challenge. It was as though another person was speaking on my behalf. "Okay," I said, "what if I do it? What's in it for me?"

For a moment, even Arvind was stunned, and didn't know how to respond. But, since it was he who had thrown the challenge, he just had to come up with an answer, or face the derision of the others. "If you come out successful, I will...er...I will...umm...I will let you ride my bicycle," he declared.

"Oh wow!" I thought to myself. A ride on Arvind's new 6-speed bicycle? Something that all of us would have given our eye-teeth for? I would have happily jumped in front of a moving train if I could get just one round on that awesome bike!

"Done," I said, scarcely thinking about the consequences. "Done," I repeated and instantly moved closer to the trellis to start climbing, lest Arvind changed his mind. The others – including Arvind – had already started putting distance between me and themselves.

Amazingly, I did manage to win the bet..and that too without being stung black and blue by the bees. For some strange reason, the bees did not harm me at all. On the contrary, when I had climbed up and my face was just inches away from the hive, they had all literally parted and allowed me to put my fist into the hive and break off a small chunk of the waxy structure, dripping with honey. I can only surmise that this curious and uncharacteristic behaviour by the bees was on account of the strong whiff of the eucalyptus oil that my mother had applied rather generously on my hands and legs to keep me from getting bitten by mosquitoes!

Anyway...we all enjoyed the honey, I got to ride Arvind's bike for all of one round, and I had become somewhat of a hero among my group of friends. Sadly, my daredevil feat did not impress my parents, when they heard of it. My mother used her cane to administer six of the best, which left my bottom sore for over a week!

****

There were several other occasions that I had taken up challenges in my growing years. Some had gone well, but some had backfired, and in some, I had even gotten into serious trouble. One such unfortunate challenge was when I was in my second year at college.

At this point I would like to elaborate a bit about my life. The year was 1962, and I had completed school the previous year. It was also the year that the Chinese had decided to attack India, followed by the debacle that our country suffered.

I had enrolled in college that very year, and joined the NCC Air Wing almost immediately, since I had been crazy about aviation all my life. There being an acute shortage of pilots in the IAF, (that is the Indian Air Force) post the Chinese War, the Government asked for volunteers from the NCC to join the IAF. Without further delay, I gave my name, and was given a set of forms to be filled. Being a minor by age, a 'Consent Clause' had to be signed by my father.

When I took the entrance forms to my father for his signature, he didn't say a word. Instead, right in front of my eyes, he tore the forms into four pieces, and tossed them into waste-paper basket. Looking me straight in my eyes, he intoned, "You will complete your Graduation, young man, after which you can become a pilot or an engine driver, or whatever you wish to be..but not before." And with that, he got up and walked away, leaving me standing with my mouth open and eyes filled with tears.

That was when I decided that I most certainly WILL become an Air Force pilot, come what may.

But from that day on, my time at college had nothing to do with studies. I attended classes, for just two reasons..firstly, remain in the NCC and learn flying; and secondly, to have the minimum percentage of attendance, so as to be able to take the examinations.

I had also become something of notoriety for creating mischief and had 'fine-tuned' the art of getting thrown out of the class, but only after the attendance was marked.

One class in which I always had great fun was the Hindi class. The lecturer who was assigned to impart knowledge of the National Language was someone who took his role very seriously indeed. His name was Mr. L.S. Shastri, and he must have been about 50 or 55 years old. Being a staunch Gandhian, he even dressed typically – in a white *dhoti* (worn in *Pancha Kachcham* style), a *khadi kurta*, leather sandals, and (believe it or not) a black *topi*! When he spoke, he sounded very funny, as though he had pebbles in his mouth. He also kept constantly moving his jaws, as though he was chewing gum, and it was rumoured that he used dentures. He also wore round, black-rimmed glasses, making him look like an owl.

There were several of us of us who regularly attended the Hindi class, not to learn the *Rashtra Bhasha,* but only to tease Mr. Shastri, and generally disrupt proceedings. For some unknown reason, I was always the 'leader' of the mischief-mongers and was expected to come up with fresh ideas on a regular basis to disturb the class.

If I remember correctly, it was sometime in the month of November, and the Diwali season was at its peak. The din of firecrackers being burst on the roads could be distinctly heard even inside the classroom. All of a sudden, the guy sitting next to me turned to me and said, "Hey Dilip, you think that you have the guts to light up a few crackers in the class?"

"What?" I said, incredulously, "are you serious? You want me to get thrown out of college?"

"Ha! I knew it," he teased, "you can't do it."

At that very moment, something snapped within me. Perhaps because I am a Taurean, I felt like a bull having a red cape waved in front of its nose.

"Don't you challenge me," I replied, "I will not only light a cracker, but I will light it below he platform, with *Shastriji* standing on it!"

"Really?" replied the guy, "you will really do that?"

My adrenalin was kicking in. "Tomorrow I will do it," I said, "So don't you bunk *Shastriji's* class."

And saying that, I chucked the paper plane that I had been making towards the black board, just as Mr. Shastri turned, explaining the difference between '*sandhi*' and '*samaas.*' Seeing the paper plane gracefully gliding towards the black-board, the entire class burst into spontaneous, raucous laughter.

Punishment for me was unsparing and instant. "Get out of my class, you rascal!" shouted *Shastriji*, and I happily stepped out.

****

That whole afternoon I spent planning my little prank. I knew it was fraught with danger, but the challenge was just too much to pass up.

By the evening, I had firmed up my plans. Fortunately, the first class the next day was Hindi, and that would give me the opportunity to carry out my plans without anyone else knowing about it.

Later in the evening I went and got a packet of Laxmi Electric Chain crackers, guaranteed to keep blasting for at least thirty seconds. Next, I got a couple of *agarbathhis*, which would be vital if my plan were to succeed. I had nearly forgotten about the match box but, fortunately, I was able to pinch one from the kitchen later that night.

The next morning, my mother was quite surprised when I told her that I would be leaving early for college. Perhaps she thought that her dear son had finally realised his responsibilities and turned over a new leaf. If only she knew how totally wrong she was!

I reached college much before any students had arrived and went straight to the classroom. The janitor was just leaving the place as I reached there, after cleaning the room and setting the desks and tables in order. He did not seem to have seen me (or at least I hoped that he hadn't), and went his way, whistling a tune..lost in his own world.

Just about five minutes before the start of the class, I placed the crackers under the platform near the black-board. I lit up the *agarbathhis* and wrapped the wick from the crackers onto them, about an inch below the glowing tip. This would act as a 'timer fuse' and I hoped the crackers would ignite in about ten minutes. I had a tough time shifting the platform by myself, but somehow managed to get everything in place, just as the first of the students started arriving.

The sound of the klaxon in the corridor signalled that the day had begun, and Mr. Shastri walked in precisely at 9:00 am. Without any delay, he sat down in his chair, took the Attendance Register, and proceeded to call the Roll Numbers.

My heart was pounding. No, not because I was scared of what I had done..it was pounding wildly, hoping that my plan would not fail.

Shastriji must have called out about fifteen Roll Numbers, and the wall clock showed 9:08 am. At that precise moment, the crackers went off! It sounded like a machine gun was being fired from somewhere near the black-board. And it kept going on and on, the sound reverberating in the classroom...thick acrid smoke spiralling from below the platform.

****

As soon as the first of the crackers burst, *Shastriji* had jumped up from his chair in total panic. He tripped on his dhoti and fell forwards, his face striking the edge of the platform. His teeth flew out of his mouth and clattered in front of the first row of desks. Surprisingly, his *topi* was still on his head. Momentarily, a thought went through my mind. "So...*Shastriji* did wear dentures, after all!"

There was total pandemonium in the class. Since no one (other than the guy next to me) knew about this prank, the other students too panicked, and ran helter-skelter. Lecturers from the adjoining classrooms rushed in, as did the college attendants and other staff. Two or three of them helped *Shastriji* to his feet and made him sit on the chair. Someone brought a glass of water and gave it to him to drink.

By now the smoke had cleared away, but the acrid smell of sulphur from the crackers pervaded the air. In the melee, someone had stepped on *Shastriji's* dentures and they had shattered...the teeth lying around grotesquely.

Just then Father Elias D'Souza – the Principal – walked in and went straight to *Shastriji*. They spoke for a few minutes, but it seemed that the Principal could not understand what the Hindi Lecturer was trying to say, as his mouth was devoid of the dentures. I thought that he closely resembled a large fish gasping for air.

It was then that I noticed that the Janitor had come in, and was looking around the classroom, as if searching for someone. Something told me that things had gone terribly wrong. As if on cue, the Janitor turned, pointed in my direction, and said something to the Principal.

Father D'Souza once again spoke to *Shastriji*, and both of them looked in my direction. I could see *Shastriji* vigorously nodding his head. It was pretty obvious that he was painting an awfully dismal picture of me!

I will not go into details of what happened thereafter. Suffice to say, I was almost expelled from the college. It was only Father D'Souza's kindness, and a generous donation to the College Building Fund by my parents that allowed me to remain on the rolls, with a suspension for two weeks.

Shastriji resigned from the staff shortly thereafter, and we came to know that he died of heart failure within a month after the incident. Although I tried convincing myself that my prank had nothing to do with his death, the feeling of guilt affected me hugely, and I promised to myself that I would not accept such challenges in the future.

****

When I managed to graduate from College in 1964, I really didn't know who was more surprised – my parents or me! But, having fulfilled my father's condition about the pursuit of my ambition to become a pilot, I lost no time in applying for the Air Force through the UPSC, and got through in my first attempt. I also cleared the Interviews and the Medical Tests, sometime towards the end of 1964. I would be required to report for training in March 1965, and until then, it was total happiness, doing nothing except playing cricket or table tennis at the YMCA, or just loafing about with my friends.

During this period, there were several times when I had come close to accepting some challenge or the other, but memories of the fiasco at College had tempered my enthusiasm for such actions. This is not to say that I had completely had some change of character – I was still game, but I picked the ones that would not even remotely cause injury or grief to anyone else.

I remember one such challenge particularly clearly, because it nearly put paid to my chances of going for my Air Force training. As I mentioned earlier, those were the days that I spent with my group of friends, literally doing nothing. My parents too had stopped being over-intrusive in my life, as they realised that shortly I would be on my own and would have to be responsible for all my actions.

During the time, I was living with my parents on Nandidurga Road, which – believe it or not – was one of the loneliest roads in Bangalore. Ours was one of the first houses to come up on the road, and the only regular 'traffic' was that of dead bodies being carried to the Muslim cemetery which was located up the road. There were just two buses which passed by during the entire day, and it would be termed a major achievement if one could coax an auto-rickshaw driver to come to Nandidurga Road.

Although none of us were really bothered by the fact that we stayed practically a stone's-throw away from the cemetery, it was an unspoken rule that everyone avoided passing by that way after dark. In those days, there was not even a wall along the cemetery, and the graves would be in full view on either side of the road. There used to be a narrow path running through the cemetery, which was used as a short cut to reach Munireddy Palya – a small hamlet on the other side of the cemetery, which boasted of the only market and a few small shops in the area. This path was used regularly during daylight hours and cycling through the cemetery was no big deal.

Sometime in the month of February 1965, a new guy joined our group. His name was Rashid, and he was slightly older than any of us. Initially, there was much resentment in accepting this newcomer into our group, but when we came to know that he had an extremely pretty younger sister (by the name of Saira), he was welcomed with open arms!

Rashid had come to Bangalore from Bombay and would regale us with very interesting stories of film stars, electric trains and Marine Drive – things which none of us had seen, except in Hindi movies. And it seemed that he was allowed to watch any movie that he wanted to...unlike us guys, who were still restricted by our parents to watching kids' films.

One day, Rashid told us that he had watched *Bhoot Bangla* – a horror movie of that time and narrated the story in chilling detail. Probably noticing that we were all listening to him with our mouths open, he derisively ended his narration by saying that he hoped that none of us would get nightmares after listening to the tale. As if adding insult to injury, he took a dig at me saying, "Hey Dilip, how are you going to become an Air Force pilot if you are so scared of ghost stories?"

"What? What did you say?" I asked, my hackles rising at his remark.

He kind of sniggered and repeated what he had said earlier.

I could feel the eyes of all the others in the group staring at me. Now it was a matter of ego, and I was definitely not going to cower down. "Listen buddy," I said, "I am not scared of spirits or ghosts..in fact I don't think apparitions exist at all. So, you don't try and show off just because you have watched some silly horror movie."

"Oh, is that so?" He retorted, "If you are so brave, I dare you to cross the cemetery alone at night, using the path. I will wait for you on the other side, just to make sure you have not chickened out, and taken the road."

I did not answer immediately, and I could sense that all my friends in the group were waiting to see what I would say. After all, I was the one who was always talking about the dangers of flying – especially after getting selected for the Air Force. Although I was not scared, I was not very keen to accept the challenge. But then again, it would have been a big loss of face for me in my own group.

At that moment, my innate personality of never turning down a challenge took over. "Okay," I said, looking him straight in the eye, "I will do it. Tomorrow you be on the other side at 8:00 pm and I will come across."

I hardly slept that night. For some strange reason, I kept tossing and turning, and thinking of the challenge. Eventually, sometime around 2 or 2:30 am, I must have fallen asleep.

In spite of sleeping so late, I was up by five in the morning, and went and sat on the balcony. Now that I had a chance to recall the events of the previous evening, I was beginning to think that I had been rather foolish to accept the challenge. After all, this guy Rashid was a newcomer, and what business had he to interfere with our group? Perhaps he was just trying to prove a point, so that he could become the 'leader' of the group..an honour which had been mine for the past three years.

I clearly had two options: go through with the challenge and prove once and for all that I was not scared and would remain the 'leader,' or pull out – giving some excuse or the other – which would certainly attract scorn and ridicule from my friends. The more I thought about it, the more I was convinced that the second option was no option at all. After all, I had just about a month before I left for training, and it would be shameful to leave in ignominy.

No. I would not chicken out. I would take the challenge, and I would win!

****

The rest of the day went by in a kind of a daze. I ate very little at breakfast and toyed with my lunch...so much so that my mother asked me several times if I was not feeling well. Naturally, I could not tell her about what I planned to do that evening, and so gave some excuse or the other for my lack of appetite. I also mentioned that I was going out to a friend's house, which would serve as an excuse for me to be out late at night.

Finally, it was 5:30 pm, and the group met as always in my room. It was rather a quiet meeting, with no one wanting to discuss my upcoming adventure. Rashid too was there but did not talk much. Perhaps the tension was getting to him too.

Eventually, we all broke up at about seven, and except for Rashid and I, everyone returned to their homes. After a few minutes, he came up to me, shook my hand and said, "I better get going. Hope that you are not going to chicken out?"

Clearly, he was needling me, but I decided that I will not give him the pleasure to get under my skin. "Me? Chicken out? No way," I replied, "I just hope that you are not too scared to be waiting all alone at the other end."

He did not reply, but gave me a look of utter disdain, and walked out of the room.

I sat in my room for a few minutes more, before getting ready for my adventure. Although it was mid-February, evenings tended to get quite cold, and so I had decided to wear my woollen jacket when I went out. It was not a very thick one, so I felt that it would be ideal to keep out the mild cold. I also took my trusty torch, as there were no lights within the cemetery (come to think of it, there were no lights even on the road!), and as it was common knowledge that there were plenty of snakes in the cemetery, I certainly did not want to run the risk of being bitten by one of them.

It had already become quite dark, by the time I was all set to go. I also noticed that the moon had not risen as yet. There was a pretty stiff wind blowing, and I was thankful for wearing my jacket. I wondered if Rashid had reached the other end, and what he would be doing. Perhaps he would be enjoying a cup of tea in one of the tea stalls, which were plentiful in that area.

I walked briskly from my house and reached the cemetery in about five minutes. There was not a soul on the road. It was pitch dark, although I could see lots of stars in the clear sky above. I knew that there was a narrow culvert between the road and the cemetery, with a stone slab placed across it to cross over, and I realised that I could very well miss it in the dark. So I slowed my pace, and squinted my eyes, concentrating on finding the stone slab. When I didn't find it for a few minutes, I was tempted to retrace my steps, and look for it again. But I decided to search for a few more minutes, and thankfully, almost instantly spotted the stone slab. I took a deep breath, and quickly crossed the culvert, and was well and truly inside the cemetery.

****

It was awfully quiet, except for the faint rustling of the trees as the wind blew through the leaves. Occasionally, the quietness was punctuated by the hooting of an owl, somewhere in the distance.

I concentrated on the circle of light from my torch, as it unerringly illuminated the narrow path. It was absolutely dark on either side...so dark that I could not even see the graves which I knew were just next to the path.

I must have walked for about six or seven minutes, and I guessed that in another five minutes or so, I would be on the other side. In my mind, I was rehearsing what I would say to Rashid, and visualising the look of defeat on his face, when he would see me walking out of the cemetery. In fact, I think that I was smiling to myself, savouring the fact that I would prove to my group once and for all that I was their leader.

Just at that moment, I felt as if something – or someone – had suddenly gripped my left foot. One moment I was striding steadily, following the beam of light from my torch, and the next, I was hurtling uncontrollably, falling over to my left. I spread my arms out, desperately trying to maintain my balance. I could not see the path ahead, for the beam of light from the torch was now shining uselessly into the dark sky. As I fell over heavily, the torch flew out of my hand, and I could hear it crash into one of the graves with a loud thud, it's light instantly fading out.

After the initial shock, I tried to orientate myself. I was lying on my back, and from what I could make out, I was not injured, as I was able to move my hands and feet. I tried rolling over to my right but seemed to be held down. Gathering my strength, I once again tried to turn, but found it impossible to move more than a few degrees. I felt my body tense, with the first signs of fear in my mind. Using all my strength and what leverage was available to me, I heaved my left leg over and tried to get on my knees. Nothing happened…it was as though I was being held back firmly by my jacket.

Initial fear quickly gave way to intense panic hitting me like a tsunami, and I think I screamed. My mind was totally blank…except that I knew for certain that something horrible happening to me. I gingerly looked around but could see nothing except inky blackness. For a fleeting moment, I thought that I felt something softly touch my neck, cold and moist. I screamed again, raw fear in my voice. I jerked my head forward, once again making a desperate effort to get to my feet, but with the same result. Although it was very cold, I was sweating inside my jacket. I suddenly felt something very warm around my inner thighs and spreading downwards on my legs. I realised then that I had wet myself.

Taking a deep breath and fighting back my panic, I forced my mind to think. Extreme fear kept clouding my mind, but eventually a practical thought did appear – I would be free if I got rid of my jacket!

Quickly I undid the zipper of my jacket and pushed myself up into a sitting position. I felt the jacket slipping off from my hands and body and the next moment, I was upright. In a frenzy, I turned to my side and rolled over and over, putting as much distance between me and whatever had been holding me. I found myself on flat ground and realised that I was back on the path. Wasting no time, I stood up and started to run blindly in what I believed to be the direction that I had come from.

I remember falling down several times, but fear and the instinct to survive made me move on. Also, by this time, the moon had risen, and the faint glow of its light helped me in seeing the path. I have no recollection of how long I took to reach the road, but eventually, I did. I stopped for a few moments to catch my breath, and then made my way back to my house. Fortunately, no one saw me come and let myself into my room using my key.

****

The next morning, I was up early as usual. Fortunately, except for a few scratches, I was not injured after the previous night's experience. I was only apprehensive that my mother would discover the loss of my jacket and ask me about it.

Thinking of the jacket, I involuntarily shuddered, remembering the horrifying minutes that I had spent in the cemetery. Strangely, now that it was daylight, much of the panic seemed to have gone, and I was beginning to think logically.

As these thoughts were going on in my mind, Rashid landed up, along with a couple of my friends. I could see from the look on his face that he believed that I had chickened out, and not gone to the cemetery at all. When I related what had happened, it only served to make him to smirk more, and to put on a superior air. It seemed that no matter how many times I repeated the story, neither Rashid nor my other friends were convinced about what I had experienced. I just knew that somehow or the other, I had to make them believe what I was saying was true, and that I had not chickened out.

"Okay," I finally said to Rashid, "what if we go to the cemetery right now, and look for my jacket or torch? If we find any of those, that should convince you that I am telling the truth…right?" He looked at the others for their opinions, and I was thankful when they agreed with my plan.

"Fine," he replied. "I only hope that this is not a wild goose chase. As it is I was quite fed up waiting for you last night."

****

In a short while, all of us set off to the cemetery, which looked sublimely placid in the bright sunshine, and not in the least bit foreboding. We crossed the culvert, and walked along the path in single file, with me leading the group. Nothing much was spoken...I guess we were all immersed in our own thoughts...Rashid surely must have been thinking of how he would become the leader of the group, when we failed to find the items.

I, of course, was very tense...my mind going over several possibilities. What if the torch or jacket were not to be found? If that happened, I would be ruined. My very credibility would be lost, and I just didn't know what I would do. Even the thought of committing suicide briefly crossed my mind!

After about five minutes, I sensed that we had reached the spot where I had had the weird experience the previous night. I slowed down and along with me, so did the rest of the group. Abruptly, I stopped, and for a moment, couldn't believe my eyes. There, about two feet away from the path was my jacket, firmly snagged on one of the branches of a large, thorny bush!! Also, clearly visible was a thick root from the shrub protruding on to the path, on which (I now realised), I had tripped over last night.

I just stood there and laughed...I laughed so hard that tears came to my eyes. Realising what had happened, the others too joined in my laughter, followed by lots of back-slapping and leg-pulling. Even Rashid seemed to be caught up in the moment, and came up to me, shook my hand and said, "Well, that is that. Just don't forget that you owe me two cups of tea this evening!"

FISH OUT OF WATER

It was one of those '50-50' evenings, that Bangalore is so famous – or infamous – for, during the Monsoon season. One was never sure if it would rain or it would remain dry for the next hour or so. Hence the 50-50 odds.

Adding to this uncertainty was the fact that in our once-beautiful City, it could be pouring down in your back yard, whereas the front yard would be bone dry. No..no..this is not a joke. Several residents have told me that they would keep umbrellas strategically positioned in the middle of their homes, so that those wanting to transit from the front to the rear of the house could arm themselves with one, before exiting through the rear door.

And so it was that on this particular day – the weather did not seem bad, but it did not seem good, either. Therefore, I was in two minds whether to go for my usual visit to Richards Park or not. On the one hand, I was very keen to go and meet all my dear friends and share a few laughs. On the other hand, I could very well get caught in a downpour..and I certainly was not in the mood to enjoy a free shower.

For a few minutes, I was immersed in this serious dilemma, and I could feel my BP gradually going Northwards. Suddenly, out of nowhere, I had an inspirational thought…"Why not I toss a coin and settle the issue?" After all, more vital matters (like cricket matches) depended solely on such a method. But since I was not a gambling man, I was averse to tempting fate, and so did not search my pockets for a coin.

At that very moment, I happened to look out of my widow, and I beheld the most beautiful sight that I had seen for quite a while…the clouds had vanished and I could see sunshine bathing the entire area in its wonderfully warm evening light. In my excitement, I very nearly let off a Tarzan yell, but quickly controlled my enthusiasm, lest my wife think that I had gone nuts. Wasting no further time, I donned my sneakers, and set off to good old Richards Park…eager to meet my (mostly) geriatric friends, as well as a few of the younger generation.

To say that I made it to the Park in good time would be a lie…as I took nearly 17 minutes to travel the one kilometre from my house to the Park. No…no…I didn't get lost en-route. Neither did my car have a breakdown. The reason for my tardy progress was solely due to the fact that there must have been at least a million-people thronging the eateries that had sprung up on MM Road to cater for the ravenously hungry Ramadan 'fast-breakers.'

Anyway, eventually I did reach the Park, and slowly made my way in to reach the benches where my friends would sit every single evening. For a moment, I thought I had entered the wrong Park…or maybe gone to the wrong benches, as I did not see any of my male friends at all. In fact, out of the three benches which used to be populated entirely by our group, two were unoccupied. On the third bench sat three ladies, who were also part of our group.

Now..I would have been well within my rights to do a smart about turn and go back the way I came. But, being a person who strongly believed in gender equality and empowerment of women, I sauntered up to them and said "Hello."

I could see that they were in the middle of an animated discussion on whether gherkins ought to be fried or sautéed. I was about to quietly slither away, so as not to interrupt, but was caught in the act. All of them unanimously said "STAY!" And I had no choice but to stay.

After a few routine sentences (pertaining mainly to the weather), the conversation trailed off into silence..at least on my part. The ladies, though, had switched tracks and were going great guns, talking about necklaces, chains, *mangalsutras*, nose rings, ear rings, finger rings, bangles, bracelets, anklets and other such adornments. I, of course, was supremely ignorant on the subject, and hence unable to contribute to the discussion in any way.

After a while, I was getting bored..but, being a gentleman, I had to pretend that I was thoroughly involved in their discussion.

It was quite a Herculean task..believe me, and my mind kept going back to one of my earlier *janams*...when I had the fortune of being born as a fish. And not any old fish..but a genuine 24 carat Gold

Fish. My family name was *Carassius Auratus*, and we were held in very high esteem by all the other species of fishes. In fact, there was a time when we would refuse to be seen in the same tank as the other 'lower' species of fish!

It was not that we were snobbish, but historically we were always accorded superior status in society. It is said that we were the 'Species-of-Choice' in Queen Nefertiti's aquarium. We were revered so much in ancient Egypt, that there was a retinue of eunuchs, specially charged with taking care of us and ensuring that our status was never sullied by anyone. To say life was great would be a monumental understatement, and we Gold Fish enjoyed our high status to the fullest for several centuries.

****

Time went by and many centuries later, I had the good fortune of being in the collection of one of the most beautiful and famous stars in Bollywood. There was not a day that I was not admired by dozens of visitors...who were more interested in drooling over me than meeting my famous owner. However, I was from the 'old school' (so to speak) and tried to be as modest as possible.

One day, disaster struck, in the form of an earthquake measuring 7.2 on the Richter Scale. I was all alone in my pure gold tank, nibbling at some titbits which my gorgeous owner had dropped into my tank. Just as I was finishing my meal, I suddenly felt the tank sway from side to side. The swaying was so violent, that massive waves started to form in the water. To me it looked and felt like a tsunami..about which I had heard of from my Uncle long ago. The wild rocking soon assumed catastrophic proportions, and I was physically lifted and flung out of the tank, falling heavily on to the terracotta tiles which covered the floor of the aquarium.

I don't know how long I would have been there..gasping for breath, but eventually, I passed out due to the effects of acute anoxia.

****

Standing all alone in Richards Park amongst the trio of yakking ladies, I remembered the oft-quoted statement 'FEELING LIKE A FISH OUT OF THE WATER', for it was exactly what I felt liked that evening.

My reverie was abruptly cut short when all three ladies stood up as one and prepared to leave.

It is common knowledge that ladies always move in groups when even just one of them has to use the Rest Room. However, since there were no Rest Rooms in Richards Park, I was rather taken aback when the trio prepared to set course in unison. Fortunately, I did not embarrass myself by asking where they were all headed.

However, my doubt was soon cleared, when all of them turned to me and said "Bye! We are going home. See you tomorrow. Hope you enjoyed your evening!"

I did not reply, because, whatever else I am or am not, I certainly am not a liar!

HAVE A HEART

"My heart is beating, keeps on repeating, I'm waiting for you..."

So sang Preeti Sagar for the 1975 hit Hindi movie 'Julie.' The song itself went on to become extremely popular on its own merit, and indeed, it can be still heard off and on.

In fact, just the other day, while I was listening to some music on the FM Radio, this very song was being played, and it set me thinking. What is it with the 'heart' that it evokes so many feelings within us? Why is it that every time there is happiness or sorrow, fear or surprise, peace or turmoil..it is always connected with the heart?

From times immemorial, the heart had been symbolized as the seat of all emotions, the repository of feelings in human beings. It was not just another organ within the human body...it was THE most important organ, which not only was vital in keeping one alive, but was also what determined the inner being of a person.

However, with the advancement of science a couple of centuries ago, the heart all but lost its importance and was relegated to being described as just another 'pump,' whose sole purpose of existence was only to propel blood through the entire body. If, at one time, the heart had been considered THE most important organ in the human body, it was now the brain, which was elevated to that position.

Remarkably, about fifty years ago, things changed, when it was discovered that the heart had a much more important role to play than to just beat an average of 72 times per minute, while pumping blood to the rest of the body. Researchers ascertained that certain impulses/commands originating from the brain were indeed 'over-ruled' by the heart. More importantly, this remarkable organ was able to modify its working to suit the situation.

I have always held the view that the heart is more important than the brain. One just has to look around to find millions of 'brainless' morons who inhabit this planet, but I seriously doubt if one would ever find a living being without a heart! And I don't say this in either poetic or philosophical terms.

To justify my opinion on the primacy of the heart, I put forward a few thoughts, which originate from my brain, but – ironically – are all to do with the heart!

At the outset, permit me to offer my 'heart-felt' thanks to those who have the patience to read my musings, and, more importantly – are 'large-hearted' enough to pardon me for any lapses. A word of caution though – being large-hearted in the literal sense of the term can be injurious to health...as any cardiologist would tell you. Hence, they caution about cardiomegaly...or simply, 'enlarged heart,' which is a very serious and potentially life-threatening medical condition indeed!

Let me ask you something. Why is it that when one is dumped by one's 'sweetheart,' one suffers from 'heartache?' And why is it that 'heart strings' are tugged, whenever one gets emotional? Or, consider the fact that we always 'heartily' congratulate newly-married couples, who have 'given their hearts' to each another (sometimes I think that matrimony is just another name for 'heart-transplant!).

If the brain was indeed the organ that ran our lives, how come we offer 'heartfelt' sympathies and condolences at funerals, or feel one's 'heart skip a beat' when one's beloved unexpectedly appears?

How many times have we heard the expression 'have a heart,' when someone utters something patently idiotic, ridiculous or unbelievable? If indeed the brain were more important, should we not say 'have a brain?'

Of course, we have all heard 'heart-warming' stories, as also stories that send 'chills to the heart.' And, isn't it strange that we exhort others to put their 'heart and soul' into whatever they are striving for..but NEVER coax them to use their brains?

When one is sad, the 'heart is heavy,' and when one is happy, the 'heart is light.' When one is forgiving of others' follies, one is 'warm-hearted,' but when one enforces the rules, one is 'cold-hearted.' Then, of course, when someone stands up for what is right, he or she becomes a 'brave-heart' – mind you – not a brave-brain! And..isn't it common to hear that 'the heart bleeds' when we hear of some tragedy? How come the brain does not bleed?

I can go on and on, giving examples to my 'heart's content'...but I guess that you have got the gist of what I am trying to say.

Which brings me to something very 'close to my heart.'

When I see the state of affairs in Bangalore (or Bengaluru, if you please), my 'heart weighs a ton.' Sometime back, I was sorely tempted to run away from this garbage-strewn, pot-hole infested, mosquito-ridden City. But in my 'heart of hearts,' I still love this place which gave me life. For me, 'home is where the heart is'.

Made in the USA
Middletown, DE
12 May 2018